I0699324

LETTER TO THE READER

As you turn the pages of this novel, you'll journey with Maddie, Lila, and Caleb through the tangled web of grief, love, and discovery. This story was born from a simple yet profound truth: "Life must be lived forward but is understood backward." It's a phrase that has echoed in my heart for years, shaping the way I see the world and the experiences that have marked my own life.

In the midst of our daily struggles, it's easy to feel lost, overwhelmed by the weight of circumstances that don't make sense. We often find ourselves asking, "Why is this happening?" or "What's the purpose behind this pain?" But the answers don't always come immediately. Sometimes, it takes years before we can look back and see how the pieces of our lives fit together, revealing a picture we couldn't have imagined.

Maddie's journey is one of those stories. She faces unimaginable loss, the kind that shakes the very foundation of her world. In her desperation to reconnect with her daughter Lila, she turns to Caleb, a man who seems to offer hope, but whose presence in their lives carries its own set of questions. Together, they navigate a path filled with secrets, heartache, and ultimately, a shared understanding that the past and present are intricately woven together.

As you read, I hope you'll find a part of yourself in Maddie's strength, Lila's volatility, or Caleb's quiet determination. We all go through seasons where life feels uncertain, where the road ahead is unclear, and we're left wondering how we'll make it through. But it's in those moments that we're often being shaped for something greater, something we can only see when we look back.

So, as you immerse yourself in this story, I invite you to reflect on your own journey. Maybe you're in the middle of a season that feels impossible, or perhaps you've just come out of one and are beginning to see the reasons behind the trials you've faced. Whatever your situation, I hope this novel resonates with you and offers a sense of connection and understanding.

Thank you for choosing to spend time with Maddie, Lila, and Caleb. Their story is, in many ways, a reflection of the truth that life, with all its twists and turns, has a purpose—even when it's hard to see.

With heartfelt gratitude,

Jessica

Praise for *Here I Stand*

"Evenly paced, well-written, and keeping the reader emotionally invested, author Jessica Leed's "Here I Stand" is a must-read contemporary women's fiction read. Engaging, heartbreaking, and heartwarming all at once, readers won't be able to get enough of Sienna's journey and the author's amazing ability to draw the reader into the narrative wholeheartedly. If you haven't yet been sure to grab your copy today."
Goodreads

"After reading 9 Years I had to find out what happened to Sienna Henderson. I loved following her story, being a teacher myself I found it totally relatable. I'm also not usually one to cry whilst reading but this one tugged on my heart strings! Amazing writing yet again!"
Goodreads

"Here I Stand is a captivating story following Sienna as she says goodbye to the past and finds an inner strength to forge out her new life. Great read, you won't want to put it down."
Goodreads

"Heartfelt and captivating story that will tug your heartstrings and stir your emotions. Well written book will engage each reader and maintain their interest until the very end."
Goodreads

"Jessica's much anticipated second novel did not disappoint. The story answered so many questions from the first book in the series, but equally it could be read as a stand-alone book. I couldn't put it down at times! Warning: it's a bit of a tearjerker! Can't wait to read the next novel from Jessica Leed!"
Goodreads

"I found this book very engaging. It was well written and took me on a ride. I felt as though I knew the characters deeply and left me wanting to go back and read Jessica's first book. This is a talented young author to keep your eyes on. I already look forward to her next book."
Goodreads

SILENT PROMISES

SILENT PROMISES

JESSICA LEED

Silent Promises
First Edition, December 2024
Published by Hillford Press ✑
Tennessee, USA

Copyright © 2024 Jessica Leed

Edited by Leilani Dewindt
Interior formatted by Glenn Sarco
Cover designed by Sami Miller

All rights reserved. No part of this book may be reproduced or transmitted in any form, by any means—electronic, mechanical, photocopying, recording, or otherwise—without prior written permission, except for brief quotations used in reviews or critical articles.

Printed in the United States of America.

ISBN: 979-8-218-52807-2 (eBook)
ISBN: 979-8-218-52808-9 (Paperback)

In the hush, a whisper weaves,
Unspoken truths in shadows flow.
In every breath where mystery cleaves,
Silent promises begin to grow.

PROLOGUE

Summer 2005
Maddie

DO YOU EVER feel like you were made for more? More than the shallow, scripted routines everyone else seems content with? I don't mean it in an arrogant way, though I know it can sound that way. It's just—there's always been this feeling inside me, a certainty, that I'm meant for something bigger. Something real. I held onto that belief fiercely, even if it meant waiting longer than most for someone extraordinary. Someone who saw the world like I did. Someone who understood.

At twenty, I found him.

They say love sneaks up on you when you're not looking for it. For once, they were right. I wasn't chasing after boys, and my grades reflected that. Sure, I had a social life—if spending most of my time in the library counted. I wasn't avoiding people; I just preferred the quiet, the company of books and the occasional like-minded soul who wandered in.

It was during one of those afternoons, the familiar hum of the library settling around me, that his voice broke through.

"Hey, you ever wonder why libraries are so quiet? Like, what's the point?"

The question landed out of nowhere, slicing through the stillness, pulling my attention away from my manuscript. I looked up, spotting the guy sitting a few tables away, his messy hair sticking up in all directions like he'd been running his hands through it. His voice was louder than the unspoken library code allowed, with a distinctly American accent that immediately stood out in the room. And why was he grinning at me like that?

I shot him a glare, hoping it would be enough to shut him up. But my heart was already racing. Great. Why did he have to be cute?

But no. He was grinning now, clearly amused by my irritation. I could practically feel the silent groans from other students rippling through the room.

With a sigh, I glanced back at my laptop, trying to pick up the thread of my thoughts. But the rhythm was broken, the flow gone. My fingers hovered uselessly over the keyboard. I stared at the same sentence I'd been working on for ten minutes, now indecipherable thanks to this guy's random question.

Before I could refocus, I heard the sound of a chair scraping the floor. *No. He couldn't possibly be—*

He was. He was walking toward me, his hands shoved in his pockets like he had all the time in the world. Of course, someone that good-looking would have that kind of confidence.

"Don't mind me, just curious," he said, sitting down across from me with an air of confidence I couldn't quite figure out.

I blinked at him, my annoyance growing. I really should say something. Anything. Don't just sit there staring, Maddie.

"Can I help you?"

He grinned, unfazed. "Maybe. Depends on what you're working on."

"School stuff," I said flatly, hoping that would end the

conversation. And hoping he didn't notice how awkward that sounded.

But he leaned forward, eyes narrowing like he could see right through me. "Really? Because it looked like something a bit more... personal."

I quickly clicked over to a blank document, hiding my manuscript. "You're interrupting."

He was too close now. His cologne—something warm and woodsy—was making it hard to focus.

"Touchy," he teased, glancing at my screen like he wasn't buying the act. "Come on, what's the big secret?"

Why was my face so hot all of a sudden? "It's not a secret. I'm just trying to work, and you're not exactly helping."

"Well," he said, leaning back and folding his arms behind his head, "I'm Dylan, and clearly, we're going to be best friends, so you might as well tell me now."

The sheer audacity of his statement caught me off guard, and despite myself, I laughed. I hated that he was making me laugh. "Best friends, huh? Based on what?"

"Based on the fact that you're the first person in this library who hasn't ignored me completely." He shot me a wink. "That's a connection, right?"

Was he flirting? No. Maybe?

I shook my head, but I was smiling now. Stop smiling, Maddie. He'll think you're interested. "You're relentless."

"I get that a lot." He leaned in, dropping his voice. "But seriously, I saw what you were working on before. It wasn't just school stuff, was it?"

My fingers tightened around the edge of my laptop. "Okay, fine," I said with a sigh. "It's a manuscript."

Dylan's eyebrows shot up. "Like a book?"

"Like a book," I repeated, waiting for him to crack a joke or make some smart comment.

But instead, his expression softened. "That's awesome. You'll get published. I can feel it."

What? No teasing? I stared at him, half-expecting sarcasm, but his tone was sincere. The confidence in his voice threw me off balance. "You don't even know me."

"Maybe not," he shrugged. "But I know when someone's passionate about something. You were working like it mattered."

His words made something inside me shift. I tried to look away, but my eyes kept drifting back to his. His face was too perfect—sharp jawline, deep brown eyes, and that messy hair that looked annoyingly good on him. Why did guys like him even exist?

We sat in silence for a moment, the noise of the library fading into the background. I wasn't sure what to make of this guy, this Dylan, who had barged into my afternoon with his loud voice, bold confidence, and that unmistakable American accent. And his way-too-perfect face.

"So, where are you from?" I asked, half out of curiosity, half to shift the subject. And hopefully make this less awkward.

"Michigan," he replied. "I'm an exchange student here, finishing my psychology degree."

I tilted my head, intrigued now. Of course, he's smart too. Fantastic. "Michigan? I've always wanted to see snow. You guys get real snow up there, right?"

He chuckled. "Yeah, we get real snow. Tons of it. You should visit sometime, see for yourself."

His casual invitation made me pause, my pulse quickening just a little. Was he serious? Wait, was I actually considering this? I forced a smile, shaking off the unexpected tension. "I don't know if I could handle that much cold."

"You'd be surprised," he said with a grin. "I think you could handle a lot more than you think."

The way he said it—light-hearted, but with an undercurrent

of something deeper—made my heart skip a beat. *Stop overanalysing everything, Maddie. You're not a teenager.*

"And what about you?" I asked, trying to steer the conversation to safer ground. "How are you handling the heat here?"

Dylan laughed. "I'm melting, to be honest. Christmas in summer? Blows my mind."

I couldn't help but laugh. *Why was everything he said so disarming?* "It's not that bad!"

"The girl who's lived here her whole life speaks," he teased."I'll get used to it—or die trying."

I shook my head, still smiling. *Probably too much.* I never actually said I'd lived here forever, but his guess was spot on.

Enough already.

He had this way of disarming me, making me forget I was supposed to be irritated. As he stood to leave, his hand brushed mine. *Oh.* It was barely a touch, but it sent a spark up my arm, and I froze. *Why am I freezing? It's just a touch.*

Get it together.

He lingered, his eyes meeting mine with a softness that made the world around us blur for a second.

"I'm Dylan," he said, reminding me again. "And don't give up on your dream, Maddie."

The way he said my name hung in the air, lingering even after he disappeared around the corner. I closed my laptop, my mind spinning. *Dylan.* His name fit him, annoyingly enough. Too perfect, too confident, and way too distracting. I had no idea then how much that moment, that one conversation, would change everything.

ONE

Spring 2023
Maddie

IT WAS NOTHING short of a masterpiece.

I couldn't stop admiring my husband's handiwork as I lined the cheese board with sliced pears, nuts, and creamed honey.

The gazebo was exactly as I had imagined, with its octagonal design and tall windows encircling the space, allowing sunlight to pour in and create a bright, inviting atmosphere. At the front, elegant French doors enhanced the charm, providing both a beautiful and functional entrance. Painted in a soft, serene blue with clean white accents, it stood gracefully in the garden, surrounded by a vibrant flower bed bursting with colour. Inside, a chandelier hung from the ceiling, casting a gentle, warm glow that gave the whole place a cosy, inviting atmosphere. It had quickly become our peaceful escape, and I knew it would be the perfect setting for hosting guests at Christmas, which was just around the corner.

Each time I looked at it, I saw more than just a structure—it was a testament to Dylan's love and the life we were building together.

As I arranged the cheeses, my eyes wandered to the vase of

red roses on the windowsill, their vibrant petals catching the sunlight. Dylan knew how much I adored them and made sure our home was never without a fresh bouquet. They added a touch of elegance to the kitchen, their sweet fragrance mingling with the aromas of the cheese and honey.

I rinsed a packet of strawberries, feeling my heart grow warm as I watched him and Lila finish off their game of Scrabble. Lila was fiercely competitive, never backing down until it was a close win. The gap between their skill levels shortened as Lila persisted for a game each night. It had become like clockwork. As soon as dinner and homework were completed, there Lila would be, at eight o'clock sharp with the board game in her hands, ready to go. Sometimes I would join in, but even though there was some level of expectation being a teacher, I wasn't that good at it. Maybe I played it up a bit, but honestly, I liked that they had this quality "father-daughter" time together. It had become a tradition, and it was beautiful to watch. Being a Saturday, this particular game had become an afternoon one.

Dylan stepped out from the gazebo to take a call. I felt myself clench. He seemed to be taking lot of calls these days.

More than normal.

Part of me felt frustrated that he would respond to such calls outside business hours, but I knew he would make it quick. I wouldn't let it get to me. He always prioritised his family.

I stood with the cheese board in my hands and watched him from inside, feeling my frustration shift into something else I couldn't quite pinpoint. Was it me, or had his body language changed since he had been spending more time on the phone? He appeared to be more slumped these days when he would usually hold himself more poised, more confidently. I was probably reading too much into it, especially with all of this physical labour he was doing. It was bound to take a toll.

I pushed open the screen door. "Did I time intermission

well?" I asked, stepping carefully on the pebble stones leading up to the gazebo entrance.

"Oh wow, Mum! That looks incredible!" Lila beamed as I placed the wooden board on the cleared table space.

"Who's winning?"

"Dad is." Lila scrunched up her nose and wiped the loose parts of her hair away from her face. "But only by a little."

"Only by a little I hear?" Dylan returned, taking a piece of sliced pear and tossing it into his mouth.

"One hundred percent. You wait till you see the next word I have ready; you won't even know what's coming for you." Lila giggled, picking up a cracker.

"Keeping me on my toes I see, sweetheart."

"Don't you know it!"

They exchanged a knowing smile and the warmth I felt earlier returned.

Dylan leaned in and kissed me on the cheek. "You couldn't have timed it better, Hun. Lila was right, this spread looks incredible."

I rubbed my husband's back in response, feeling the heat from his shirt warm me instantly. I closed the door to trap the cool air from the AC and settled into a seat next my family.

I looked across the table at my daughter. I still couldn't believe how fast she had grown up. How was she fifteen already? It felt like only yesterday that I was bouncing her on my knee.

Lila pulled her legs in under her and dug the knife into the brie cheese, her expression unchanged from a moment ago. She was a happy child; she always had been. Together, raising Lila had been a dream. She rarely threw a tantrum and was always the first to follow the rules, often reminding people to do the same. Now that she was a teen, I was waiting for a rebellious streak to present itself, but had yet to see it. She was transitioning in other ways, though: starting to wear a bit of makeup these days; a touch of foundation and a coat of mascara on her already full lashes, but thankfully her dress style was still tasteful.

I reached for Dylan's knee under the table and gave it a little squeeze. He curled his fingers around my hand and sent me a tired smile. That was another thing—he was looking tired these days. But despite how weary he looked, he still had boundless energy.

After ten minutes, we had demolished the platter completely. Dylan dusted his hands off and further angled his tiles away from any prying eyes, his mind already back to the game he was playing with his daughter.

"So…you've got a big one coming, do you?" he asked Lila with a sheepish grin.

"Yes …." she started, pretending to look scared and looked at her letters again. "But I'm feeling good about this!"

Dylan shook his head with a mischievous smile. "Game on."

"You two have fun. I'm looking forward to hearing how close this one will be," I said as I took the empty cheese board from the table.

We certainty liked our cheese.

"Oh, I've got this one in the bag, Mum," Lila said, her eyes focused on the Scrabble board as she manoeuvred her hands above it as though she was about to cast a spell.

"So competitive you two." I laughed, opening the door with my elbow, feeling the heat hit my face.

"Will you get some writing done?" Dylan asked, his eyes holding the same pleading expression as always.

"Yeah," I started, nodding slowly. "I'll knock out some words."

And I would. It's not that I've stopped writing over the years, because I haven't. I am still convinced that I will write until I'm physically not capable of it. I like to think that means I'll write well into my old age, permitting I'm dementia-free. But even if my mind does happen to go, it will be an entertaining read for those who try and make sense of my jumbled thoughts. I've finished one of my many half-attempted manuscripts. Zero published novels… but minor details.

"I look forward to hearing about it later," Dylan said with perhaps a little too much enthusiasm. God bless him. He was always my number one supporter, never ceasing to encourage me since the first day we met. Little did I know how hard it was to be traditionally published, and to be quite frank, I had no idea how to go about it. Once Lila was born, the writing naturally took a back seat as other things in life became a priority.

But I never stopped writing.

The ideas never stopped flowing. One book soon turned into three; an unexpected trilogy took form as they sat there on my laptop, hidden from the world. Together with my articulate husband who really ought to write a book of his own, we had recently begun working on my book proposal. Even though this project required way less words, it was the most daunting part. I had one chance to impress a literary agent or publishing house with my letter of intention. Did I mention that you have only about seven seconds to grab their attention? Because that was all you had. After just seven seconds, their opinion is formed on whether or not they want to invest in you and your work or toss it aside like they did with the majority of proposals they received.

The odds weren't really in my favour, but that's why it was so important that I nailed this thing. With all the research we had done to make this dream a reality, I knew that in time, it was possible.

Dylan made me believe that.

TWO

Spring 2023
Lila

LOST. SERIOUSLY THOUGHT I had this one in the bag, but no—Dad pulled out a word I didn't even know existed, and that was it, game over. Refusing to accept defeat, I insisted we go for a run. Dad has longer legs, sure, but his endurance these days? Not so hot. Mum says I'm wearing him out, but honestly, he's the one spending every spare second building and fixing stuff. If anyone's wearing anyone out, it's him.

And I say that with love.

Stepping outside, I popped my earphones in, feeling the prickling of goosebumps on my arms. Weird to get those in the heat, right? I laughed, watching my arm hairs stand at attention like they were surrendering to the sun. I smoothed down the fly-away parts of my hair, giggling at the sight.

"Ready to go?" Dad shut the front door behind him, no earphones in sight. I could never understand how anyone could run without music.

"Ready as I'll ever be," I said, trying to sound more confident than I felt. Honestly, if I weren't so competitive, I'd be on the couch with an ice cream.

Turning left out of our street, we followed the sidewalk to the entrance of the *O'Kinley Trail*. I loved this trail, stretching over 40km, though we'd only explored a fraction. That was my goal by year's end: to reach new trees instead of the same old landmarks.

We exchanged a knowing look, and with a nod, we were off. Few others braved the track in this heat. About a kilometre in, I noticed Dad falling behind, despite his strong legs.

I shot him a smirk, silently telling him he was slowing me down. He managed a weak smile, but something about it didn't sit right. He was sweating heavily, struggling to catch his breath.

"Dad, you okay?" I asked, pulling out an earphone.

"Yeah, sweetie," he muttered, coming to a sudden stop. He leaned forward, hands on his knees, staring at the gravel track.

"Is the heat getting to you?" I realised how my question might sound like teasing. I felt bad. "We can stop if you need to."

Dad wiped sweat from his neck. "Nah, let's keep going." He straightened up, hand on his lower back.

"Are you sure?"

"Yes, let's keep going."

I popped my earphone back in and tried to regain my rhythm as Dad picked up the pace beside me. I didn't expect us to go much farther; in another kilometre, we'd turn back home. Plus, I was desperate for water—the sun was brutal today.

I love this time for thinking. Some people swear by the toilet or the shower, but running gets my thoughts swirling. My dance concert was coming up, and I couldn't stop pondering who'd snag the lead roles. We're doing our take on High School Musical, and I'd been rehearsing non-stop. I was determined to nail those moves! Our class was packed with fantastic hip-hop dancers, so the competition was fierce. We hadn't had a formal audition yet, but Ms. Stringer hinted she'd announce the cast soon.

I picked up my pace, deep in thought. It'd been almost three weeks since she mentioned it. My gut said she'd tell us tomorrow night. She has to, right? Tickets were already on sale for the December 12th show—that's only seven weeks away. And we'd barely learned the choreography! I hoped Ms. Stringer knew what she was doing.

Turning the corner, sweat trickled down my neck. We were taking the shortcut home, no question. Today's lack of breeze made every drop cling like a leech.

Can't wait to shower when I get home.

Ryan was supposed to call later, and I wanted to feel fresh. I figured I'd blow-dry my hair and let it fall naturally today; he said he prefers it that way. Don't want to try too hard—maybe just a touch of concealer for these breakouts around my chin. Ugh, when did puberty get so tough?

Not that it should matter; you can't really see them on video calls anyway, thanks to the quality. I'd just angle the camera near the window for that flattering light. That always works. Feeling better already. I wasn't usually this insecure, but ever since Ryan Hensley started noticing me, I found myself overthinking things I never cared about. Silly, considering we've known each other since kindergarten. He's seen it all— like that time I face-planted during athletics and left half my skin on the track. I still have the scar. Actually, he's seen worse. Like that one time two years ago when we…

"Lila?"

Dad's voice was faint, barely audible over my pounding footsteps and the music blaring through my earphones. Ignoring it once, I kept my eyes fixed ahead, determined not to break my stride.

"Lila."

This time, the urgency in his voice cut through my concentration. Slowing my pace, I turned, dread settling like a stone in my stomach.

"Dad?"

Twenty metres behind me, my father lay on the track, doubled over as if struck. Panic gripped me as I jogged back to him, each step heavy with dread. How many times had he called my name?

"Yeah, can you give me a hand?"

He sounded breathless, weak. I helped him up, his hand trembling in mine. Why couldn't he stand on his own? Had he injured himself?

"What happened?" Fear tinged my voice. I'd never seen him fall, never seen him anything less than strong and composed. Now, he looked frail, vulnerable.

"Dad?"

"I'm okay, sweetie." His attempt at levity fell flat, his eyes betraying the pain he tried to hide. "Just getting old. Can't keep up with you anymore."

I wanted to believe him, but his strained expression told a different story. I brushed aside his joke, my heart sinking at the sight of him struggling.

"You're not old, Dad. You're fitter than me on your worst day."

His smile was strained, eyes narrowing as he steadied himself against the pain. He deflected my concern, gaze drifting away.

"Did you trip on something?"

"Must have." His gaze flickered to the distance, avoiding my scrutiny. "No blood, see? I'm good to go. Maybe we can walk the rest?"

"Is your stomach hurting?" I pressed, unease gnawing at me. This wasn't like him, to downplay discomfort.

"Sweetie, I'm fine." His hand on my back lacked its usual reassurance. "Let's head back, make some lemonade."

He knew I was worried. I could see it in his eyes. But seeing him so vulnerable didn't sit right with me. I couldn't shake the image of him on the ground.

Something was very wrong.

THREE

The Backstory
Maddie

STILL DON'T KNOW why he singled me out. Out of all the people he could've approached, all the girls with more charm and confidence, it was me he chose to sit beside that day. Why? I've never been the girl guys noticed—never knew how to flirt, or even talk to them without feeling like my words were tripping over each other. It just didn't make sense. But somehow, none of that seemed to matter to him. With him, I didn't seem to have this problem. He saw me, really saw me, and for reasons I still can't fully understand, he chose me.

Every time we happened to be in the library, he would ask how my writing was going. It wasn't like the questions would come in the way, either. Each question would be deeper, more intentional.

Even more playful.

"So, what's the latest masterpiece about?" he asked, a playful glint in his eye.

I rolled my eyes, trying to hide my smile. "Oh, you know, the usual—star-crossed lovers, dramatic twists, heart-wrenching endings."

He chuckled. "Sounds intense. Do you ever write happy endings?"

"Sometimes," I admitted, "but where's the fun in that? Besides, life isn't always about happy endings."

He gave me a thoughtful look. "True, but it doesn't hurt to dream a little."

I nudged him with my elbow. "And what about you, Mr. Serious-Internship? Do you ever dream?"

"All the time," he said softly, his eyes locking with mine. "Mostly about us."

My heart fluttered at his words, a warmth spreading through me. In that moment, I realised just how much he had become a part of my life, my dreams, my everything.

He was the first guy I had met who cared more about knowledge, literature, human connection—things that had depth. At twenty-four, he was almost four years older than me, but I could connect with him in a way I had never connected with any guy before. His frontal lobe must have been more developed or something.

And for whatever reason, he seemed as crazy about me as I was about him.

I don't know how it happened—I guess life is an accumulation of moments in that way—but we became inseparable. I didn't think too much about what that moment would look like when it was time for him to return home. Six months had never flown by so quickly as they had with him. At the same time, I didn't realise it was possible to fall in love so quickly and so hard, all in the same space of time.

My parents were beyond excited that I had finally met a boy at the ripe age of twenty. I think they were somewhat relieved that I was invested in something other than studying and writing. They did wonder how serious it was and what the plan was. It was a question I never quite knew how to answer. It very quickly became a giant question mark looming over our relationship. Yes, a *relationship*. Crazy stuff. Especially considering he wasn't here to stay. I had never given much thought to what a long-distance relationship would look like, let alone a relationship in general. I had never had a boyfriend before.

But despite the physical distance, we landed on a plan. Dylan would complete his internship in America, and then in a year or two, he would come back to Australia to live. Most Americans never want to leave their country, but Dylan didn't have any objections.

Stereotype broken.

I had no doubt that this was the man I was going to marry. I may have been young, but I have never been so sure about anything in my life. They say when you know, you know. And well, I knew.

It is safe to say that long-distance sucked. I was optimistic about it in the beginning, but four or five months in, it began to take its toll. Managing the time difference wasn't the obstacle; it was the small wins, the milestones no matter how big or small, that were spent apart.

I longed for him in a way where I began to question myself. I had always been independent, never relying on anybody to make me happy. It wasn't that I was relying on Dylan for my happiness—not at all. I had grown to enjoy what it meant to share your life with someone, to really let your guard down and let someone in. To be vulnerable. I learned more about myself with him than I could ever have imagined.

I became restless as that reality settled over me, often spending many evenings wide awake, wondering if maybe we had been crazy to do this to ourselves. Especially when the time apart began to override the time we had actually spent together.

And if that wasn't hard enough, what happened next added a deeper layer. Just weeks before Dylan's graduation, his parents were killed in a car accident.

My future in-laws, people I had never met.

There are no words to describe how excruciating that time was. I hated more than anything that I couldn't be there for him during the most pivotal time of his life. I almost became desperate, glued to my device, every device, checking up on him every ten seconds.

Grief has a way of doing unexpected things to people, and during this season, Dylan shut down completely. I wanted to get on a plane even though I had no idea how I would swing it financially, but he insisted that I stay put, no matter what I suggested. I was certain he was going to break up with me. It was as though overnight we became strangers, and there was nothing I could do about it.

It was two months we never got back, two months we never spoke about, all these years later. Even now, it was a time that stood untouched in conversation. Then one day, after very few responses from him, and not even fully knowing if we were still together or not, Dylan called me out of the blue. He had booked a one-way plane ticket to Australia. It was a slow road to healing, but with a lot of work, he reached a place where the pain became manageable.

Dylan proposed just ten months later.

With a miracle visa situation, he completed his internship at my parents' practice, and we married the month after I graduated. I landed a teaching position at a private school in Melbourne, working for barely a year before I gave birth to our beautiful daughter, Lila.

You could say it was all very unexpected; nothing transpired the way we had imagined it. But that's the thing about life: we often have very little control over its speed or the events that unfold.

Little did we know that we would learn that truth the hard way.

FOUR

Summer – January 2024
Lila

I THINK EVERY KID looks forward to summer. Actually, every human being. I get that not everyone gets the luxury of school holidays, but they do get Christmas and New Year's. Every family, of course, celebrates this differently. But in our household, we always jam as much as we can in those six weeks. Dad has never had an issue taking leave, aligning it with the time off Mum and I both get being at the same school.

Every year, on December 27th, we spend time at my cousin's holiday house at the beach in Sorrento. My mum's side of the family is big and, better yet, all of us are similar in age. Sure, us "kids" have to share a room to make us all fit, but it's hardly an issue as we get along so well. It's always ten days, never a day more, never a day less. Sometimes we might leave and come back on slightly different dates. But other than that, it's been our tradition for as long as I can remember. But that didn't happen for us this year. It's not as though my cousins were sick, the holiday house was double-booked, or torrential rain was forecasted. There was no excuse for us not to have gone. But according to Mum, there was. I might as well tell the story.

It went something like this:

"We thought we would take the caravan and go to the Grampians as a family."

Grampians? I mean, it was random. We were definitely a beach family, not a rock climbing one. Apparently, I was wrong. Somehow, somewhere down the line, I had missed Dad's apparent desire to climb a rock and abseil down one. As far as I was aware, he had a fear of heights. I pushed for my parents to invite my cousins. If we couldn't all spend it at the beach, I didn't understand why they couldn't all join us for this little adventure. Had my family had some sort of falling out that I didn't know about? It was the only thing that made sense. Actually, no, I take that back—it didn't make sense. We have never fought; I had never seen my parents fight with them before. Actually, I don't think I've ever seen them fight with anyone before.

So, as we went off to explore nature, the rest of the family continued to roll out our tradition at Sorrento. I spent most of the trip on my phone responding to messages and swiping through their photos at the beach, wishing I was part of them. I wouldn't have minded having a collection of cute photos for Ryan to see, either. I felt like I was finally getting somewhere with him. It was probably the first time I felt disconnected from my parents as frustration and maybe even jealousy of everyone's fun holiday got the better of me.

As we climbed the many rocky trails during the day, I was picturing myself playing volleyball on the sand. As we stopped to take photos of waterfalls, I dreamed I was riding the waves. As Dad abseiled down a cliff with an enthusiasm on par with a kid riding a bike without training wheels, I could barely celebrate his victory. I probably sound like a stubborn brat, I know. I didn't mean to have an attitude. I really didn't. I wanted to enjoy this "family time," as Mum would put it, even though the rest of our family was all together, happily building their tans as our pale skin stayed hidden by the mammoth-sized trees that seemed to block out every ounce of sunlight. If anyone was being exclusive, it was us.

By the time our last day came around, I was actually starting to have fun. I still don't understand what inspired the break of tradition this year, as I didn't feel like the experience brought us any closer for this change of heart to be justified. When I asked my parents if it would be bush or beach next year, they looked at each other and gave me this look that has only left me confused. But as it turns out, I'd have to wait till next year to find out where our family trip would be.

If Dad's sudden desire to abseil down some rocks wasn't weird enough, Mum had a sudden urge to start running too. I'd put it down to a mid-life crisis. I mean, surely that's what it was? I googled some of the symptoms, and it fits the description perfectly.

I would have joined them for a run today, but it was safe to say my body had pretty much had it after six intensive days of summer school, and I needed to rest. When I say, "summer school," I don't mean I'm some academic nerd, hungry to get ahead. I'm talking about a dance workshop type of summer school with guest teachers from across the state. It was a pretty sweet experience, I learned a lot, and probably sweated more. Already after a week, I feel stronger and more inspired than ever before. I don't want to become a professional or anything, but it was fun to be a gangster and have all the moves down. Each year, school puts on a production, and I basically lead the dance group each time. I don't say that to brag, but it's true. I liked getting my teaching skills on; who knew, maybe I'd be a teacher like Mum one day. But highly unlikely.

I wanted to be a journalist.

Anyway, today was a chill day at Ellie's house. We spent

most of the afternoon in her pool and her mum literally just dropped me home.

"Is anyone home, dear?" Ellie's mum asked as she pulled into the driveway.

I took my canvas bag from the back seat and opened the car door. "They should be or will be soon," I said, stepping out and feeling the heat hit the wet patches of my dress. "They've gone for a walk I think."

"Would you like me to wait?"

"No, it's ok Mrs. Waters, thanks. They'll be home any minute."

After waving goodbye, I took the spare key from the small zip compartment of my bag and unlocked the front door. It took about half a second to notice that the air conditioner was off.

Strange.

They would keep it on while they went for a run, or walk, or whatever. I guessed they weren't expecting me home this soon, but Ellie's family was expecting guests, so I kind of had to scoot. I took the remote from the wall to get the cool air circulating.

"Mum?"

No answer.

I stood in the passageway with only the sound of my dripping hair hitting the tiles. Now I had to figure out how I would fill my afternoon. I had watched every Netflix series and movie known to man, so that was checked off the list. That binging happened in the first two weeks of holidays.

After changing out of my wet clothes, I made a decision. I was going to make a collage board of all my favourite pictures over the year. And no, the Grampians wouldn't make the cut. I had come across some inspiration on *Pinterest* and thought it was a pretty neat idea. My room was overdue for a makeover anyway. This would be fun; it would kill some time and spark my creativity.

I sat down in the lounge room and took out my laptop. After sifting through about five hundred photos, just forty-nine made the cut. I flicked dad a quick message, asking if I could use the printer. No answer. It's not like I hadn't used it before, but I always liked to ask before I waltzed into his office. I liked to think I was a respectful kind of girl. Besides, dad's office was a bit of a mess, or an "organised mess," as he liked to call it. I guessed psychology was one of those professions with a ton of paperwork.

After another half-hour had passed without a response, I sent my photos to the printer. I was ready to get into it. I had no doubt that I would be cutting and arranging photos for the rest of the afternoon. I got my Spotify list cranking and jumped to my feet. Already I could hear the clunking sound of the printer warming itself up for what would be a pretty big print job. I just hoped there was enough toner in the machine. That was something I could never figure out how to replace.

The printer started spitting out photos and to my relief, all of the colour was intact. With thirty-odd pages of full-resolution photos to print, I suspected this would take a while. I took a seat on dad's black leather chair and curled my feet up underneath me. Gripping the edge of his varnished desk, I built up some momentum and let go, instantly making myself dizzy, like a kid on a merry-go-round. I got about four consecutive spins in before I lost control and face-planted into a nest of papers. How I got my entire body involved in this, I don't know.

Immediately, I could hear the tear of a few papers under my palm as I stabilised myself.

Crap.

With the printer still working away, I lifted my hand to uncover the damage. A few receipts and scribbled notes appeared from underneath it, but nothing with any fancy letterheads or stamped documents had been ripped. I slowly released a breath and neatened them back into the "organised mess" I had found them in. My eyes were drawn to a brighter document, a pamphlet maybe, one that was purple in colour. I pulled it from where it rested hidden behind a bunch of papers.

Pancreatic Cancer – What to expect

I unfolded my legs from under me and brought the pamphlet close to my face and continued reading.

This information sheet tells you what to expect during your treatment.

The heat of the room suddenly got too much. I found myself sweating as I straightened, feeling my back stick to the leather of the chair like double-sided tape.

1. Initial investigations and referral

Referral? I assumed this was a work thing. I guessed it was part of his job—to refer clients if he suspected they had cancer.

The sound of the printer clunking away seemed to get louder. I inhaled, not realising that I had stopped breathing. What was this all about? Dad was a psychologist, not a doctor. With my heart fumbling in my chest, I glanced over the headings further down the page.

2.Diagnosis and Staging, 3. Treatment 4. Living with cancer.

The tiny text in between was too overwhelming to process. I ran my hands over the other piles of paper, searching for anything similar in nature. That's when I spotted the second thing.

I picked up the envelope stamped with a logo I was familiar

with, the one with the heart and the little blue hand wrapped around...

Austin Hospital

"… Lila?"

I jumped, sending the envelope flying out of my hands.

"Gosh, dad, you scared me."

He reached for the envelope that had landed by his foot. He looked at it, then back at me.

"What are you up to?" His voice sounded strained, but his expression glowed with curiosity. He glanced at the printer at the exact moment it finished the job.

"Doing some printing. I texted you."

He looked down again at the envelope in his hands. "Sorry, sweetie, I haven't checked my phone."

I studied him. The picture didn't look right. He was in a pair of chino shorts and a polo top. On his feet were a pair of sandals.

"How was your run?" I asked, knowing full well that he couldn't have gone for one. Not in that outfit.

Before he had time to answer, Mum came to the door.

"Oh, here you are." She almost sounded relieved. She looked at me and tilted her head. "What are you up to?"

"How was your *walk*?" I asked, ignoring her question.

They both looked at each other and I could literally feel the tension. My face was tingly as I retrieved the photos from the printer, keeping my focus on them. I wasn't going to allow them any time to have a conversation with their eyes with my back to them. They were capable of that sort of thing.

Dad turned the envelope in his hands, looking all nervous.

Something wasn't right, and now my mouth felt what my face was feeling.

I knew my parents. I had grown to know their many expressions, and the look they were giving each other right now was foreign territory.

"We ended up going for a drive," Mum started, her voice small. "I'm sorry we weren't back before you got dropped off. I hope we didn't worry you."

I looked at dad. His eyes were on the floor. Mum was shifting uncomfortably side to side as she eyed the envelope that was dangling by dad's side.

"Should I be worried?" My voice was wobbly, but I couldn't help it. Something inside of me was screaming red. "What's this about?" I held up the purple pamphlet from the desk.

My parents looked at each other again, making some sort of communication with their eyes, and not with me.

"Dad?" I cleared my throat. "Do you have a sick client or…" I was losing control. "Is someone we know sick?"

"You shouldn't be going through your father's things," Mum started, her voice almost frantic.

"Mum." I held up my hand to her. "I'm asking dad."

"Lila…" he started, looking more uncomfortable than I had ever seen him. I stared at him. His eyebrows were twitching.

"What's going on?" I said with more force, more power behind my words. I stood to my feet and stretched out my hand, basically shoving the pamphlet in their faces. My bottom lip starting to tremble. "What is this about?"

Mum stepped forward and placed her hand on mine, lowering my arm down. "Why don't you come into the living room where it's more comfortable?"

She seriously looked like she was about to cry, and that wasn't like Mum. She was basically a warrior, always so inhumanly positive, never rattled by anything.

It didn't help that dad's eyes were diverted to anything and everything, other than at me. I didn't like where this was going. I didn't like her tone, and I certainly didn't like how neither of them could answer me directly.

That's when I snapped.

"No, I'm not moving anywhere until one of you tells me

what's going on!" I sounded like a brat, a toddler chucking a tantrum.

But I was scared.

"I have many sick clients, sweetheart," dad started, finally locking eyes with me. "But this isn't about them."

I waited for him to expand, but he didn't.

I cleared my throat, feeling a burning sensation take hold. "…Is it about you?"

Dad's eyes tethered, and in that moment, I knew.

"Yes, it is. I'm not in good health at the moment, baby girl."

That was it. I burst into tears.

Dad rushed to my side and wrapped his arms around me, holding me far less tightly than he usually would whenever I was in pain.

Where had my strong dad gone?

"Your father is going to be ok, darlin," Mum said, stroking my hair the way she did when I was about four.

I didn't believe her.

"Pancreatic cancer is really serious," I managed between sobs. "But you'll get better right?" I looked at dad with pleading eyes. "Right, dad? You'll fight this thing, won't you?"

"Yes, honey, he will."

I shot Mum a look, not really knowing why I had suddenly become so mad at her.

"I'm asking dad!"

She pursed her lips together and dropped her eyes to the floor.

"I will always fight, baby girl." He released his grip and smiled, but it didn't reach his eyes. "I'm sorry we didn't… I'm sorry I didn't tell you earlier. Your mum and I haven't wanted to worry you, not until we became more informed of the… well… until we knew what we're looking at."

"You haven't been out running just now, have you?"

Dad's jaw clenched. "No."

"You've been at doctor's appointments this whole time? What about our boycotting the beach this summer? Was that somehow related to this?"

Mum looked up. "Sweetheart, you have to understand…"

"What, Mum? I have to *understand* that you've been lying to me?" Something had gone off inside of me and I couldn't stop. "You've both hidden this gigantic secret from me, and you want me to *understand?* For how long?"

Dad let out a defeated sigh. Hot tears spilled down my face as I nestled into dad's chest, feeling them soak into his top. Mum stopped playing with my hair.

Everything went way too quiet.

"I was diagnosed a couple of weeks before Christmas." His voice came small, beaten,

"What does that mean?" I buried my face harder, deeper into his chest. "I don't know what that means."

"It means that we caught it early enough to look at what treatment I need to help manage this, sweetie."

It should have given me hope, but it didn't. There was something about dad's answer that derailed me.

I lifted my head back up, feeling the air conditioner finally hitting my flushed face like a slab of ice. "To help manage, or to get better?" I swallowed but my entire throat felt stuck. "You'll get better, right?"

We stared at each other for a while, all three of us. My heart was racing at an uncontrollable speed, but I was determined not to miss a second, not wanting to miss a word of what he was about to say.

I must have held my breath, because I felt like I was going to pass out as I waited. After what felt like an eternity, with glassy eyes, he finally opened his mouth.

"My days are numbered, kiddo."

FIVE

Autumn 2024
Maddie

NOTHING ABOUT THE last couple of months had been normal. I had taken time off work to spend what doctors had told us would be Dylan's final weeks in his battle with cancer. It was excruciating to watch as it attacked his body a little more each day.

Now that we knew more, the signs had been there all along. From his suppressed appetite to the chest pains that led to his fall while running with Lila—these had only been the beginning. Initially, the doctors prescribed him gastric reflux tablets, thinking that was the solution. Next, we were told Dylan's potassium levels were low, hence the cramps, so he was prescribed iron tablets. But the pain under his right ribs and back only continued to grow. It got to the point where he could barely sleep lying down and had to move into the spare room at night.

That was when it started to hit home.

He wanted to be close to me, to hold me tight as we lay in bed at night. Of course, I wanted that too, but it came at a cost.

I hated knowing that I was hurting him with every touch, yet the physical distance as we slept separately only hurt us more.

But the news only got worse.

Blood tests showed high liver enzymes, leading to an urgent ultrasound and bronchoscopy. Tumours began to present themselves on Dylan's liver, jaundice plaguing his appearance as his skin yellowed. Watching this silent killer attack my husband's body from inside and out was devastating. It was one thing to know he had cancer of the pancreas, but being told by countless doctors that there were no surgical options was devastating.

Although his body was deteriorating, his spirit was very much alive. He was nothing short of a fighter, striving to live each day as normally as possible. He was determined to work from home, continuing sessions with his loyal clients via Zoom when he could. By this stage, everyone knew about his cancer. I imagined the news would only add to his clients' psychological stress, knowing that the ongoing service they were investing in had an expiration date.

We were told he had four months. That was it.

There was nothing we could do other than simply wait. During the waiting, Dylan was determined to spend as much of it at home as possible. I felt the need to keep him preoccupied, engaged in anything and everything to make this time bearable for not just him, but for us as a family. My parents called me out on it, telling me I was acting in denial as though everything was okay. Maybe I did behave as though everything was rosy. I didn't want to talk about the obvious truth, the reality we were facing. Why would I want to spend these last few months consumed by what was to come? How would that help anyone?

The thought alone made my stomach curl. I wasn't acting out of denial. I was well aware that in a matter of time, our lives would be changed forever. But I was determined not to live as though my husband was gone until we had to. Why would I want to ruin the present, the precious time we had left, by focusing our attention on what we couldn't control? I had to be strong for Dylan. I had to be strong for our daughter, whose spirit was already broken.

Ever since Lila learned the news of Dylan's diagnosis, she had shut down completely. It was as though we had suffered a loss ahead of time. Our precious daughter who was usually bursting with life, became distant, withdrawn, and uncommunicative. The beginning of the year had been rough. For someone who loved to learn and socialise, Lila could barely get out of bed.

"Come on, sweetheart, you'll be late for school," I would say as I found her each morning, her head fully submerged under the covers.

"I don't feel well," she would groan.

It was the same excuse every day, just worded differently each time. I didn't feel well either. In fact, I felt sick to my stomach, but I couldn't voice that.

"You'll feel better once you eat something and get some sunshine," I said this time. "It's beautiful out there." I pulled back the duvet, exposing her to what was truly a beautiful day. "Come on, up you get."

Lila didn't move but gripped her pillow like a child, seconds away from a meltdown.

"I really don't want to go to school, Mum," she said, her voice small and deflated.

I sat on the edge of the bed and smoothed her hair back. I drew a breath. "I know, Lila, I get it, I do. But you'll feel so much better staying busy than being in your head."

We hadn't talked much about Dylan's cancer, but it was obvious that the change we were seeing in Lila was her way of processing, or lack thereof.

It wasn't that I was avoiding a difficult conversation. We

had tried to sit her down more times than I could count. But ever since that day we found her in the office where she had learned the truth, she had been dismissive of every attempt. I could understand her anger, especially the way she had found out, stumbling across that pamphlet before we had the chance to tell her. We had a plan, but we also wanted to have all the answers before we dropped such a catastrophic bomb.

Dylan had wanted to tell her earlier. The time he had fallen while running with Lila was one of those times. It had left her confused, and it killed him to hide such a secret. It killed me too, more than I probably showed, but I was adamant for Lila to have a summer that was as close to normal as possible.

Life had to go on. There was no denying that. And today, that started with getting my daughter to school. We were just weeks away from launching our new high school facility. The nine million dollar grant from the government had expanded our facilities, bringing us a new gymnasium, a two-story complex with open-spaced classrooms, and a recording studio. It really was a milestone for the college, so much so that they wanted to create an opportunity to celebrate it. Showcases of dance, singing, and drama were some of the items planned to take place between the speeches.

Lila, being the head of the middle school dance team, was meant to lead her group for the event. I use the word loosely because she hadn't shown up for the past couple of rehearsals. Other girls had volunteered to take over, but according to Ms. Maxwell, the dance coach, the group wasn't responding well to the unexpected change. The biggest change being Lila's announcement that she wouldn't take part in it, that she was opting out of the whole thing.

Lila was a born leader. It was something she was naturally gifted at. She was warm and kind, with an ability to make people feel loved and valued. Sure, I'm her mother and may be a bit biased, but she really is a lot like her father. Not only did they share similar qualities, but she was also the spitting image of him. And really, I couldn't be prouder. But everything that made my daughter who she was, was lost. I wouldn't let Lila give up on one thing that I knew gave her so much joy.

"Come on, sweetie, there are people relying on you, people who want to see you." I had no idea if it was the right thing to say, but she pulled herself up and sat upright in her bed.

"They don't need me, Mum. No one cares if I show up or not. Life goes on," she stated smugly.

My body clenched. Yes, life had to go on, but she was acting like he was already gone. Why did we have to grieve prematurely?

I combed her long brown hair down her back with my fingers. She didn't seem to resist my touch, but her eyes glared at me. She was waiting for me to respond, waiting for me to convince her to get up and get going.

"You're absolutely right," I said, standing up. "Life does go on, and yours is out there waiting for you." I opened the blinds, filling the room with light. "But first, I made your favourite Nutella crepes for breakfast." I was pulling out all the stops.

And today, it worked.

SIX

I DIDN'T SHOW IT, but I was kind of excited. I loved performing, even though it was a little weird that my classmates and teachers would be watching me during school hours. I mean, I'd done a ton of school musicals before, but this was different. Maybe because this time, not every kid was involved. Instead, it was an isolated performance where the spotlight would be purely on eleven girls waving their arms and legs about as the rest of the school sat in the audience in their school uniforms. Okay, so maybe it was more than that.

Ryan would be there.

He had never seen me dance, but I could tell he was looking forward to it. We had gotten closer over the summer, even if it was mainly through texting. I hadn't had the courage to ask my parents to drive me anywhere as there was no way I was going to tell them that I was crushing on the boy whose mum was the receptionist at Dad's psychology clinic. Yep, Ryan's mum worked with Dad.

I knew secretly they would be pleased that if it was any guy, it was Ryan. He came from a good family and would make an excellent choice for a first boyfriend. We hadn't talked about being in a relationship as such, but I could tell it was coming. I knew it was only a matter of time until he asked. I had hoped that maybe he would approach me more at school, but I think he got nervous every time he saw me. He had this thing where he pretended to be preoccupied with something every time we got within two feet of each other. I'd caught him looking at me, shooting a knee-buckling smile my way every now and then. But I guessed he was just as shy as I was. I don't think I'm really that shy at all, but I was using it as an excuse lately because I was just so damn sad.

I'd hardly wanted to talk to anyone.

I swallowed hard, feeling the excitement replace with a different feeling—one of overwhelming sadness. Mum was right; I needed to be here. I needed to keep my mind busy, otherwise I would dissolve in tears. I hadn't talked about it with Ryan, but I suspected he knew, seeing as his mum, Sarah, worked with Dad and everything. Maybe he didn't want to upset me, and I was glad. I would rather keep our little bubble going even if it meant we knew very little about each other. Truth was, I would be mortified if I broke down in front of him; he was that perfect. No joke, he really was.

And the text I just received from him only proved that more.

Hey Lila girl. Sorry I didn't get the chance to wish u good luck up there 2nite. You'll smash it. Just getting comfy now & looking forward to seeing u do ur thing.

Lila girl.
Maybe he already saw me as his girl.

A shot of adrenaline mixed with nerves shot up my spine. Never mind the fact that he had plenty of opportunities to wish me luck—I must have passed him about ten times at school today. That wasn't the point. The point was that Ryan Hensley was thinking of me and looking forward to seeing me dance.

I inhaled and extended my winged eyeliner so that my eyes popped just that little bit more.

This was it. We had one shot to get this right, and to be honest, I wasn't feeling that confident. I had missed a few practices, but I had always been quick to pick up choreography, which was a relief, seeing as Ellie and Maci had made a few changes in my absence.

"Is that a smile I see, Lil?" Maci dumped her makeup bag next to mine and began applying foundation to her face.

I placed the lid on the liquid liner and closed my mouth, feeling it deflate from its widened position. I was careful not to make a mess with my makeup as I took out my mascara. We were the first-ever students to use the new bathroom facilities. Everything was white, clean, and pristine.

"Maybe," I said, not denying it. I didn't need to cover anything up, did I? She knew I was crushing hard over Ryan. But I was almost certain that I wasn't the only one—he was, hands down, the most gorgeous-looking year nine boy in the school.

"He's here," she said, his name not needing to be mentioned. "Pretty close to the front too."

Just like that, my smile returned. "Yeah, he just texted. Ugh, I'm kinda nervous he'll be watching."

Maci flicked her long chestnut brown hair over her tanned shoulder and leaned in closer to the mirror as she took out her makeup brush to powder her perfect face. Ryan was easily the most handsome boy in school. And Maci would have to be the prettiest girl. Sometimes I caught myself watching her. Especially moments like these where she looked like a doll and a model, all in one.

"He'll love it. You're the best dancer at our school, Lil. Let's be honest, you'll blow him away."

I muffed a laugh under my breath. "I doubt it."

I secretly hoped she was right.

"It's obvious he's in love with you," she said, sounding different.

My eyes landed on her in the mirror. I couldn't help but notice the way she pursed her lips together as she applied more hurried strokes on her face than before. Was that jealousy I was detecting? If anyone should be jealous of anyone, it should be me, of her. Was it possible that she liked Ryan too?

I dismissed the thought.

"Anyway…" She met my eyes in our reflection and placed down her brush. "Let's try and get everyone together in the next ten minutes or so, yeah? I'd like to run over it at least once before we go on."

I nodded and picked up my phone to respond to Ryan. At the same time, a text came through from Mum saying that they were leaving home. They had reserved seats in the second row. Normally, I would write back without thinking, but these days were different. I clicked out of the message and began forming my reply to Ryan instead.

I wasn't mad at my parents. I just didn't know how I felt towards them for the most part. I don't think I trusted them the way I used to after lying to me for weeks, if not months.

Who really knows if it was even longer than that.

I wish they could see that I wasn't a kid anymore. I wanted to be treated like an adult or at least be given the opportunity to process my emotions in my own way. But instead, I had been put on the spot; placed in a situation where I had to process Dad's cancer in the heat of the moment, in the space of like three seconds that awful day when they had had months. Or weeks. Or whatever.

Either way, it wasn't fair.

Like clockwork, Maci called our group together to warm up and get a practice in. I tried to ignore the niggly feeling that she was acting like the leader of the group when my position never changed. Sure, I had missed a few rehearsals, but that didn't mean our roles had changed.

I watched as she took the reins with Ellie, hyping the girls up as though we were some kind of cheerleaders about to step into a full stadium. It was just way over the top, but I bit my lip and took it on. What was ten minutes in the grand scheme of things?

After tonight, this whole thing would be done and dusted anyway.

The audience was full. It was hard to predict exactly how many people had shown up for the opening, but if I had to guess, I would say there were close to seven or eight hundred. Somehow, being on the same level as the audience and not on stage made the whole performing thing more exposing. We had rehearsed in the space before, but I didn't realise the first row would literally be inches from my face.

As we made our way onto the stage, I did a quick scan of the audience. My heart quickened at the thought that Ryan would be watching my every move. I felt good about our costume choice in the end. We had ended up going with high-waisted black leggings and a pale blue top. Mine was more figure-hugging than I would have liked, but it didn't reveal my stomach. Thankfully. That would have been way awkward with parents watching.

As I took my position, our eyes locked. A swarm of butterflies unleashed inside my belly and for a moment, I was floating. In the past, one of us would break contact right about now, but this time, he kept his eyes firmly on mine with a massive grin on his face. I could have died. When the music started, I forgot everything else and got lost in the moment as the music and movement raided my body. Dance always had the ability to do that to me, cute guy or not.

As I took my final pose, we found each other's eyes again.

Like many others in his row, he had stood to his feet with applause. I shifted focus to try and spot my parents, but I couldn't see them anywhere. Second row, didn't Mum say they were?

I shifted my eyes across each person from left to right, but they weren't there. The lights dimmed, and we cleared the podium. An unpleasant feeling began to take root, and just like that, an overwhelming sensation suddenly came over me. I felt vulnerable, like a little girl who lost her mummy in a grocery store.

The next thing I knew, Ms. Maxwell gently took my arm and led me off stage. Her stricken face gave me little to work with as she walked me away from the girls, away from everyone.

"I don't want to alarm you, Lila, but I've just received some news."

No.

I wasn't ready.

My eyes welled with tears, and I felt like I was going to vomit. "What news? What's going on?" At least, that's what I think I said. I don't remember hearing the words come from my mouth, but she kept talking, so I assumed they had made their way out.

"Your mum just called. She's at the hospital. Your dad collapsed and…"

I have no idea what she said after that. I don't remember hearing the rest. All I remember was collapsing to the ground as a flood of people rushed over to console me. But there was nothing anyone could do to make it okay.

Not now.

Not ever.

SEVEN

Present Day
Maddie

THE FINAL BELL rang, and as usual, I made my rounds through the campus before heading back to my desk, where a pile of papers awaited me. I could have gone straight to the common room, knowing my daughter would be there like always after school, but I had to be discreet. My movements had to appear intentional, like the clockwork routine I followed every day at 3:25 p.m. It might be pessimistic of me, but I was waiting for the day when she wouldn't be there at 4:15 p.m., waiting for me to finish up.

She had become unpredictable.

This time, I approached from a different angle, using a different entrance that gave me a new view into the room. From this vantage point, her back would be to me and she wouldn't likely see me. She always sat at the same table in the far-right corner. It's not like I was avoiding my daughter; in fact, I was desperate to connect with her. But she was beginning to notice my check-ups, and I didn't want her to feel spied on and find a new hangout place without my knowing. I couldn't handle that.

All the changes had already become too much.

I worked my way back to my office and took a seat, feeling the weight of the week—or maybe just life—hit me like a ton of bricks. I took a steady breath in, wondering if there would come a day when things would get easier, when I would feel lighter. It had been almost four months now, and the gaping hole in my chest was just as vast. It was a hole flooded with many emotions, including an all-consuming concern for my daughter, who no longer spoke to me. Or to anyone, for that matter.

I opened my laptop to find two emails that confirmed I wasn't the only one feeling this way.

Dear Madelaine,

I hope this email finds you well. I was wondering if you have time for a quick word after school. Unfortunately, Lila refused to do her oral presentation for a group assignment today and as a result, ruffled a few feathers among the members of her group. I'm concerned about her. Happy to come to you if you have a spare few minutes to talk.

This particular email was from Lila's Geography teacher, Alicia. Somehow, I knew exactly what oral presentation she was talking about. I shouldn't have been surprised, but I was. My daughter wasn't perfect, but she had a perfect record of staying on top of things. She had been that way since kindergarten. Lila was a studious student—if there was such a thing. She was more studious than I had ever been, and I had always been basically attached to my books.

I sank a little deeper in my chair, trying to think this through. Weren't Maci and Ellie in her group? That's where Lila had been the other night, hadn't she? Practicing for their presentation. At least, that's what I thought I had read in her text message. But it didn't stop there. The second email was from the school welfare officer, also about my daughter.

This one was more formal. The tone of the email made me look like a naive parent who was doing little to support her daughter. I finished reading it, feeling a surge of tears build in my throat before landing heavily at the back of my eyes. Counselling. It was official; we had gotten to the stage where my fifteen-year-old daughter was advised to see a professional on a regular basis.

I combed my fingers through my hair and let out a sigh. I wouldn't cry. Instead, I would set up an appointment and hope there wouldn't be a fight to get her to go. I would book her in at my parents' clinic. It was a familiar environment, and hopefully one where she would feel safe, even if I couldn't for the life of me remember the last time I had set foot in there. Nine months? Maybe longer.

Gone were the days when the clinic had been my second home. I used to be in and out multiple times a day, running errands for my husband or simply popping in for a sneaky kiss when I could snag one. We always lived like it was our honeymoon days.

I closed my laptop, ignoring all other emails awaiting my reply. I inhaled sharply, feeling somewhat short of breath. Gosh, I missed him so much. The truth was, life was evidently falling apart without him. Dylan had been our refuge, our rock, the glue that held us together. Now that he was gone, everything seemed to unravel in a downhill spiral that only became more knotted with time.

Thankfully, we hadn't navigated this nightmare alone. Our friends and family had been amazing and continued to be. I don't think I cooked a single meal for about three months after his passing. We hadn't had an appetite to enjoy most of it, but that was beside the point. We were taken care of as my focus poured onto Lila.

And was still very much 100% on Lila.

A good day meant we could hold eye contact for at least five seconds. On a really good day, I might coax a single sentence from her during my efforts at small talk. Unfortunately, that's where things had ended up. It was tough to face the fact that the once well-run ship of our relationship had run aground and fallen apart.

I peered at my watch, knowing I needed to catch Alicia before she packed up for the day. I should have known better that this behaviour would transfer into the classroom. That it wasn't bound by the four walls of our home. I had trusted what I had always known about my daughter. I had taken Lila's word as truth for what had clearly been a series of excuses.

I took out my cell and dialled Alicia's number.

EIGHT

Lila

WITH MY LOCKER open wide enough to shield my face, I peered through the crack where the hinges met the door. I had to keep a firm eye on her. It wasn't even like she was hiding it anymore—the way she stepped in sync beside him, all giddy. I mean, it was obvious. I pretended to gather my books just in case I got accused of spying. I would act dumb as the horrible scene unfolded in front of me. Maybe I shouldn't even bother trying so hard to be subtle. If someone caught me, I don't see how it would further taint my already compromised reputation. And it hadn't taken long to get there.

These days, kids didn't know whether to laugh at me or keep their distance. In most cases, people just left me alone. No one knew what to do with me, and honestly, I didn't really blame them. Not even I knew what to do with me. But more importantly, I didn't know what to do about what I was seeing. She was meant to be my best friend.

They were just lingering there against the wall, inches apart, without a care in the world. It was as though they were completely unaware of their surroundings. I could vomit. Maci flirtatiously brushed the wall with her hip as Ryan propped a foot up behind him in a try-hard casual way. Part of me wanted to slam my locker door shut and break up this moment they shouldn't even be having.

How dare they.

I collected my books for real this time as I contemplated the idea. But then what? What was my plan after that? I would just place myself in a situation where I would storm off with them looking back, whispering after me. It was pointless. I just had to endure it.

It hadn't always been this way, but everything these days had a way of changing quickly. It felt like forever ago when I was the one in Maci's position. Okay, so, I was never pressed up against a wall like that—that's just suffocating. Smothering. *Possessive.* But I was likeable—and more importantly, liked by Ryan. He liked me, and I liked him. A lot. Maybe that's why this was such a bitter pill to swallow. Or more so, one of betrayal.

Maci was very aware of my feelings for Ryan—she had actually encouraged it. Now when I think about it, everything I ever shared about him had fed her own agenda. She had been a good friend. Used to be a good friend. She was there for me when Dad died, and I had pushed her away through all of it. For months, she sent me morning messages and phone calls, checking in on me. She had been consistent, and her efforts had been solid. I couldn't really blame her; the distance had been entirely my fault. She would write me essays filled with encouraging words and invite me out to even the smallest things as she reassured me that she would always be there. And I ignored all of it. Not in a mean way—I was just in a bad way. It wasn't personal. I didn't want to talk about it with her or with anyone. I don't fully know why. Maybe because the moment I did, my father's death would be stamped as processed, and I would be expected to put it behind me.

I wasn't ready to do that.

How could I possibly think of moving on when he was everything to me? My dad was worth more than that, and I wasn't about to disrespect him. I refuse for him to become nothing short of a memory. Not when he was living inside of me, and I planned to keep it that way. I think about it all the time—the way I pushed Maci away. By doing so, I had pushed her into the arms of Ryan. As far as I was concerned, she could have him. His emotional intelligence was on par with a five-year-old. When everything went down with my dad, he basically didn't know what to do.

He didn't have the capacity.

I might have felt like a shell of a person, but he actually was one. He didn't have depth. Other than a couple of messages back and forth, he had left me alone. I had taken a month off school, and not once did he call me. Not once did he turn up at my doorstep to add to the collection of flowers or food baskets that everyone else who cared had left for us. Then one day, he stopped texting altogether. He ghosted me. Honestly, they could have each other. I wouldn't consider Maci a friend anymore. She barely met the bare minimum criteria.

It's not like we've had a big fight or anything. There hadn't really been anything specific at all. Some people grow apart, and even though I thought that couldn't happen to us, in reality, it had. The geography presentation we were about to make was our last crack. And the chances of pulling it off were unlikely, seeing as we had only gotten together once over the past three weeks to rehearse it. Maybe the two of them had gotten together on their own. I'm sure of it, seeing they were detailed people like me. I wish I cared—I just didn't anymore. The bell rang, indicating that fifth period was about to start.

You've got to be kidding me.

Maci and Ryan still hadn't moved from their position against the wall, but I had no choice but to shut my locker. It was like clockwork, the way it happened. It had to be intentional—how Ryan's lips brushed hers the second I was moving in their direction. I stood still in my tracks, more than likely becoming an annoyance to those wanting to get to their destination. A few annoyed comments came from behind me as I stood in the middle of the hallway, but I didn't care. I could feel my face grow hot as I stared on, frozen like a deer in headlights. That's when Maci saw me.

"Lila…" She looked as though she had been slapped. I hoped she felt awful because this honestly was a slap in the face. Ryan looked down awkwardly and tugged on her arm as if to signal for her not to worry about it. But for whatever reason, she broke contact and came after me. I increased my pace, not caring what I looked like as hot tears began to splash down my face. It shouldn't have affected me so much; this had been coming from a mile away.

"Lila," she said again, brushing my sleeve. I didn't look at her—I couldn't. I lowered my head and reached for the door. I had to get inside, take a seat, something. But the door was locked, the way it always was without a teacher present. I gripped my books tighter, not knowing where to look.

"I'm sorry, we didn't mean to…"

"Didn't mean to what? Get with the guy I liked or parade it in my face?" I couldn't help myself. It just came out. It was the most words that had come out of my mouth in months. By the look on Maci's face, she was just as surprised.

"No, I… Let me explain." I had clearly put her on the spot. By now a few more students had joined us, including Ellie, who was basically her wingman these days.

"Hey, Lila," Ellie's voice came more high-pitched than normal.

"Hi," I mumbled, shifting my focus off Maci's red face. Ellie's eyes bounced between us.

"Everything all good?"

I pursed my lips together to hold back the many words caged behind my tongue. What a stupid question. Of course, everything wasn't "all good." As if she didn't know how this whole thing with Ryan was hurting me. Ellie and Maci looked at each other, not even attempting to hide the silent exchange between them.

I felt sick.

These girls used to be my best friends, and now they were treating me like I was nothing. Like a complete loser. Maybe they were right. Maci whispered a few words and dashed down the hallway, probably to get her books. I hoped she showed up late. That should teach her not to…

"We've asked if we can go first today. You know, get the presentation out of the way." Ellie tossed her hair over her shoulder and breathed in sharply. "Thoughts?"

They had asked already? Without me? I shouldn't be surprised.

I nodded, then realised I hadn't even voiced a word to her yet. "Sure," I said with more confidence than I felt. I wasn't prepared. Not at all. Probably the first time ever. The thought of that alone made me want to cry. I had no doubt that they had memorised their parts, having rehearsed to a tee.

"Cool." With her spare hand, she formed a thumbs up. I stared at her. Did she really just do that? I could tell that she knew she had hurt me. We had always joked about the "thumbs up" emoji in the past, being the most passive-aggressive gesture ever. It was something we swore we would never use on each other. Until now, apparently.

"I hope you know what you're doing. It isn't exactly fair that you haven't shared the load."

No way was I going to let that slide.

"What do you mean? We're speaking on three slides each. That was the plan." I was mad. I may not have practiced with them, but I knew my part. Sure, I didn't know it by heart, but I could improvise well.

"See, that's where you have missed so much," she started with a matter-of-fact tone. "We decided to do more and complete the extended response. To, you know, strengthen our presentation. I know personally I could do with some bonus marks on this one."

We?

"Anyway, Maci agrees with me. So that's the plan." She shot me a sheepish smile. "Just sayin'."

My head started spinning. How was this not communicated to me? Were they trying to set me up to fail? The extended response had a whole additional section to it. What was I supposed to do?

In that moment, our Geography teacher, Mrs. Daigle, arrived and inserted her keys into the classroom door.

"Alright everyone, please come in quietly and take a seat." The door spewed open, and everyone quickly filled the room. Ellie powered ahead to the back of the room and placed one of her books on the space that was free next to her, the way we always did to reserve seats for each other. Although this time, she only reserved two. For her and Maci.

That was when something inside of me snapped.

NINE

Maddie

THERE WAS BEAUTY in having parents who owned a psychology clinic. It meant I could make an appointment whenever I wanted. Not that I had tested that theory—this was technically the first appointment I had actually gone ahead and made. The downside was that although confidentiality was a thing, the business was a family one. Everyone knew everyone—how confidential could that really be?

The clinic hadn't changed much. Staff retention was strong, as was the interior design. When I saw the name *Caleb Peters* pop up on the online booking system, I had to scratch my head. *Peters.* It wasn't a surname I recognised, but I hadn't been in for months. It's not like I was updated every time someone new was hired. I hadn't even considered that someone would have had to step into Dylan's position. It made sense, especially when he had so many faithful clients needing expert opinions they probably wouldn't find elsewhere. He was that good. He had won awards for his practice, expertise, and professionalism. But I wouldn't allow myself to dwell on that—it just made me too sad. The clinic would never be the same again, and neither would we.

I had to change my thinking, take another perspective. Whoever this Caleb Peters was, it wouldn't take long to find out. We only had to give him a go. This could actually be a good thing. I don't know how well Lila would have opened up to someone who knew her from as early as the days when I would bring her in as a newborn. A warmth spread through my chest as I reminisced. My daughter was loved deeply. The clinic had become her second home. She spent much of her early years there, sitting in her daddy's office, working on her homework after school. Not because she had to, but because she wanted to. She was daddy's little girl, and everyone wanted her around. Her smile lit up the faces of everyone she met. Her sweet mannerisms and discerning mind captured the hearts of those who worked there. Her handwritten cards and pictures must have ended up on the magnets of multiple fridges. "What an angel she is. You must be so proud of her," people would say. And it was true.

I might be biased, but it was true. She was.

A wave of nausea washed over me. It was like playing back a movie; one where you are familiar with the characters but can't fully relate to them as they are fictional. But this flashback was anything but fictional. This was my daughter, and I was determined to see that spark again.

I clicked on Caleb Peters' name and scrolled through his availability over the weekend. I had formed somewhat of a plan. We would do brunch together, and I would take her to her appointment myself. The good thing about weekends was that only a handful of staff would be rostered on, so we could avoid a lot of the small talk and empathetic looks sent our way. Without diving too deep into Caleb's profile to learn his credentials or even what he looked like, I went ahead and booked the appointment. I felt somewhat lighter after taking that step. That was what our life focused on these days: one small step at a time.

That was, until I changed tabs. As I stared at the screen, the whole "small step" thing suddenly felt less comforting. I curled my legs up in my chair and felt my weight slump down into it. My eyes prickled with tears as the hundreds of pages of words hit me like a tsunami.

I had to do this. I had to find a way to get this thing published. As I closed my eyes, I could almost hear Dylan reminding me of the same thing. He had been encouraging me to get this thing completed for years, no matter how much I doubted myself. And now he would never see my dream come true.

I opened a blank word document and typed "Book Proposal" at the top of the page. The truth was, I knew what to do. I had been researching what the "perfect pitch" looked like for over a decade. We both had. It was time I honoured my dream and put this thing together. My fingers began to type as my letter of intention poured out of me. My tone had to be confident, convincing—but not desperate. If my opening statement didn't have an impact, then the rest simply wouldn't be read. That's how the game was played. Ruthless.

After two hours of plugging away at it, I pressed my back against the chair and felt something I hadn't felt for a long time: a sense of accomplishment. It would need many rounds of editing, no doubt. But I had done it. After all this time, I had done it. In that moment of victory, the front door slammed.

"Lila?"

Silence.

I glanced towards the study door, hoping to hear more clearly. Gone were the days when my daughter would willingly find me at all hours, bursting with the details of her day even after our drive home. I would fix her a banana smoothie— almond milk, cacao, and extra honey—and we would sit on the patio, sipping our drinks—Lila with her smoothie, me with my extra hot skinny latte. Now, I can't remember the last time

I bought a banana. I had never been a fan of the fruit. Lila's love for it made up for my lack of it. That was another thing that deeply concerned me. Anything that resonated with the life we had before our hearts were ripped apart had been left behind. I may have given up on the banana smoothie idea, but I wouldn't give up on my daughter. No matter how distant she had become.

I rose to my feet and followed the hallway until I reached her room. Her door was open wide enough to glimpse inside. With her back turned towards me, she lay on her side, propped up by an elbow, her fingers moving furiously across her phone screen.

"Good walk?"

I had only assumed she had gone on one by the activewear she was wearing. This particular outfit highlighted just how stick-thin my daughter was getting. She had always had a smaller frame—maybe it was the angle that made her already narrow waist look like her stomach was sucked into her spine. My heart dropped at the sight, silently praying she was eating throughout the day. Her fingers stopped moving, but she didn't look up. With her back still facing me, she shrugged.

I nodded in response, already accepting defeat. Today wasn't going to be different than any other day. Maybe my daughter found the small talk just as painful. Every attempt at conversation only confirmed the massive step back we had taken in our relationship, which had once been filled with more words than the dictionary itself.

"I've made an appointment at the clinic," I started, not knowing how this would land.

With her head still down, I could almost hear her hold her breath.

"Caleb Peters is his name," I continued. "He must be new on staff."

"Do I have to go?" Her voice was monotone as she looked at me. Empty. Her eyes were empty.

"I'll drive you there," I suggested, as though offering to drive answered everything.

She didn't budge.

"I would like you to go," I added, making it clear she didn't really have a choice.

The look in her eyes transitioned to a pained expression. "I'm not a psycho, Mum."

"Oh honey..." I opened the door wider and took a seat on the edge of her bed. "Of course you're not. No one is calling you a psycho."

Was this her preconceived idea about the profession all along?

She sat up, keeping her body a safe distance from mine. I glanced at her phone as she fiddled with the plastic cover. The screen was illuminated, and I took a sneaky peek. The thread of lengthy messages I saw could be a good thing—or not. There were a lot of words on that screen.

After a long moment, she spoke. "Everyone hates me. So, I must be a psycho."

"What do you mean everyone hates you?"

"Mum, stop," she said, yanking her head away from my hand in her hair. I hadn't even noticed I was stroking it.

"Sorry." I brought my hands in close. "What do you mean everyone hates you?"

"They just do," she mumbled under her breath.

"I'm sure that's not the case, sweetie..."

"See?" She scrambled off the mattress and, with force, threw her phone somewhere among the pillows at the head of her bed. "You have no idea. You just don't get it, Mum."

"I want to. Help me understand," I said, ignoring the fact that I had never had an argument with my daughter before—if this was what this was. All I knew was that what I was seeing was completely foreign to me.

"It's too late." Tears streamed down her face as she erratically tossed the pillows aside in search of her phone with alarming possessiveness.

With her back turned, I gently reached for her arm. She shook it off like I was some kind of wasp.

"It's never too late, Lila. There's nothing you could do or say that would make me think otherwise."

After finally retrieving her phone from the mountain of pillows, she turned to face me. Her mascara had bled out. There was a look in her eye—a haunting look I had never seen before. She took a shaky breath in and narrowed her eyes. What she said next confirmed that I had made the right choice.

"I wish I had died with Dad."

TEN

Lila

ERE IT GOES. My first-ever counseling session. I stared blankly at my phone, scrolling through meaningless apps, pretending to be engrossed. I wasn't allowed social media. Not until I'm sixteen. It is so lame.

The hum of the car engine was the only sound between us. Silence had become our new normal. She'd run out of words. So had I. Now, all we had was this unbearable quiet, stretching between us like a canyon we were too afraid to cross.

Out of the corner of my eye, I could see the expression on my Mum's face. Her jaw was clenched as though she was physically in pain, and her hands were stiff on the steering wheel. She was staring ahead like a zombie. I returned my focus to my phone. I felt like I was bleeding from the inside, so hollow. Was internal bleeding even possible when it came to emotion?

I shouldn't have said what I said. It was a little dramatic of me. I didn't want to die. Well, at least I didn't think I did. I just wanted the circle of pain to stop running laps in moments like these, highlighting the strangers we had become.

We pulled into the all-too-familiar parking lot, and I felt like I was going to be sick. I had only good memories of this place. But that was about to change, wasn't it? Why would Mum take that away from me? We could have gone anywhere else.

Thankfully, there weren't many cars around. I knew what Ryan's Mum's car looked like, and I couldn't see it here. I don't think I would have had the guts to walk in if she had been working. Not that I had the energy to explain that to Mum. Besides, I never told her about us. She doesn't even know about Ryan—the good or the bad.

"Would you like me to come in?"

There was absolutely no way she was walking in there with me. I was a *teenager*. But instead of voicing that, I calmly shook my head and stepped out. I just wanted this whole experience to be over and done with.

Nothing had changed with the place; not that it would in the space of a few months. The only changes were the ones taking place inside of me, and perhaps outside of me as I hitched up the waist of my jeans. They had been inching down with every stride these days. I was getting skinnier, and it was gross.

Guys like curves, not bones.

There was a different woman at reception as I approached the desk. I had never seen this woman before, but she seemed to know who I was and spared me the clipboard that usually needed to be filled out in advance. Probably because I was under eighteen. I don't know.

I barely made the seat warm before a man popped into my radar, looking way too happy to be dealing with depressed people.

"Lila Evans?"

I glanced at the person I was being forced to confide in. He looked nice enough if you could judge a person on their looks alone. Other than his stubble being ten shades too dark for the hair on his head, I guessed he seemed alright. He sounded like he had some sort of accent, Canadian maybe. I nodded, confirming that he had the right patient.

Patient.

The term alone sounded like I belonged in a psych ward.

At the same time, the front door swung open. Sarah waltzed in and took her place at reception as the woman who had greeted me collected her belongings. After exchanging a few words, the woman left. And there we had it; it was just me, Ryan's mum, and my dad's replacement, whose name I had already forgotten.

The muscles in my throat tightened as I angled my body away from the woman I had fantasised about being my mother-in-law one day. Maybe she hadn't seen me. Maybe I could avoid her completely. Just as I was plotting how this could possibly play out, Ryan came trotting in.

"So, you'll pick me up at four?"

He walked behind the desk where his mum was, like it was his territory, and pulled a phone charger from the wall.

"Yes, or close to. I'll message you if anything changes." I heard Sarah muffle as she set her belongings down to set up for her shift. I stood frozen as Caleb waited for me to follow him to one of the back rooms.

Only, I couldn't move.

My throat began to swell, spreading wide over my body to the point where my arms began to tingle. I couldn't feel the muscles in my face. I knew what a panic attack felt like and assumed another one was setting in. I breathed in, hoping to steady myself, but it only made my body seize up more.

"Lila? Are you ready?" Caleb's eyes were on me; not as cheery as before. Maybe he suspected something was off.

Something was definitely off—I couldn't breathe.

What made it worse was that I held the attention of everyone in the room; well, the only two people that I had hoped would never catch me in a psycho clinic. I didn't want to look, but somehow my eyes landed on his.

I was convinced he would laugh, seeing as I was the laughingstock of the school these days. But his face held a confused look, almost as if it was the last place he expected to see me. That expression lasted about a second. Next thing I knew, he was raising his eyebrows at me. And was that a smirk I was seeing?

I wanted to slap the smug look off his face. Who did he think he was?

Sarah seemed to have caught on now. She came by my side, clearly seeing how uncomfortable I was. This wasn't a natural reaction. I knew that, but that didn't stop me from being frozen, looking like an idiot, unresponsive to anything Caleb had said to me.

"Sweetie, are you ok?" she whispered and gently touched my arm.

It was the first time she had ever seen me like this, and I was mortified. Thank the Lord it was a quiet day and no one else was in the waiting room. I opened my mouth to reply, but it felt like I had been stung by a pack of bees. The silence suddenly became deafening. The clock on the wall sounded like London's Big Ben when it struck a new hour. The snort from Ryan's mouth—or at least I thought he snorted—felt as good as a punch in the face. Sarah's concern made me feel like I was five. And Caleb—I was sure I had made it to the top of his high-alert list if he had one.

I had to leave.

I pulled free from Sarah's arm and darted for the door, refusing to glance back as I ran in the opposite direction of where Mum had parked moments ago. I didn't stop until the clinic was far behind me. Only then did my throat loosen, and I could finally breathe again.

ELEVEN

Maddie

IT WAS ANOTHER kick in the gut.

I stared at the email as my students quietly worked on their essay responses. I should have been circling the room, but my mind was entangled in this bombshell. I read it once, twice, and then a third time, hoping I had missed the part where they said my manuscript had "potential," that it offered something they couldn't overlook. It never came.

Dear Madeline,

Thank you for submitting your work to the agency. After careful consideration, I'm afraid I do not feel I am the right agent for this work, and I am therefore unable to offer to represent you. I'm sure you can appreciate the need for an agent to be totally committed to a work to sell it enthusiastically to a publisher; to do otherwise is not in the best interests of the author.

Unfortunately, because of the volume of submissions I receive, I cannot offer any critical comments on your submission.

The letter went on. The way it was signed off was just disappointing. It was such a generic response—the woman hadn't even bothered to mention the title of my novel in her reply. After having sent my book proposal only a week prior, I had to question if she even read the chapters I submitted at all. Turnaround was never this fast.

I exhaled loudly, catching the attention of a few students. Their heads lifted from their papers.

I managed a tight smile as pairs of eyes landed on me. "Ten minutes to go. By now, you should be working towards your final paragraph."

My eyes returned to the email. Sure, it was a blow, but I heard it normally takes months to hear back from agencies. I also heard rejections were a very normal part of the process and would roll in by the masses before a single offer is made—if any at all. I mean, isn't that what happened to J.K. Rowling? Wasn't she rejected twelve times, or something like that?

I wouldn't allow myself to get down about this. There would be one person who would like my work, and that's all I needed.

Just one.

With ten minutes to go, my year six students were hard at it. They had found their rhythm, which was basically a teacher's dream. It was also convenient as it bought me some time to submit my curriculum planning documents to the Head of Junior School. It was a routine procedure despite it being almost impossible to get things done. The end of the semester was a crazy time, but luckily mid-year reports were behind us now. So, that was something.

I opened the tab on my laptop and brought up the English planner. It was a detailed document with the learning modifications and differentiation attached to it. Admin would be impressed; it was overly done. Way more than what was required, but that was the perfectionist in me.

Reading over it triggered the thought that I needed to send a parent email about the last week of term. Somehow, we had arrived there already. Just one more week to go.

With my mind racing a million miles per hour, weighed down by the proposal rejection and my ongoing concern for my depressed daughter, I made a terrible mistake. One that could potentially cost me my job.

I only realised after I sent it, but once I did, blood rushed to my head, and I felt like I was going to pass out. There must have been some kind of physical response as more heads shot up around the room, staring at me.

"Five minutes to go," I said hastily.

"Miss, are you okay?"

The voice came from Luke. One of my sweet students. He was one of the good ones; behind academically, but had a heart of gold, and that's all that truly mattered in the type of world we were living in. His eyes held concern as though he could detect something was upsetting me. Which wasn't truly a surprise after everything with Dylan. I hadn't regained my spark since then, but I hadn't been asked any questions, either. I had to respect that their parents must have told them not to talk about it at school. The death, that is.

But this was, of course, something totally different, and just maybe everyone's sympathy for me would somehow mean that this mistake would be overlooked. That I would be given grace.

I lifted my eyes from my screen. "Fine, thanks, Luke." I gave him a confident nod. It seemed to be enough for him to turn his eyes back to his paper, even though his hand wasn't moving as fluently as most of the rest of the class.

I swallowed hard and clicked into my sent items just to double-check. Yep, I had sent the entire student modification and differentiation notes, with individual students' names and everything, to my parent contact list. Along with notes from learning services. Highly confidential stuff. Highly, highly private information. How could I be so careless?

Maybe I was overthinking it. Maybe it wasn't so bad.

I clicked into the attachment I had sent, hoping that the student notes were magically gone from the document even though they had been there five seconds earlier. I scrolled down to find that they hadn't. Flagged students were noted by first and last name on the document, for every family in my class to see. Not only that, but I also hadn't even Blind Carbon Copied the email addresses when I sent it out, meaning everyone's personal details had been exposed. It was a major confidentiality breach.

I was going to be crucified for this.

I must have been focused on it for a while as I googled how to unsend an email (turns out there is no such thing) as my students began to get chatty the way students always seem to do when a teacher isn't looking at them. It's amazing how they think that by doing so, the teacher's ears are suddenly turned off. I never understood the logic behind that.

I glanced at the time. I had given them ten minutes longer than I had said as I was consumed by my dilemma, fretting in my thoughts. No wonder they were restless.

By the grace of God, somehow, I managed to get through the rest of the lesson without thinking too much more about the consequence that no doubt lay before me. In sixteen years of teaching, I had never made such a stupid mistake.

By the time the period was over, I already had several emails waiting for me in my inbox. Three from parents who had seen my email go out, and one from Brad, the Head of Junior School.

Sure enough, there were questions. Two of the three parents had thankfully overlooked the massive error I had made, and instead had asked if there was something additional that they needed to be doing at home for their child (probably to avoid their child's name ever being added to the list). But then there was another parent who was clearly upset, made obvious by the many misspelled words and poor grammar that comes with writing in a rage. I would know; I had drafted a few emails of similar nature in the past, only deleting them before they ever got sent out, realising how passive-aggressive I was coming off.

Come on, we've all been there.

And then there was the email from Brad. He wanted to speak to me immediately. It was barely a question—it was an order.

Feeling nauseated, I closed my laptop and, with it tucked under my sweaty armpit, I made my way to Brad's office, fearing the worst.

TWELVE

Lila

HE WAS LOOKING at me, but I wouldn't meet his eye. It wasn't that he was intimidating or anything; in fact, he was lovely. I just couldn't do it.

I've watched enough movies where psychologists ask questions like, "How does that make you feel?" Honestly, I was waiting for Caleb to ask something similar while jotting down notes in a little black book. But those types of questions never came, and there didn't appear to be any notebook, either. I guess he didn't need one considering I was yet to open my mouth. Not much to note down. It's not like the room exuded warmth anyway; with its hospital-white walls and matching furniture, it felt like the evil queen's castle from *Narnia*.

Although, I would much rather be there.

I don't know why they removed the yellow couch that had been here for years. It was the comfiest thing. Sure, it had become a little worn and tattered over the years. Mum had changed my diaper on that couch as a baby as many times as the zipper from my school dress had gotten caught on that velvet material. It didn't matter that it had gotten a little shabby; it just meant that it was loved. At least it was bright and yellow and felt a lot more comforting than this.

Instead, the leather couch I was sitting in was white with a series of uncomfortable studs that had a way of digging into my back no matter where I positioned my bum. They must have had a revamp, or quite the opposite I'd say. It all looked so outdated, like I had stepped into a scene from Downton Abbey.

"What's your favorite thing about winter, Lila?"

I finally looked up. I felt bad for the guy; he was really trying, and I was giving him nothing. With one leg over his knee, he gave his overgrown stubble a little scratch.

There was a lot about winter that I loved. It had always been my favourite season. Where to start... I loved curling up in my pink knitted throw blanket Mum made for me when I was seven as we listened to the fireplace crackle on those colder nights. I loved how at eight o'clock on the dot, Dad would emerge from his recliner chair and make the best hot chocolates with heavy cream and a touch of cinnamon, night after night. I loved how Dad and I would put on our matching blue and white football beanies right before we took off on our runs together, howling like wolves as the frosty air hit our eyes, making them water. We would stare at each other with tears streaming down our cheeks, adamant to not be the first to blink.

Dad always won that challenge.

It sounds weird, but it was our thing. In more recent times, I also loved how we would sing all the best '90s classics at the top of our lungs in the gazebo as we played Scrabble together, making bets on whether or not Mum could hear us from where she was inside the house.

But instead of saying any of this, I just shrugged.

My lack of response didn't seem to bother him.

"Let me tell you about mine."

He uncrossed his legs and clasped his hands together, as if preparing to reveal a secret. "When I was in college, winter was snowball season," he began, his accent hinting at Canadian roots (I think). "My friend and I used to have snowball fights all the time. We'd build huge forts with the most elaborate designs, like something you'd expect to see in that movie—what's it called? *Frozen*?"

I stared at him. I had no idea what this had to do with anything.

"Even with all the defences I created, my friend always levelled them easily with a well-placed mortar snowball." He went on, smiling at the memory. "Do you know what a mortar snowball is, Lila?"

I actually did know. Dad had done the same thing with me about three years ago when we went to Mount Buller that one time. But I shook my head anyway.

"A mortar snowball is kind of like a mortar shell. It's a really big snowball—we're talking like bottom-of-a-snowman size—you have to throw at an upward angle to hit your enemy, if you like to call it that," he went on with way too much enthusiasm. "If you make them right, they explode in all directions when they hit the ground, making an impressive reaction in whatever or whomever you hit."

I couldn't help but think that Mum was paying for this guy to reminisce with me about his snowy college days. I had no idea how these sessions were meant to go, but this felt very off base.

"I think for me, looking back," he started, crossing his legs again, "I appreciated we could make fun out of anything. We didn't need a lot, and we certainly didn't have much back then. Neither of us did, my friend and me. But somehow, we found joy in the simplest things."

Something in that struck a chord.

I shifted my weight in discomfort on the horrible couch. I

don't know what it was about what Caleb had said, but it made me think of Dad all over again.

The man must have noticed because he reached over to the little wooden table next to him and uncovered a notebook from its single drawer.

There it was. I knew it was a matter of time until the notebook came out.

"I've got an idea." He opened the book to a blank page. I stared at him as he took a moment to scribble something down. Once he was done, he presented it to me. Reluctantly, I took it.

"I want to get to know you a little bit, so I've written down a couple of questions for you. Once you're done, you're allowed to ask me two questions. Any question you want."

I must have screwed my face up at him; I couldn't be sure, but I could tell he sensed my attitude.

It didn't seem to bother him as he broadened his smile and passed me a pen. "I'll answer it honestly too, I promise. But don't go too hard on me just yet. Let's warm into it."

I managed a half-smile back, trying hard to be polite. This was ridiculous. Positioning the book on my lap, I peered at the two questions:

What is a particular quality in a person that makes you feel safe?

Parents make mistakes, like all humans. What is one thing you wish your mom had done differently? Big or small.

It was weird to see "mom" spelt like that.

"Let me remind you that there is no right or wrong answer," he said, his eyes on my page as I lowered the pen. "And anything you put down is safe with me. This is a safe space, Lila. No one is judging."

I wanted to believe him, but I was sceptical. I mean, I didn't feel unsafe, but I'm not sure that I trusted that anything I wrote wouldn't just be relayed back to Mum. I mean, that second question—it was weird.

But I did what he asked. Six months ago, I would never have imagined I would have written half of the content that I put down, but apparently, it was safe to do so.

I passed back the notepad a few minutes later and waited for his reaction. There was no way this Caleb guy would be satisfied with what I wrote. I was making his job hard when he was supposed to be "fixing me."

He took a few moments to read what I wrote, his face unchanging.

"Thank you for that. Now it's your turn."

I frowned at his response. Was that it? Wasn't he going to try and dissect what I had written?

If he expected me to talk, it wasn't going to happen. I pushed my back against the couch and started to play with the skin peeling away from my nails. I could feel him watching me as he passed the notebook once more to me.

"Now it's your turn. Two questions for me."

I really couldn't be bothered with this game. But seeing as I had already made the decision that this would be my first and last session, I thought I might as well cooperate a little bit longer. I did owe it to him for wasting his time by doing a runner the first time I met him. I wonder if mum ever got billed for that session I never attended. Probably not. She didn't even seem mad that I did that.

I went ahead and changed the first question but kept the second one the same.

"Hmmm," he said, reading them. "Well, I would like to learn about what makes you, you. I'd like to learn what your hobbies are, what makes you happy and sad, and whether you hate McDonald's pickles in a burger as much as I do." He searched my face as he said that last part—hoping to make me laugh.

I didn't.

"Question one: What do you hope to learn about me?" he said, reading my first question for him. "That's a good one. I would like to learn the dreams a bright girl like you is bound to have inside of you." He paused as he considered the last part. "I'm not sure if I've answered the question exactly; perhaps I've been greedy and have asked for too much." He casually took a sip of water and lowered the tall cylinder glass down. "But like I said, there is no right or wrong to this."

I waited for him to move on to the second question, but instead, he spent the next ten minutes talking about some meditation exercises and strategies that I could try over the next week. I didn't know why, but somehow, I felt frustrated that he hadn't answered the second question. He promised me two, even if my own efforts had been pretty lousy.

I stopped him mid-sentence by pointing to the notebook that lay closed on the table and raised my eyebrow at him. The smile on his face dimmed, but only for a second. He understood what I meant. He opened it back up and stared at the question I wrote for a long moment as though he was reading a thesis.

"This next question is, well, quite a personal one." he started as he scratched his stubble. "Question two: Parents make mistakes, like all humans. What is one thing you wish your mum had done differently?" he read aloud; his voice much softer than it had been all session. He stalled a bit as he cleared his throat.

I straightened myself up in the chair.

"I wish she had done everything to keep me close," he answered, looking at me in a way that made my stomach do some kind of weird drop, like an octave in a song. I waited. I thought there would be more—that he would elaborate on what he meant by that. But he didn't. Nor did he bring up what I had written in response to the same question he had posed to me.

Caleb seemed to sense my confusion and curiosity. He paused for a moment, and I could see him gathering his thoughts. "When I was six years old, my mom was struggling with her own.... stuff. And it was incredibly hard for me. I felt abandoned and unloved, and I couldn't understand why she wasn't there for me, not only physically, but emotionally."

I felt something. Caleb always seemed so strong and put together, but I could see the pain in his eyes as he spoke.

"But here's the thing, Lila. Despite everything, I know now that she loved me in the best way she could at the time. She was dealing with her own demons and couldn't always be there for me the way I needed. It took me a long time to understand that her actions weren't because I wasn't important or loved, but because she was fighting her own battles."

His words hit me hard. I thought about my own mum, how distant she sometimes seemed, and I felt a lump forming in my throat. I could see the vulnerability in his eyes, the remnants of a wound that had never fully healed. It made me think about my own relationship with mum, the times I felt distant or misunderstood. Maybe we weren't so different after all.

Caleb leaned forward slightly, his voice gentle and reassuring. "I guess what I'm trying to say is, sometimes our parents make choices that hurt us, not because they don't love us, but because they're dealing with their own pain and struggles. It's okay to feel hurt and wish things were different. Your feelings are valid, and it's important to talk about them."

I nodded, absorbing his words. It was a lot to take in, but it made sense. While I could appreciate his own vulnerability, my situation wasn't the same.

It was different.

Caleb seemed to sense my confusion and reluctance. He smiled gently and said, "Lila, sometimes the answers we seek aren't as straightforward as we'd like them to be. It's okay to feel uncertain or sceptical. These things take time, and trust isn't built in a day."

I nodded, feeling a mix of frustration and a strange sense of understanding. Maybe he wasn't like other psychologists I'd imagined. Maybe he genuinely wanted to help.

Caleb cleared his throat, and the focus shifted. How about we wrap up for today, and you think about what we've discussed? Reflect on your answers and any feelings that come up. We'll pick it up from here next time."

I felt somewhat relieved that we weren't going to unpack what I had written as my response to the same question.

That alone would require a full session.

I nodded as he walked me out of the office. The sterile white walls of the hallway seemed a little less intimidating now, a little less cold. I couldn't help but replay the session in my mind, particularly Caleb's story about his mother. It was strange how his vulnerability had opened a door to my own thoughts and feelings.

Outside, the world felt a little less heavy. Just by a tiny bit.

THIRTEEN

Maddie

GOT LUCKY. IF it hadn't been for having the best boss in the world, I would have been in serious trouble. Not that it had been a straightforward process—far from it.

After a particularly confronting meeting with Brad, it was clear that steps had to be taken regarding my misjudged error. While Brad handled much of it, there were still a few parents I had to call and explain myself to. I felt like a child being scolded by an adult, stumbling through apologies and explanations. By the time I hung up, though, it seemed forgiveness had been granted, largely due to the strong relationships I had cultivated with those parents.

The silver lining was that a disclaimer statement had finally been added to the bottom of every staff email for future protection. I was grateful this addition had been made without highlighting my little blunder. Now that a couple of days had passed, it seemed the incident had been put behind us.

Or so I thought.

Normally, I'm on top of things, but Luke's sudden moodiness had me perplexed. I understood it was the end of term and everyone was checked out, but Luke's typically bright and kind demeanour had always been unwavering—until his name appeared in that document.

Brad had handled the incident, even contacting Luke's family, and it had slipped my mind completely. But clearly, it hadn't slipped Luke's.

As my students stood to collect their math books, I circulated the room, keeping an extra eye on Luke as he took longer than usual to find his book in his tub.

"Can the red group please come to the floor," I announced out of habit. In every class, there's a wide range of abilities; the red group consisted of five or six students who benefited from extra support. Luke was one of them.

As we settled into a circle on the floor, I noticed Luke lingering near the back desks, chatting with a couple of rowdier students.

"Come join us, Luke," I encouraged, but his body language today was different—he seemed detached, unresponsive.

"Should I get him?" Nicholas, a student, asked.

"No, it's okay. Let's give him a minute," I replied louder, watching Luke ignore me from across the room. Our eyes briefly met before he looked away, clearly presenting a different version of himself today.

He never joined us on the floor, resisting with an attitude that seemed to appear out of nowhere. Eventually, he insisted on working from his desk, which I allowed. But by the end of the lesson, as I corrected books, it was clear he hadn't understood a single question.

Thirty seconds before the bell, I found an opportunity to pull him aside, asking him to water the peace lily plants in our classroom—a duty he fulfilled weekly. He was on his third or fourth plant by the time the class left for lunch, leaving just the two of us.

"What's going on, buddy?" I asked, getting straight to the point. Our relationship was built on openness like this.

He lowered the watering can onto the bench, reluctantly turning to face me as I approached.

"Nothing," he muttered, fiddling with the handle nervously.

I sat on the edge of a desk, exhaling slowly. "I know you know."

His jaw tensed, but whatever he planned to say, he held back. Grabbing the watering can again, he turned his back, moving to the next plant.

"I made a mistake when I sent out those confidential teacher notes in that email. I'm deeply sorry," I admitted. Over the years, I'd learned that students respond better when teachers are honest and acknowledge their faults—it shows them we're human. I didn't know what to expect from Luke, but he remained resistant.

"We all have things to work on and are constantly learning. Me included," I added.

"That's cool. I just didn't realise that..." he began, then stopped abruptly.

"Realise what?" I stood up. "Hey, Luke, look at me for a moment," I said gently. I had to make things right with him.

"I didn't realise I was so... dumb," he burst out, slamming the watering can down with frustration, making me jump.

"You're not 'dumb' in any way. You're a clever boy, so gifted," I assured him.

"Oh, please, Mrs. Evans. So clever that I have my own special set of instructions from the rest of the class?" His eyes were sharp, his shoulders defensively rounded.

"We all have strengths in different areas. It doesn't mean that—"

"What strengths? Apparently, I need help with everything!" His hand movements were erratic, causing the watering cylinder to slip from his grasp, spilling water on the floor.

He stared at the damp carpet, grabbing an armful of paper towels from the dispenser and dropping them on the floor, methodically soaking up the water. I knelt beside him, offering to help.

"It's okay, I've got this. Thank you, Luke," I said softly.

He stretched his arm, covering the area where I was working. "Just let me do it," he snapped.

Standing up, I watched him scrub the floor as if cleaning wine spilled on white carpet. When he finished, he tossed the soaked towels in the trash.

"Thank you for cleaning that up," I repeated.

He lingered by the bin, then looked up at me. "Sure." His eyes darkened. "Thank you for completely humiliating me. But I'm glad to know I'm not the only one."

"Like I said, Luke, I've done my best to make things right with those affected," I replied, feeling my frustration rise. Being upset about what I'd done was one thing, but this was getting personal.

"I'm not talking about that," he spat, his eyes full of bitterness.

My stomach sank. What was he talking about?

"Oh, I assumed you heard."

He sounded almost smug, as though he had leverage over me. But I wouldn't let an eleven-year-old intimidate me.

"I'm not sure if I have," I responded calmly, though inside, I was anything but calm. Kids often made up stories to fit in or make themselves look good, but there was a malicious tone in Luke's voice that unsettled me.

"You sending your daughter to counselling because you can't even fix her," he accused. "I heard she even ran away."

This was crossing a boundary.

"Luke, I understand you're upset. You have every right to be," I said, taking a deep breath. "I'm not sure what rumours you've heard," I continued evenly, though my blood boiled. Clearing my throat, I hardened my tone. "But what happens between my daughter and me is none of your business. Just as it's no one's story to tell."

He took a step back, shrugging nonchalantly. "It didn't come from me. Maybe you should talk to Ryan," he suggested, his voice wavering slightly.

"Ryan *who*?"

"Hensley. Ryan Hensley. You know him."

I stared at Luke, trying to mask my confusion with a steady gaze. Ryan Hensley—a name I recognised vaguely but couldn't quite place in this context. My mind raced, searching for any connection between Ryan and Lila.

Luke shifted uncomfortably under my scrutiny, his eyes darting away momentarily before meeting mine again. His earlier bravado seemed to waver, replaced by a hint of apprehension.

"What's Ryan got to do with Lila?" I asked, trying to keep my tone casual despite the tightening knot of worry in my stomach.

Luke hesitated, as if debating how much to reveal. "Just... stuff I overheard," he finally mumbled, avoiding my gaze.

"Overheard from whom?" I pressed, my voice firmer now, my concern mounting with each elusive answer.

"Just... around," Luke replied vaguely, his discomfort palpable.

I took a deep breath, trying to steady my thoughts. Lila had been acting a bit strangely lately, but nothing that wasn't of our new norm. Could Ryan somehow be involved in whatever was bothering her?

"Look, Luke," I began, leaning in slightly to convey the seriousness of my tone, "if there's something going on with Lila, something you think I should know about, you need to tell me."

Luke shifted again, his eyes flicking nervously towards the

door. "I... I shouldn't have said anything," he muttered, his voice barely above a whisper.

"Luke, this is important," I insisted, feeling a surge of frustration mixed with concern. "If Lila's in trouble, I need to know about it."

Luke hesitated, torn between loyalty and guilt. "I heard... things," he finally admitted, his voice barely audible.

My heart sank. Lila had been more distant lately, and now Luke's cryptic words added another layer of worry. "What kind of things?" I asked, trying to keep my voice steady.

Luke shook his head slightly, his expression troubled. "I shouldn't have said anything," he repeated, more to himself than to me.

I sighed, realising Luke wasn't going to give me more. "Alright," I said softly. "Thank you, Luke," I said sincerely, placing a hand on his shoulder briefly. "I appreciate your concern."

As the bell signalled the start of the next class, Luke hurried off, leaving me alone in the empty classroom, my mind racing. There was clearly something concerning involving Lila and Ryan Hensley, and I couldn't shake the feeling that I needed to uncover more.

FOURTEEN

Lila

AGAINST ALL ODDS, I had made it back for another session. But honestly, it wasn't the worst thing in the world. As sad as it was, it was one of the few times each week when someone seemed to genuinely care about how I was doing. Even if he was getting paid to do so. I had to remind myself of that.

It was his job.

We had decided to stick with a Saturday session, which I was relieved about. I hadn't run into Ryan again, and Sarah seemed to have kept to herself upon my arrival, offering polite smiles here and there. I couldn't help but wonder what Ryan had told her about me. After the way I bolted out of there the other week, like a frightened patient, he probably didn't have to work too hard to convince her I was unstable. I had apparently done that myself.

With Caleb sitting across from me, I knew today would involve unpacking some of my more concerning responses from our last session together. I still hadn't contributed much verbally, so that would be interesting.

"I have to say," Caleb began, crossing one leg over the other in his usual manner, "you have quite a way with words. Do you enjoy writing, Lila?"

I didn't need to ask which words he was referring to; we were revisiting last week's questions.

I stared blankly at him, and he seemed to understand my silence. I had nothing against him. In fact, I liked the guy and wanted to trust him, but what good would words do?

He offered a kind smile and folded his hands together, a gesture he seemed fond of. "It must run in the family... the writing."

My stomach sank. How did he know my mum was a writer? I assumed he meant my mum, since Dad was long gone from this world. But then again, in a small town like ours, everyone knew everything about each other. He probably had been given the rundown. That's all it was.

"Unless you can bring back my dad and heal me at the same time, you're as useless as the rest," he read aloud, articulating every word I had written.

I squirmed in the uncomfortable white leather chair. Hearing those words out loud sounded much worse than when I had written them down.

"Change comes from within, not from others' requests," he continued, reading my response to the second question. "My wishes and hopes feel useless. If you must know, I wish my mom would stop pretending everything is okay, just like you do with your cheerful childhood tales and your belief in finding joy. My mom is trying so hard to be strong, but I see through her fake smiles and forced laughter. It's exhausting pretending everything's normal when our world fell apart. Maybe for you, it's easy to talk about finding joy, especially when you're probably earning a lot of money, but I'm drowning in grief, and positivity won't change that."

I was surprised at how much I had written, and so quickly. I guess there was a lot to pour out.

My stomach settled when I realised he didn't seem angry, or at least he didn't look angry. His kind eyes only seemed to soften even more, making me feel somewhat guilty.

"Thank you, Lila. You've helped me more than you know," he said, uncrossing his leg and, predictably, crossing the other.

"You should never apologize for your emotions. Remember that. They're what make us human. Proof that I don't need to 'revive' you."

Leaning forward, he rubbed his hands together. "Like you said, Miss Lila, wise beyond her years, change can only come from within. And from what little I've learned about you; you have the capacity to do that. That's where I come in."

He smiled and straightened up, uncrossing his legs so both feet touched the floor. "If you give me the chance to let me in, that is. I think you would be surprised how much we could learn from each other."

It was a strange comment for a psychologist, suggesting he could learn from a teenager when he was supposed to have all the answers.

Did Caleb need fixing, too?

Pressure began building in my chest. For someone I hadn't spoken a word to yet, I felt conversation on the tip of my tongue. I parted my lips, struggling to form coherent words. I hadn't voiced a complete sentence in some time; I wasn't sure my mind remembered how to.

But Caleb took the lead. "We won't do the two-question thing again. But I'd like you to think about this between now and our next time together."

I glanced at the table, expecting the notebook to come out again, but he didn't reach for it.

"Over the next week, I encourage you to look deep inside yourself, Lila, and ask this question: What is it about your dad's passing that you haven't been able to forgive?"

Something inside me turned fiery red.

How dare he.

Who was he to say I held a grudge? How unfair that he assumed I blamed Dad's cancer on someone. He had it all wrong.

He had me all wrong.

I felt my nostrils flare, blood pounding in my ears like after a marathon. I worried a panic attack might hit, but this time, I could breathe fine. Something else was happening. An uncontrollable anger surged, and there was nothing I could do to stop it.

So, I let it out.

"You promised no one would judge, but clearly you are," I spat like venom. My jaw twitched as I struggled to control my words. "How could you jump to that conclusion? That I owe someone something, as if I've done something wrong?"

His smile vanished. He looked more curious than taken aback as his dark eyes searched my face, trying to understand.

I bit my lip hard enough to taste blood. I didn't understand myself. Why was I so angry? But more than that, I hated that I'd opened up to him. Now he had all the power.

"I'm not saying you owe anyone an apology, Lila," he said calmly, measured. It only made me angrier. I didn't need calming. I needed understanding.

"You did!" I shouted, tears streaming. I hated myself for it. This man didn't deserve my tears any more than anyone else. "You just said that," I added, lowering my voice.

I buried my face in my hands, shaking my head. This was humiliating, but I wouldn't run out of the clinic again. I couldn't recover from that. Caleb would have to handle my breakdown one last time.

Because this was it. I wasn't coming back. Period.

With my head down, I heard water filling a glass. He placed it beside me with a few tissues.

"Here, whenever you're ready," he said in his usual soothing voice, making me feel like a spoiled brat. He sat down again, and we sat in silence for a few moments until I gathered the courage to lift my head from my hands. Without thanking him, I grabbed the glass and drank it all in one go.

But as the silence stretched, Caleb's presence felt less imposing. He didn't push for more words or explanations. Instead, his patience gave me room to breathe, to let my thoughts untangle in the quiet of his office.

I wiped my eyes with the tissues he'd provided, feeling the sting in my cheeks where tears had dried. The air seemed heavy with unspoken words, hanging between us like a fragile thread. I wanted to break it, to speak, but fear held me back.

Finally, Caleb broke the silence. "Lila, I understand you're feeling overwhelmed right now. It's okay to be angry. Grief is messy, and it doesn't follow a straight path."

I sniffed, trying to compose myself. "I don't want to talk about forgiveness," I muttered, my voice hoarse.

Caleb nodded thoughtfully. "That's alright. We can explore that when you're ready. But for now, I want you to know that I'm here to support you, no matter what emotions come up."

His words felt genuine, not like empty assurances. Despite my anger, a part of me wanted to believe him. Still, in ten minutes, I'd be out of this dreadful chair forever.

The moment couldn't come soon enough.

They were whispering about me; I could feel it.

The weekend had come and gone, and here I was in the common room as usual during lunch, the rain pelting down outside on the last day of term, spoiling all the outdoor activities the school had planned. I hugged my blazer tight around me, watching it overlap like an oversized sheet of wrapping paper. It wasn't that I was starving myself on purpose; I just wasn't ever that hungry. Stress often suppressed appetite, and with dance no longer filling my days, I lacked the motivation for extra energy. Both reasons seemed to apply to me now.

"You serious? How hilarious," came a voice from the other side of the room. I had become adept at pretending naivety to the gossip that surrounded me. Drawing attention to the snake-like behaviour only encouraged more strikes.

I turned the page of my book and buried myself deeper into the beanbag. Maybe I was paranoid; maybe they weren't whispering about me at all. It had been a few months; I was old news. Believe it or not, the world kept turning. But I couldn't get lost in the pages.

"Oh my god, you for real?" came another voice. "Legit," added a third. "I heard she's like obsessed with the guy."

They giggled, except for one snort that made me lift my eyes from the page. "Shhhh!" hissed one of the year seven girls, turning away so I couldn't see her face. I returned to my book, unable to process one sentence from the next. Why couldn't they just leave me alone? I wasn't hurting anyone.

"I think she heard us," said another, stifling a laugh with her hand.

I didn't know their names; they didn't know me. So, what was their deal?

Without engaging, I stood and scanned for a new spot, but the room was now crowded with sweaty teens jostling for couches, cushions, and beanbags. Turning a corner, I spotted Ellie and Maci cozied up on a swivel chair, legs crossed, skirts hitched high, while Ryan and some guys hovered nearby. It was the first time I noticed how tarty they'd become, flaunting toned legs in freezing weather. For whom? For some try-hard boys whose voices hadn't even dropped?

Far out, I sounded like an old fossil.

The question now was: do I bother acknowledging them

for the sake of forgiveness? Wasn't that what Caleb meant when he told me to discover what I'm meant to forgive? I assumed that's what he meant.

Maci froze as soon as she saw me, proficient in avoiding eye contact when necessary. Today, her gaze darted away as soon as mine met hers. Ellie, the loyal sidekick, ensured control wasn't lost.

"Good book?" Ellie ventured.

I nodded, disliking how she made reading sound dorky. She used to love books. We used to exchange them. We practically had a mini book club. It was disconcerting how much she'd changed, both of them really, in just a few months.

Ellie gave a thumbs-up when I didn't reply, tempting me to slap the book over her bare legs. The sound would've been satisfying. Instead, I offered a half-smile and kept walking, ignoring Maci's continued avoidance. She could look if she wanted. I didn't care. I couldn't stand the sight of either of them.

"So, what's he like?" came another voice.

I kept my eyes on the exit, more determined than ever to leave the room entirely.

"I don't think she's listening, dude," someone else giggled.

Glancing back, I saw countless pairs of eyes fixed on me, like a pack of blood-sucking leeches. If there were a volume button, it had hit its lowest setting. What was going on?

Then I heard Ryan's voice. I didn't need to see his face to recognise it.

"She doesn't want to say, man. Desperate times call for desperate measures," he muttered. "I heard she writes about him in her journal."

"A journal? This Caleb guy sounds fab. How do I sign up?"

More giggles echoed around the room. Ryan, ever the coward, bowed his head to avoid confronting me, snickering under his breath. I wanted to punch him. I wanted to punch all of them.

My eyes locked with Maci's, and I glared at her, wondering if our once effortless ability to understand each other with just a look had faded away. Was the shame on her face not just about betraying our trust but also about realising what a complete jerk Ryan truly was? Damn straight he was. With each passing day, it became increasingly evident to me.

But I wasn't about to let them tear me down. I had to be stronger than that. I couldn't afford to fall apart now.

The mental pep talk sounded reassuring in theory, but in reality, it quickly crumbled under the weight of my emotions. Anger surged through me, mingling with hurt and frustration. My hand, seeking an outlet for the turmoil inside, found a metal stapler resting on the edge of the table nearby. Without pausing to think, I gripped it tightly and flung it across the room with all the force I could muster.

The stapler sailed through the air, the metallic clang as it struck Ryan's face echoing sharply in the otherwise silent room. Time seemed to slow as I watched him stagger backward, the stapler dropping to the floor with a clatter as he collapsed heavily onto the linoleum.

A collective gasp rippled through the onlookers, who had been frozen in shock by the sudden turn of events. Some whispered nervously to each other, while others stared wide-eyed at me, unsure of how to react.

I stood rooted to the spot, my heart pounding in my chest. What had I just done? The realisation of my actions began to sink in, accompanied by a rush of conflicting emotions. Guilt gnawed at me, even as a small part of me felt a twisted satisfaction at seeing Ryan silenced, if only momentarily.

Maci's eyes widened in disbelief; her earlier composure shattered. It was clear she hadn't expected me to lash out like this. Her gaze flickered uncertainly between me and Ryan, as if unsure where to direct her sympathy or her condemnation.

Ellie, always quick on her feet, broke the tense silence

that hung in the air like a heavy fog. "Holy crap, Lila! Are you crazy?" Her voice was a mixture of shock and concern, tinged with a hint of disbelief.

I swallowed hard, my throat dry. "I…um…" was all I managed to choke out, my voice barely above a whisper. The weight of my impulsive action settled heavily upon me, and I struggled to maintain my composure.

Ryan groaned from the floor, holding a hand to his now reddening cheek. His eyes bore into mine with a mix of pain and accusation. "You're nuts, Lila," he spat out.

The room seemed to close in around me, the walls pressing in as the truth sank deeper. The stapler lay innocently on the floor, seeming to mock me. I had let my emotions get the best of me, and now I had to face the consequences.

As the seconds ticked by in heavy silence, I realised there was no going back. Whatever shred of normalcy I had clung to in this chaotic school year had just shattered along with Ryan's pride.

FIFTEEN

Maddie

"**S**HE DID *WHAT*?" That had been my reaction when a woman from reception pulled me aside during the few minutes I had to eat my lunch. I hadn't made it to the staffroom in weeks; it had been that busy. Yet, the moment I settled down to eat my ham, cheese, and tomato sandwich, I was back out of my seat.

Surely, I had misunderstood. Lila didn't throw staplers at people. She had never thrown *anything* at anyone before, not even her pacifier back when she was an infant on all fours. As I was told this horror story, I saw Ryan appear from the first aid room, clutching an ice pack to his face, nodding to whatever the school nurse was saying. I felt my stomach drop. For someone who had withstood countless injuries on the football field, I would have thought this would have been a scratch in comparison. But by the way his body was curled over, it was obvious he was in agony.

I tried to visualise how the scene had unfolded, what had led to my daughter's impulsive action. According to eyewitnesses, they had all been discussing Hollywood celebrities, making comments about who they found "hot." Apparently,

Ryan made a prediction of who he thought Lila would like, and it caused her to lash out.

But somehow, this story didn't sound right to me. Lila wouldn't have cared less about that sort of stuff. Surely, he must have said or done something to provoke her in a more personal way. But why? Ryan was a good kid. He came from a good family. After having Sarah on staff for almost a decade at the clinic, and being friends for years before that, I knew that much. But I also knew under peer pressure, anything was possible. As I was being told one side of the story, all I could think about was the other side. There had to be more to it, and after Luke's comment the other day, I was certain this was true.

The drive home had been more vocal than usual. If it had been any other day, I would have been internally celebrating this change.

"You don't get it, Mum, he deserved it," Lila said all too calmly when I asked what had happened.

My eyes diverted from the road for a second as the words came out of her mouth. I was somewhat relieved to find that her expression was far less composed than her tone, showing me that my Lila was still somewhere in there. It was a miracle she wasn't suspended for the incident; just a warning and stern talking to. I thanked her squeaky-clean track record and the ongoing compassion we had received since Dylan's passing for that.

No matter which angles I came from, I still didn't seem to come any closer to uncovering what led to the chunk in Ryan's face. Each time I felt we were on the verge of getting somewhere, her bottom lip would quiver, and I would find a way to close my sentence.

After dropping Lila off at her grandparents for the night, an end-of-term tradition since kindergarten, I made my way to the clinic. Lila was scheduled for an appointment with Caleb tomorrow morning, but I would cancel it. She needed a break, and I didn't want to cut her time short with my parents. I was hoping that Sarah would be on shift so we could talk about the war that took place between our two children.

And thankfully she was.

"Maddie, hi," she said rather tentatively as I strolled in, too exhausted to process what or how I should be feeling.

"Hey, Sarah, it's good to see you." We met halfway and embraced each other in a hug over the counter.

"And you! End of term for you? That must be a good feeling!"

She was uncomfortable. I could tell she didn't know how to act around me. Was it because I hadn't seen her since the funeral, or because of what happened today?

Maybe both.

"It will be good to have a break," I answered truthfully, because honestly, I didn't feel too good about anything at the moment. "Are you well? How is Tony and the family?"

It came out automatically. Clearly, I knew how one of her children was doing, seeing as my daughter had put him in that position. The look on Sarah's face confirmed the oddness of my question. I wasn't playing dumb; I just didn't know how to transition into such a topic. Luckily, the waiting room was empty being so near to closing time.

I'd get straight to the point.

"I'm so sorry about what happened at school today," I said, lowering my voice before allowing her the chance to answer my question. "I'm not sure how it happened; Lila won't talk about it."

The tension in Sarah's shoulders dissolved. "Oh, please don't be sorry, it's not your fault. Lila has been through a lot."

"She has, but it doesn't justify what she did."

"I know that," she said understandingly, and tilted her head. "I love my son, and as parents, we always want to see the good in them. But I'm sure he isn't all innocent in this."

"Ryan is a good kid."

"Yes, he is." Her eyes shone with a kindness, making me wish I hadn't allowed so much time to pass. Of course, Sarah would take this so graciously; it was who she was. How could I have thought for a moment that she would be any different?

"I'm actually wanting to cancel her appointment with Caleb tomorrow if I can."

Sarah's fingers found the keyboard and began clicking buttons. "Done." She looked up with a smile. "Did you want to reschedule her? There are some openings on the following Saturday."

"Yeah, let's do that. Saturdays seem to work well."

"And so would coffee sometime," she said, lowering her hands. "I miss you, Maddie."

My chest expanded with warmth. I hadn't realised how much I missed her, how much I needed this. "Coffee would be nice." I leaned in closer to the counter. "I miss you too. And again, I'm sorry."

"What are you sorry for?" she said with a gentle laugh.

"For letting so much time pass. And, well, your son's bruised face."

"No stitches were needed."

"That's hardly beside the point…"

"Maddie." She took my hand in hers. "It's okay."

"It's not." I squeezed it back. "But…thank you."

In that moment, an unfamiliar face appeared from the room behind reception.

I took a good look at him, making the connection that it must be him. The new psychologist. He was tall in stature, a little rough around the edges with dark features; the contrast of his thick light chocolate brown hair and dark moustache being the most prominent. He was dressed well—maybe too formally in my opinion—more formally dressed than Dylan ever had been. He was wearing navy suit pants and a blue and white checkered shirt with a collar so triangular it took the form of two Egyptian pyramids on either side of his collarbones.

With a smile all too big, he reached for my hand. "Caleb Peters."

"Hello there," I said as I shook his. "I'm Maddie."

Hello there? Really?

"Hello there, Maddie," he mimicked back.

I smiled at him, having no doubt that my smile was a fraction of the size of his.

Sarah cleared her throat. "Maddie is Lila Evan's mother. One of your Saturday clients," she clarified, adding to the introduction.

"I could have guessed as much."

"How so?" I challenged him.

"Your daughter is the spitting image of you," he said with a laugh, almost spitting himself as he said it.

Sarah nodded, looking up from her screen. "So true. I've always thought the same! Lila has always looked more like you." She shot me a smile and brushed past us to begin locking up.

Compared to Dylan, she means.

I swallowed. They were both wrong. Whenever I looked at Lila, all I could see was Dylan. How could I not when she had the same dimple in her left cheek, a centimetre from where her lips curled? She had the same long legs, his charisma—and up until today, Dylan's gentleness.

"Well, there you go," I said, casually dismissing my thoughts.

Caleb placed one hand over the other and lowered his hands. "I look forward to spending some more time with Lila tomorrow." He seemed so put together, so...

I couldn't quite place it.

"I'm sorry, we have had to reschedule. I hope that's okay?"

Hope that's okay?

Why was I asking him for permission? I guess it was late

notice and naturally, that would peeve many people. I was just instinctively being polite.

"I will allow it," he said as the muscles around his mouth formed a smile different from his last.

I stared at him, not completely sure if he was trying to joke or not.

"That's not a problem at all," he said, changing his tune. "I will get Sarah to fix you up with another time."

"Oh, she has fixed it up already. Next Saturday."

"Perfect. Thank you for that."

I nodded. "Absolutely."

"How has Lila been this week?"

I pursed my lips together. Had Sarah filled him in about the stapler fiasco? "She hasn't had the best week," I answered without giving much away.

"Yes," he started with a distant look in his eye. "I was concerned after the way our last session ended."

I glanced over my shoulder. "How did it end?" I asked as I watched Sarah zooming around with the usual close procedures. She was over in the waiting room now, rearranging magazines.

"Did you want to take it in here?" He gestured to the room he had come from.

I followed him into the all-too-familiar office, trying my best not to turn my nose up at the furniture that looked like it had come fresh out of the early nineteen hundreds.

What happened to the yellow couch?

I took a seat on a hard white leather couch, feeling a slight squeak as my weight pressed down onto it. I might as well have sat on a plank of wood.

Caleb took a seat on something similar.

"We had a rocky start, but I managed to get her talking, which was a breakthrough. But I think the challenge I put forward to her hit a tender spot."

I felt my weight lift right back out of the couch. "You got her talking?"

He must be good; not many people were able to achieve that these days.

"Well, yes. But she was quick to get defensive."

I nodded, feeling myself sink back down.

"Of course, it's my responsibility to let you know if I believe she is a threat to herself or others, and I will certainly do that, but I don't believe we are at that point. There's some work that needs to be done. I'm sensing around forgiveness."

"Forgiveness?"

He looked at me thoughtfully. "Yes, forgiveness. Whether it's towards someone or something, I'm yet to understand with Lila. But we are working on the uncovering phase to find where this anger has come from and why it has transpired… peeling back the layers."

His eyes glimmered with empathy as he spoke, making me feel at rest; confident that my daughter was in the right hands.

"It's much easier to be angry during this stage of grief. And it makes you feel as if you can do more because it's more action-oriented. Feeling sad—and just sitting there feeling sad—sucks. For anyone. It feels really vulnerable, and it hurts. But when you do it, when you let yourself be immersed in it, then you can move through it. Fully own your pain," he went on. "There's no point in attempting to forgive someone before you have truly let yourself feel and express your pain."

Was he still talking about Lila here? Because somehow his words were stirring up the broken shards inside of me.

I smoothed my lips together, not realising how dry they had become. "So, until that point, until she makes that discovery, she will struggle to find peace?"

His eyes held their sparkle as his head slowly elevated up then down. "You're onto something here, Maddie."

Maybe he was onto me more than he understood. Could

psychologists read people that easily? Of course, they could. Most experts think that 70 to 93 percent of all communication is nonverbal. No wonder he could read Lila so well.

"My late husband taught me a thing or two."

"A very talented man, Dylan."

My heart rate accelerated. Dylan's name hadn't been mentioned in months—only I was allowed to bring him up. It was a conversation I would always put a stop to and one I certainly never initiated.

Wait.

"What makes you say that?" I knew I sounded defensive. But of course, I knew this to be true about my own husband, but what did this man know about him?

"Well," he started, "he didn't win two APS awards for nothing."

Dylan was renowned in his field and had been the recipient of two Australian Psychology Society awards over the years. Really, I shouldn't have been so surprised that this was public knowledge.

This guy was probably a fan.

"That's kind of you to say," I said as my eyes found the wall behind him where Dylan's achievements once hung in frames. Now it was bare like the other three sides—all in desperate need of colour, a plant.

Something.

"I'm sorry for your loss," Caleb said, turning slightly to follow my glance and study the blank wall with me.

"Thank you." My heart dropped at the reminder. "I appreciate that." I brought my eyes back to him before any more questions came. "I best be off and let you get home." I peeled myself off the couch. "It was nice to meet you, Caleb."

"It was lovely to meet you, Maddie." He reached for my hand, yet it felt different this time when he shook it. "I do hope to see Lila next Saturday. After our last session, I wasn't so sure."

"You got her talking," I reminded him. "Whether she agreed with you or not, you got her to talk. We will get there."

"Yes, we will." As I turned to leave, Caleb called out, "Maddie, if you ever need guidance or have concerns... please feel free to reach out."

As I turned to leave, Caleb's words resonated with unexpected intensity, their impact cutting through the haze of my thoughts like a ray of sunlight breaking through storm clouds. His genuine concern seemed to stir emotions I had kept tightly wrapped, triggering a cascade of memories and feelings that I hadn't fully confronted since Dylan's passing.

I hesitated in the doorway, the weight of his kindness settling in my chest like a comforting warmth. It wasn't just his offer to talk; it was the way he had listened, the way he had acknowledged the complexities of Lila's situation without judgment. In that brief exchange, he had shown a depth of empathy that felt rare and precious.

"Thank you," I murmured softly, my voice barely above a whisper, still unable to meet his gaze. It wasn't just gratitude for his words, but for the unexpected solace they brought amidst the turmoil of recent events.

Caleb nodded quietly, his expression reflecting understanding and a quiet strength. "Take your time, Maddie. Whenever you're ready."

His words hung in the air, a gentle reassurance that I could unravel the knots of grief and confusion in my own time. It was a stark contrast to the hurried pace of life I had grown accustomed to, where every day brought new challenges and demands.

I managed a weak smile, touched by his sincerity and the unspoken promise of support he offered.

With a nod of thanks, I finally stepped out into the corridor, the echo of Caleb's words lingering like a fragile thread of hope in the darkness that seemed to cling to me.

98

S I L E N T PROMISES

the echo of Caleb's words lingering like a fragile thread of hope in the darkness that seemed to cling to me.

SIXTEEN

Lila

H E WASN'T GOING to get away with it.

As I lay in the gazebo, my book resting on my stretched-out legs, I began thinking of ways to make him pay. I know that sounds sinister, but I wasn't the revenge type of person—or at least, I hadn't been.

Until now.

Ever since Ryan publicly humiliated me, something ugly inside me took form. I couldn't believe that someone I believed to be good could create such a lie. What was his purpose for hurting me when he already had what he wanted—he had Maci. He was popular before her and liked by everyone. So why the need to be a bully? Unless, of course, he wasn't a good person at all.

But it wasn't just Ryan. It was like everything, all the hurt I'd pushed down since Dad died, was rising up and spilling over. He'd been gone for almost a year now, and somehow, I'd convinced myself I was okay. That I didn't need anyone. But I did need him. Maybe if Dad were still here, I wouldn't be spiraling like this, trying to get back at someone who wasn't even worth my time.

Anyone can put their best foot forward when they want something, like the way he did when he was trying to win me, but now he had shown his true colours. That's why I was determined for others to see them too.

It was about time that Maci knew the truth.

Putting my book aside, I sat up and reached for my phone. I knew exactly what to do. I jumped onto the *Play Store* and downloaded the Instagram app. I wasn't allowed to have Instagram, but I knew all about it—everyone at school seemed to be on it, Ryan included. It was easy to confirm this with a simple Google search, as his profile wasn't private. His most recent post, from a week ago, showed him with a few friends sitting around a mountain of food. Maci was in it, her body glued to Ryan like a magnet on the couch. Anyway, I wasn't going on as myself. I would make my identity someone else. Someone by the name of *Ivy Griffin*.

My hands shook slightly as I added the details to bring this person to life. Even though no one was watching me as I sat alone in the gazebo, I found myself looking up every few seconds as if scared to be caught. Surely this wasn't a crime. If anyone could be whoever they wanted to be on social media, which seemed to be the case these days, then I didn't see how this was any different. After some scrolling on the internet, I found some photos that would make the perfect "Ivy." I wanted to select photos that had the "girl-next-door" type of vibe—a girl who was naturally stunning—so stunning that Ryan simply wouldn't be able to look past. With a rush of adrenaline, I found what I was looking for.

Her name was Amalie Müller, a seventeen-year-old from Germany. She may have been a couple of years older, but she looked more like my age. She had long sandy hair, bright blue eyes, flawless skin, and legs for days. She wasn't a model, which I was careful about—not wanting her to be easily identifiable. But she might as well have been a model, or an influencer, with the way she was posed in every photo with the perfect filters and immaculate fashion.

I downloaded half a dozen photos and uploaded them onto her brand-new account, adding many hashtags under each photo to bank up the likes. I used quirky captions under each photo to make her look really down to earth and an all-round legend to be around. I had to make her look desirable and likable in every possible way, without making her look too skanky. The girl-next-door kind of girls were not skanky—they were genuine, funny, and classy. It was important that I nailed this. At the top of her profile, I wrote:

Ivy Griffin

New account

15

Dreamer

Melbourne, Australia

After half an hour of adding random accounts to rack up Ivy's friends list, I pulled my phone back and studied the profile. It looked legit. The lack of photos wouldn't be a big deal. Or that they had been uploaded all at once. I wasn't going to wait weeks between each upload. Now it was time to add Ryan and get chatting. I have to say, I was a quick learner. I had this social media thing down in no time.

After just ten minutes, my friend request was accepted. Not only that, he had liked my most recent photo; the one where my hands were resting on a ledge at a lookout, my back against the camera but my body angled in a way where I was showing off curves in all the right places, making it look as though I had legs for days. I mean, *her* body, curves, and legs, I should say. She wasn't me.

Obviously.

My heart raced with excitement. This was good. The

response was immediate—far quicker than I had expected this to go. I returned the favour and tried not to cringe as I "liked" his most recent photo too—the one with Maci in it. If I was to take on this chick, I had to embody her like an actor would play a character in a movie. I had to think and write like Ivy Griffin—not Lila Evans. And that started now. Which was precisely why I stepped out of my comfort zone and liked not one, but three of his photos. The next thing I knew, a message landed in my inbox.

It was time to get the ball rolling.

I had been dreading the school holidays. The thought of hanging out with Mum at home for two weeks felt unbearable. Don't get me wrong; I love my mum dearly, but there was nothing to talk about. Every time she tried to make conversation, it felt awkward and forced. It felt so unnatural that I would find ways to avoid us crossing paths, only making an appearance when needed, but sporadically enough to get her off my back.

But it really hadn't been that bad, especially now since Ryan was showing interest. What started with the usual "Hi, thanks for the add. How do I know you?" quickly progressed. Seeing as Ivy was tanned with many photos taken in nature, I decided to go with the narrative that she was moving from a small town called Katherine in the Northern Territory to Melbourne in the next month. Her "new account" was her way of putting her past behind her as she got ready to embark on her new adventure in a city that was far more populated and, well, more civilised. Out of all the states, I knew that Ryan had never been to the Northern Territory, so I didn't have to worry about them having any mutual friends.

I made sure she was full of questions, wanting to know all

the hot spots in Melbourne and what school was like here. It was funny to watch how quickly each message was "seen" and then replied to. Ryan was asking questions too, so I made sure I sent him photos of the town I found off the internet, passing them off as my own. So far, he didn't seem suspicious, which only fuelled me more as I thought of ways to become bolder with my questions.

I had a few selfies of Ivy that I hadn't put up on her account but had downloaded to my phone. Holding my breath, I mustered up the courage to send a photo of her lying on the couch with her ginger cat nuzzling her perfect heart-shaped face. I followed up with the caption:

I'm so bored, what do you Melburnians do for fun?

My heart was racing as I saw that he had received the photo instantly, but unlike every other time, he didn't reply right away. I groaned as I flipped onto my stomach on my bed, throwing the pillow over my head as I buried my face into the mattress. I couldn't look. How humiliating. I should have held back a day or two before I began sending selfies. I had gone in too deep, too soon. I hoped I hadn't ruined it.

Ping.

I flipped myself back around and brought my phone to my face to find that he had sent one back with the follow-up message: I could easily tell you, but I would rather show you myself when you get here.

I snorted as I read it, slapping my hand over my mouth to soften my giggles. As good-looking as Ryan was, he could not do a selfie. His face looked way bigger than it actually was, and what was with his hand positioned under his chin? It looked way too posed. So unnatural.

Surprisingly, I was getting way too much joy out of this.

"…What are you laughing at?"

I looked up from the screen to find Mum at my door with a strange look on her face. Almost a smirk if I was reading it correctly. She looked pretty ecstatic to see me this way. Come to think of it, I hadn't laughed in a very long time. I lowered my phone to hide the screen and did my best to compose myself.

"Just a funny meme," I said, thinking on my feet.

"Oh yeah? Who's sending that?"

"Oh, no one. I just came across it on the internet."

Mum's eyes narrowed, but she said nothing. Could she tell I was lying? I smiled at her, hoping it would distract her from asking any further questions. A smile was worth a million dollars these days.

And sure enough, it was enough to satisfy her.

"It makes me happy to see you like this," she said, gazing at me like it was a pivotal moment in history.

"Thanks, Mum." I didn't want to spoil what this meant for her. If only she knew the truth, her smile would quickly turn into something else.

"Are you ready?"

Peeling myself off the bed, I slipped on my boots. I wasn't ready for Caleb Peters or that horrible chair, but sometimes you have to do what you have to do.

If it's any consolation, it did make it easier knowing for a fact that I wouldn't run into Ryan again. Mum had caught up with Sarah, and without them knowing about our history or his secret relationship with Maci, they assured me that we wouldn't cross paths at the clinic again.

I kept the details of the incident with the stapler to myself—knowing that whatever I said to mum would get back to Sarah and then Ryan. I wasn't going to give him the satisfaction that he had hurt me; therefore, it was important I didn't focus any attention on it. Besides, if they had known that I was being teased for "crushing" on Caleb, then maybe I would be assigned to some other psychologist. I really couldn't be bothered starting all over again with someone else–although a different couch would have been nice. But on the flipside, if I hadn't been attending these sessions in the first place, then I would have received a harsher consequence for what happened in the common room that day.

Period.

I had to be here whether I wanted to or not. It was just one of those things.

Today's session seemed to focus around the holidays and how this time could help me find "rest" from all the noise and distractions. Caleb began to talk about what his school experience had been like for him back in the day before social media, but I wasn't really listening. All I could think about was the buzzing in my coat's pocket as I felt Ryan's messages come through, one after another.

Ping, ping, ping.

His eyes flickered as my phone went off. It was the first time it had ever been a distraction in our sessions.

"Do you think boys and girls present themselves differently online than in person?"

"Oh, absolutely."

That was a no brainer. The exchange between Ivy and Ryan being a prime example. It was timely conversation to be having on this topic–and one I was interested in.

"How is it different?" he asked, looking pleased that I had contributed something. As long as he saw this as a breakthrough, then maybe I would graduate from the sessions sooner.

"You can be whoever you want to be online."

"How do you mean?"

"Well..." I pushed my phone deeper into my pocket.

"People only post what they want others to see. They take a million photos in the same pose before they are finally happy with it. But then that's still not enough. They edit or photoshop it so it's perfect. Texting isn't much different either; that goes through just as many drafts in order to nail a combination of words that makes them look fun, quirky and cute. It's all an illusion."

I was speaking from my recent experience, of course.

Caleb nodded, his smile never leaving his face. Did this guy seriously have any other facial expressions? I wondered what it would take to change that.

"A very thoughtful observation, Lila, thank you." He scratched his chin and crossed his leg over his knee. "These posts and photos you're talking about, arguably conform to the opinions of other people, because anything different will likely be judged and criticized. Would you agree?"

Everything he said was so… structured; so philosophical. It was so… *annoying*.

"Sure," I said, not really having anything else to contribute. I had probably already said too much. If I wasn't careful, he would be able to sense what all the pings in my pocket were about. I knew he could hear them.

"I get that social media is a platform where everyone wants to show their best lives, but it's important to see the flipside–like you said. So often people can fall into the trap of conforming to a world of popularity which stems from insecurity."

"I don't have social media," I said a little too defensively, feeling my phone go off again.

"I'm not saying that you do." His voice was kind, unjudging. "I want you to know that bullying, whether you have experienced it or not, comes from insecurity. Remember; hurt people hurt people. Something to keep in mind."

I stared at him as I let the words digest. Hurt people hurt people–something I hadn't really thought about before. A dark cloud came over me. This was about the forgiveness thing again, I could tell. Did Caleb know about the incident, and this was his way of wanting me to forgive those who hurt me? He knew. He had to. Was it possible he even knew about the lovely Miss Ivy?

"I'm assuming you know what happened at school?" It was best I asked.

"No?" He uncrossed his leg. "What happened at school?"

He looked oblivious, which made me feel a bit better. He didn't know. I was safe.

"Nothing," I muttered.

"Okay," he nodded, not seeming to mind that I was withholding information from him. We sat in silence for a while.

"Can I ask you another question?"

"It hasn't stopped you in the past." My hand flew to my mouth, but I didn't apologise.

Caleb let out a honk of a laugh. "That was quick of you." There went his hands–clasped together again as the other leg went up.

I stared down at my shoes, embarrassed. I don't know what had come over me. Maybe it was this thrill I was feeling from impersonating Ivy Griffin that made me feel confident, stronger, fearless. And the messages. I had never received so many messages from Ryan before. Not even when we were almost together.

"I know you like to dance, but is there anything else you like to do, to express yourself? Favorite pastime? Personally, I like to run, even if I can't run as well as I used to."

"I like to run too."

"Do you?" he asked, his eyes beaming. "Where do you recommend the best places to run around here? I'm still fairly new to the city."

"There are a few good running trails, but we always stuck

to…" I swallowed down hard. "We always stuck to the same trail. The one at…" I couldn't finish. Not when it all came rushing back this fast. Every detail.

"Lila?"

"Come on slow poke, don't give up now, we're almost there!"

"…Lila."

I dug my fingers into the couch, feeling the leather tighten beneath my grip, my nails not sharp enough to pierce it.

"Dad? Dad, are you alright?"

"Yeah, can you give me a hand?"

How could I have not *seen* it? Just seconds before it, I had mocked him, calling him slow. Dad was weak, unable to carry his own weight and where had I been? Thinking about myself; my head in the clouds dreaming about a stupid boy.

"Dad?"

"I'm ok, sweetie." He managed a smile and tried to bring *himself into a standing position. "I'm just getting old. I can't keep up with you, you're too fast for me."*

He wasn't getting old; dad was one of those people who got better with age. He was dying and I had only sped up that process. I knew he looked tired, I knew he had less energy than normal, but all I had cared about was our routine; clocking up those kilometres, seeing if I could go for longer than the last. I should have known dad was sick. But it had all been about me. I had been too concerned about myself. I had been selfish. If that day hadn't have happened, who knows how much longer we could have had with him.

"Hey, what's going on in there?"

The next thing I knew, the chair opposite me was empty, and there was a weight on my shoulder, grounding me in the present. I felt the heat of Caleb's hand, an unexpected comfort that clashed violently with the storm raging inside me.

"What?" I asked, my voice barely a whisper, lost in the whirlwind of my thoughts. The word felt heavy, like it had to push its way out of my throat. I wasn't even sure if it reached his ears.

I slowly released my grip from the couch's sides, noticing the deep dents my fingernails had left in the leather. How long had I been clutching it like that? Time seemed to blur, tangled in the intense emotions and memories swirling through my mind.

"I lost you there for a moment. Were you having a flashback, Lila?"

He crouched down to meet me at eye level, his gaze steady and concerned. But I couldn't look at him. I couldn't bear to see the understanding in his eyes. I stared at the floor; my vision hazy with tears that refused to fall.

"It was all my fault," I said, the words choking out of me, each syllable laced with agony.

"I'm not sure I'm following… What was your–"

"It was all my fault," I repeated, my voice breaking, my throat burning like it was filled with lava. This time, the words were louder, more forceful, demanding to be heard.

The weight of my guilt crushed down on me, suffocating me, making it hard to breathe. My fingernails found the leather of the couch again, and I dug in, trying to anchor myself as the memories flooded back with brutal clarity.

Back in the present, I felt the tears finally spill over, hot and angry, streaming down my cheeks. "I killed him," I confessed, my voice trembling, the words tasting like poison on my tongue. "I pushed him too hard, and it made him worse. I didn't know, but it's my fault."

Caleb's hand squeezed my shoulder gently, a silent reassurance that I wasn't alone, but it did little to ease the crushing weight of my guilt.

"You didn't know, Lila," he said softly, his voice soothing. "You couldn't have known."

But his words felt empty, meaningless. They couldn't

change the past. They couldn't bring my dad back. And they couldn't erase the guilt that consumed me.

"I should have known," I whispered, my voice barely audible. "I should have seen it."

Caleb moved closer, his presence a steadying force. "Grief can make us see things that aren't true, Lila. You didn't cause your dad's illness. It wasn't your fault."

But deep down, a part of me couldn't accept that. A part of me would always carry the burden of that day, the memory of my dad's smile fading, his strength waning. A part of me would always believe that I had pushed him too far, that I had failed him when he needed me most.

"I'm so sorry, Dad," I whispered to the memory of him, my heart breaking all over again.

And as Caleb's words washed over me, the relentless storm of guilt surged stronger, whispering the harsh, unyielding truth I couldn't escape: the weight of my father's death was a shadow I could never outrun.

"It doesn't matter what you say," I said, my voice steady but my heart in turmoil. "I know I did this. I'll never forgive myself."

SEVENTEEN

Lila

A s THE NEW term began, I felt different.

It wasn't that I had been seeking out the faces of those who had mocked me. Even if they were, I wasn't scared of it. A new confidence had grown inside of me, and I had Ivy Griffin to thank for that. I'm not crazy, I know she isn't real—well, she was real somewhere in the world. But you get what I mean. She was real in my head.

And I had created her.

It was empowering to have control over what her life looked like, who she was, and how she spoke. I now understood why Mum used to love writing so much. It was a world where she had the freedom to create her own realities. And in a messed-up world like this one, that was a glorious thing.

Some would say what I was doing with the fake profile was messed up, but I disagree. I wasn't hurting anyone—I was trying to teach a lesson. How that lesson would unfold, I was still working out the details. But so far, after two weeks of messaging, I had Ryan right where I wanted him.

By now the selfies were constant, and after last night, we had even sent each other voice messages using voice recorder. It was the perfect way I could make this "Ivy" girl more tangible without exposing the real face behind the many messages. It was fun to play with my voice, manipulating it in a way where he wouldn't suspect a thing. I had never stared at myself in the mirror so much as I practiced.

It was exactly what I needed to keep my mind off dad. I couldn't fall apart–not now when I was on the verge of exposing Ryan for the person he was. I had to stay focused; I couldn't crumble. I had to think, speak and dress like Ivy, the stunning girl from Germany, in order to redeem myself and make this term a tolerable one. It would only take a moment of vulnerability to undo all of it.

The Instagram profile wasn't enough. I had to do more. I had to carry Ivy's essence into every facet of my life, like an actor embodying a character; and that included here, at school. Which was the reason why today, on the first day back at school, I had packed a spare uniform to change into.

It took a bit of digging, but I had trenched out my old school skirt from three years ago. It was both a fortunate and unfortunate scenario: Unfortunate because it made me realise that between then and now, I still had zero curves, but fortunate as the lack of these meant that it could still button up around my waist with ease. My long, gangly legs had been the only part of my body that began growing at a disproportion rate since grade five. It kind of worked out in my favour as it allowed the skirt to land midway down my thighs, instead of at the knees the way we had to wear it. Instead of the usual pair of navy stockings I always resorted to, I decided on the knee-high white school socks–something I never wore being the biggest cold frog to ever exist. But after careful observation in the mirror, I had decided that it if I folded it under a centimetre or two, it made my legs look longer and leaner.

As for the makeup, I was careful not to go too overboard otherwise the whole look would backfire. A bit of eyeliner and a neutral eyeshadow was all it took to make my eyes pop as I unfastened my hair and let it drape down my back. With Mum working on the other side of the campus, I knew I would be safe. At the end of the day, I would excuse myself to the bathroom and change back into my regular uniform, and ta-da!

The plan was flawless.

What did I want to achieve other than living and breathing the fictional Ivy Griffins? Well, the events of the day spoke for themselves. Part of me expected the whispering and gossip to continue, but the holidays must have worked as a buffer, as now I seemed to have become old news. And just like that, I resumed my prior status where I was slotted back into being the girl that no one talked to. But being talked to is one thing; being noticed is another. I have to admit, I was slightly apprehensive as I walked out in what felt like a costume.

As I walked down the long hallway of C block, I pretended not to notice the sets of eyes that rested on me. The transformation was subtle; not enough to transpire whispers, but distinct enough for shoulders to turn.

By the time I reached my locker, I was invincible. I placed my phone down on the top of my bag behind me and began to organise myself for the day. Our lockers were way too small and narrow for the number of books we needed. It was quite ridiculous. But somehow, I made it work.

"Hey, Lila."

There she was, lingering against the wall behind my locker door. I didn't expect her to acknowledge me or communicate at all.

How long had Maci been standing there?

"Hey, how were your holidays?" My tone was upbeat as though I was unbothered, unaffected. I tossed my hair, sending it flying over my shoulder in one great sweep. The look on her face was priceless; I bet she didn't expect me to actually answer.

"Great." She looked at me tentatively, eyeing me down like a hawk. "Took it easy, went on a few day trips here and there."

"Sounds super!" I said way too cheerfully, pretending to be oblivious to her eyes scanning up and down my body.

"New uniform?"

"This?" I took the edge of my skirt and scrunched my face. "Nope."

She nodded and finally met my eyes. "Well, you look… good."

I could have jumped up and down. This was huge–this was everything. But I had to contain my excitement. I had to play it cool.

"Thanks," I said casually, casting a quick glance down the hallway. Ryan's absence surprised me; they were rarely seen apart. As I turned back, I noticed Maci hadn't moved. Her presence here suddenly felt more significant than just passing by. Perhaps it wasn't about my transformation after all. Maybe she wanted to talk.

"Everything going well?" I asked, trying to break the tension that hung between us.

Maci hesitated, her eyes flickering with uncertainty. "Do you know…" She trailed off, her mouth twitching with unspoken words.

I waited, sensing she was wrestling with something. But just as quickly, she withdrew. "Never mind," she said abruptly, her voice edged with forced cheerfulness. "Everything is great."

There was a shift in her demeanour, a fleeting glimpse of regret in her eyes before she turned to leave. Blinking rapidly, she hurried down the hallway, leaving me standing there, frustrated and unsure of what had just transpired.

I slammed my locker shut with more force than necessary, the echo reverberating down the corridor. I had been so close— almost had her opening up. Yet, once again, Maci slipped away, closing off whatever she had wanted to share.

But I knew this wouldn't be the end of it. There was something brewing beneath the surface, something Maci wasn't ready to reveal yet.

There was a rule that mobile phones were to always stay locked away, but no one actually followed that. This was fabulous, giving me plenty of windows of opportunity to keep Ryan fastened to his phone. I could tell that he was falling for this girl. Heavily smitten. It sickened me how easily someone so pretty could draw anyone in. It disgusted me that he could be this way with two girls at once, proving repeatedly why I had to see this project of mine to the end. His messages came frequently and unprompted, landing in my inbox like fireworks.

Ping, ping, ping.

It got so annoying I had to turn my notifications off, but I did not back down; I did not change my tone. I had to pretend I was just as smitten as he was.

At recess, I found a quiet place near the rose garden and pressed down on the voice recorder. "Hey you. How's your day going? Well, I survived two periods of History but all I could think about was the future and what it will be like when we're in the same city as each other. Two weeks, Ryan. Just two weeks to go. I can hardly wait–yay!"

With a shot of adrenaline, I released my thumb and watched it land in our message thread. Now I had to find a way to witness the look on his face when he heard Ivy's husky voice. Apparently, guys liked that.

As predicted, he was hanging out at the base of the stairs with a few of his mates, Maci and Ellie lurking just metres from them in their awkward attempt to be part of the group without actually joining it. I took a seat on one of the picnic chairs, giving myself a clear view of his poised body language as he pretended not to notice the girls looking on nearby. Rolling my eyes, I took out a book and lifted it to my face–studying it probably a little too hard. I brought it back an inch and let out a breath. There, much better.

It didn't take long until the phone slipped out of his pocket. He didn't even try and hide it as he brought it to his ear, stepping away from his friends to create some distance. He must have played it more than once because he held it there for a while. Anyone could have seen his smile from a mile away–I would know, I was witnessing it. I don't think I had ever seen his lips stretch that wide, his "try hard" posture completely forgotten about as Ivy Griffins swept him off his feet a little bit harder. It was completely fantastic.

Wait. What was this?

I felt like I needed binoculars so I wouldn't miss all the details. The space between them closed in as Maci approached Ryan. My heart quickened. I don't know what happened between them during the holidays, but tension seemed to be flying as hand gestures made an appearance into their conversation. No–the term "conversation" didn't cut it. It didn't appear to be two-sided at all as Maci's mouth did all the talking and Ryan backed away like a puppy being scolded.

My jaw dropped as she snatched his phone from his hands, turning her back to him as he frantically tried to retrieve it. I would have thought more people would be enjoying the show, but they probably assumed they were playing as she took off with his phone in a game of cat and mouse. How much had she seen? Had she seen their messages? I had never seen Maci completely freak out like this before. I almost felt bad.

Eventually, Maci passed the phone back to him. Their bodies came together, closing the distance that they had just placed between them. He placed an arm around her, nuzzling in, her head nodding to whatever he was whispering in her ear.

I shook my head in disgust. He had her wrapped around his little finger. He had fooled her, almost like the way he had once fooled me. It was a letdown for sure, but I wouldn't let this discourage me.

I had a bigger and better plan up my sleeve.

EIGHTEEN

Maddie

I T WAS TIME. Sometimes, to move forward, you have to revisit the past. This was one of those moments. Intellectually, I understood this truth, yet emotionally, I wasn't prepared to confront such a stark reality.

I had come to terms with Dylan's absence–it had been a gradual process, slower than expected, but I had reached acceptance. No longer did I anticipate his return at precisely 5:52 p.m. or catch glimpses of him through the gazebo window engrossed in a game of Scrabble. The stack of sweaty polo tops in the laundry, the outfit laid out meticulously for events, the half-asleep reminders to switch off the bedside light–these routines had faded. Yet, in my dreams, he remained vivid, a presence I knew would linger in my heart indefinitely.

Photographs possessed a unique power to refine memories, much like the way proper lighting transforms artwork. Despite my passion for photography, I hesitated to shed light on these memories, wary of what shadows might emerge. Healing often comes through pain; I understood that deeply. But facing the reality of our fractured family, irreparably split, felt overwhelming. Could the shattered pieces of our life ever be pieced back together?

Dylan's own past trauma, losing his parents during those formative years, had left deep scars, obscuring not just months but years of his life in a mental fog, like an eternal slumber. His pre-Australia life remained largely a mystery to me—mere fragments of a small family and academic success. Always an achiever, well-liked, with a lifelong dream of moving Down Under—these were the pieces I knew.

As humans, when posing for photographs, we beam, exuding light and joy. Reflecting on this, I understood why large segments of Dylan's life remained unphotographed; a significant part of his story left untold.

What I did know was this: Dylan was undeniably the strongest person I had ever known. He loved fiercely, as though untouched by heartbreak. Melbourne suited him effortlessly. Our life together, chronicled in countless photographs, appeared seamless, picture-perfect in every way.

Carefully, I retrieved the cardboard box from the office cupboard, the same one we used sixteen years ago when we moved into this house. Its corners were frayed from countless moves, the bottom threatening to give way under the weight of memories.

Supporting it with both hands, I placed it on the desk, a surge of panic rising within me. Inside lay bundles of photos, tied together haphazardly, reminiscent of scenes from *The Notebook*. Tears welled in my eyes as I flicked through each photo, each page of our story.

My fingers hesitated over the photograph capturing those early, hopeful days in our new home. I closed my eyes, transported back to that moment.

"Yes, I can see it now."

"What do you see?" I chuckled, leaning into Dylan as we

stepped into another empty room, its bare wooden floors and pristine white walls brimming with potential.

Dylan wrapped an arm around me, surveying the space with a determined gaze. "This will be your writing room."

"My writing room?"

"Yes. Can't you see it? Baby, it's perfect."

A smile spread across my face as I envisioned the possibilities. "It is kind of perfect, isn't it?"

"And so will be the many books you'll write one day."

My heart swelled. "You really believe that?"

"Without a doubt." He kissed me tenderly, and as we held each other close, our dreams began to unfold. Dylan metaphorically opened windows of opportunity.

"So much natural light, too."

I nodded, looking out the window. "And a pretty decent view."

Dylan's eyes twinkled with amusement. "Oh, I was going to say, that pile of dirt out there is... inspiring," he teased sarcastically.

"That looks like some excellent soil," I teased back, squeezing him playfully. The backyard resembled a bulldozer's playground, but in our dreams, potential was all that mattered. "Moist enough for a perfect garden someday."

"It would." His expression softened. "And that tree," he gestured to the one dominating the yard, "would make a perfect treehouse. A swing set could fit nicely too."

My heart raced. "Really?"

"Oh, I can see it. Maybe even a trampoline for the little one?"

We had often discussed starting a family, but in that moment, it felt tangible, real. My heart overflowed with joy and anticipation.

"A gazebo. I want a gazebo too." If we were dreaming, I might as well voice all my wishes.

"Two writing rooms now? Aren't you greedy." With a playful grin, he lifted me, spinning me around.

"I think we can make that happen. What do you say?"

Wrapping my arms around his neck, I stood on tiptoes, pressing my nose against his. "You make me so excited for the future," I whispered.

He smiled, leaning in closer. "What kind of gazebo are we talking about?"

I grinned, picturing it perfectly. "An octagonal-shaped one, with tall windows and French doors, painted pale blue and white. We'll have a garden bed circling it, flowers everywhere. And inside, a chandelier hanging from the ceiling, casting a soft glow."

His eyes lit up. "Sounds like a dream."

"It is," I said softly, feeling the warmth of the vision envelop us both.

I opened my eyes, letting the photograph slip from my fingers. Everything we had envisioned had come to pass over the years—the treehouse, the gazebo. But the writing room, that dream remained unfulfilled.

As I stood there, memories flooded back in vibrant detail. I recalled the laughter echoing through the halls as we planned our future together. Each room held the promise of our dreams, each corner filled with the warmth of our love. It wasn't just about the physical spaces; it was about the life we had imagined, the life we had built. Dylan's optimism and unwavering belief in me had been a beacon of hope, guiding us through both the challenges and the triumphs.

I traced my fingers over the photo, lingering on the image of us standing in that bare room, surrounded by possibilities. The years had passed, and while some dreams had evolved into reality, others remained suspended in the realm of what-ifs. The writing room, with its imagined shelves filled with books… still felt just out of reach.

NINETEEN

Maddie

As much as I hate admitting it, I was waiting for this day to come. I knew something was off. I could feel it.

I was hopeful that there had been a shift; her eyes sparking up as her fingers danced on her phone. It really did give me the impression that the old Lila was beginning to show signs of life again—even though I had noticed that she was wearing more makeup than usual. Not only that, but I could also hear the joy in her voice as she slipped into the gazebo to take phone calls, unaware that I was watching. Of course, I knew about it. I was a mother—I noticed everything. Even her grades were bouncing back, which could only mean one thing: she was healing.

Well, that was the conclusion the hopeful side of me came to. But when I got the call from the clinic telling me that she hadn't shown up to her appointment, it confirmed the "off" feeling I had tried so hard to ignore. It didn't make sense. She was doing well with Caleb—I was sure of it. The incident with Ryan was well in the past, and a colleague had told me she was even talking to Maci again. Apparently, they even had a shopping date arranged for today. In fact, it was the reason she was adamant about catching a train into the city before her appointment.

As soon as I finished my call with the clinic, I called Lila, hoping to locate her whereabouts. But when all four of my attempts went straight to voicemail, I began to panic. I wanted to trust my daughter. If she had been late, I might have understood. But there was no excuse for missing an appointment without a phone call, especially when her phone had been fully charged on the counter when she left the house that morning.

Frustration took root. I should have driven her. The appointment should have come first, her shopping date second. How did I know she was where she said she was anyway? I felt sick. I hated that we had entered such a season where I was questioning her every move. Maybe she could sense my mistrust in the same way my gut knew something wasn't right.

But just as quickly, my thoughts took a turn, and a haze of fear closed in. What if something had happened?

I turned my phone over in my hand. Maybe her battery was flat, and she was on her way to the clinic now. I would meet her there—that's what I would do. It was beginning to rain anyway. I didn't particularly like the idea of her waiting outside in the cold and wet. She probably didn't have an umbrella. Grabbing my keys, I sighed a breath of frustration and made the journey in.

I don't know what I was expecting when I pulled into the car park. By now, the rain was coming down harder, and the car began to fog. I cranked up the heater and reached for my phone. No new notifications and no Lila in sight. With the car still running, I released my seatbelt, squeezed my eyes shut, and prayed my daughter was okay.

A knock came to my window, completely startling me. I unwound the window a couple of inches, surprised to see Caleb.

"Mrs. Evans, hi, how are you?"

I can't say I was expecting to see him in this way.

"Maddie. You can call me Maddie," I replied abruptly, ignoring his question.

"Sorry, Maddie." He squinted as the rain from his dark hair fell over his eyes. He angled his umbrella as he bent himself in half to peep through the sliver of space I had made for him.

I knew my tone was sharp, but I had bigger matters on my mind. He may be my daughter's psychologist, but I wasn't about to let essentially a stranger into my car. He didn't seem bothered by the rain or the fact that the wind was so strong that his umbrella held absolutely no purpose at all. He was drenched.

"Lila hasn't shown up?" I said, realising how silly that sounded. "I assume not, otherwise you wouldn't be out here."

Caleb's eyes widened. "You didn't get our call? I'm sorry, Maddie. I wasn't aware that you had been out here waiting. Lila never showed up for her appointment."

"I got the call," I snapped. "I just thought that maybe her phone died and that she had gotten the time wrong or something." I inhaled a deep breath. "I thought I would come in case she showed up."

He scratched his chin, his expression bringing no comfort as his smile left his face.

"Do you think it's possible she is with that boy?"

I had absolutely no idea what he was talking about.

"Sarah's boy," he added, as though he could read my clueless mind.

I couldn't watch him suffer out in this rain. I could barely hear him against the roar of the downpour. I reached over to the passenger side and opened the door.

"Get in."

"Huh?" He pressed his head all the way against the glass, so his nose was peeking into the warmth of the car.

"Get in before you get pneumonia."

He nodded, almost looking relieved as he slid into the seat.

"The boy, Ryan." His voice softened as he ran the palms of his hands together. "Do you think there's a chance she's with Ryan?"

"The boy she threw a stapler at? I highly doubt it."

Caleb's eyes widened. "She threw a what?"

I shouldn't have smiled because it wasn't funny. At all. "You heard me."

"Ok..." He relaxed into the seat and stared ahead at the windshield, which was now completely fogged up. "Wow."

I nodded and joined him as we stared ahead. The rain was coming down in pellets, making it impossible to focus on anything more than a meter ahead of us as we sat in my parked car. It was the first time I realised how weird this was: my daughter's psychologist just randomly hanging out in my car with me. I barely knew the man.

But I was curious to learn his thoughts.

"What makes you think Lila is with Ryan?" I doubted his prediction, but then again, I wasn't the one sitting in on his sessions. Maybe he knew something I didn't.

"I can sense there is something going on between those two."

"I think that might have been the case once upon a time. But now," I scratched my chin and looked down at my phone again, contemplating calling a third time, "I just don't see it."

"But she is talking to someone," he said, moving his feet about under him.

"What do you mean, as in, a boy?"

"That's my guess from the way her phone was constantly going off in our sessions." He inched his long legs closer to his body.

I needed to do a better job of monitoring her phone.

"You can press the lever back," I said, pointing to the side of his chair, "so your legs can breathe."

Before giving him a chance to respond, I went ahead and did it for him anyway. He launched backward in his seat in one swift motion. Now he had space.

"Things seem to be better with her friends, or at least with her best friend, Maci. If she is messaging anyone, it would be her," I said, watching him as his hands reached under the seat and he began to fiddle with something. "Sorry, I have so much junk in this car." It was true—anyone would think I camped out in here. It perfectly resembled the state of my life right now.

Chaos.

"I'm so sorry," he started, with his arm reaching behind his seat. "I think I did this."

His hand reappeared. And there it was. The all too familiar manuscript—the one I had completely forgotten I had printed back in the day.

I stared at the front page where half the title had been ripped off, exposing just my name in a font I had changed at least ten times since then.

"Honestly, it's fine," I said, taking it from his hands, remembering the first time I had presented my husband with the first draft. "It's well and truly… redundant." I tossed it into the back seat, not really knowing why I was so quick to dismiss what once had been my pride and joy.

He watched my lousy throw as it landed somewhere on the floor. In a matter of time, it would get lost and buried with something else.

"Please tell me you still write."

"Ah… well, don't you have a good eye."

"I did manage to tear a lot. But your name is still intact." He gritted his teeth and began searching for it again. "Now I'm curious. What's the book called?"

"Good luck finding it back there," I said with a laugh, watching him. Now that I thought about it, I couldn't remember the last time I had properly cleaned out this car. As bad as it sounded, Dylan had always done that for me.

"What makes you think it's a book?"

He shrugged. "I thought it would be a good guess."

I swallowed. I didn't really want to go back there again.

"*Say It Again.*"

"Oh, I like that." His head popped back up, his hand emerging seconds later with something brown and sticky hanging from his fingernails.

"Oh, wow." I stifled a laugh at the sight of his right hand. "I should be the one apologising."

"What is that?" he said again, laughing as he inspected the goo as though it was some unknown specimen.

I stifled a laugh. "I actually have no idea. How embarrassing."

"It's quite a scavenger hunt back there. I found it, but I won't bring it back out," he said with a gentle smile. Using the edge of his woollen sweater, he wiped his finger. "But I do want you to tell me about your book."

My eyes scanned for a tissue, but I had nothing. Well, nothing I could find to help remove this thing from his finger. I was relieved the manuscript would take a backseat.

Literally.

"It's a story that follows the journey of a girl who escapes poverty and makes a life for herself in London." I stared out through the windshield as a flicker of lightning hit the sky. Part of me wanted to share more; it was a story so complex with plot lines that once kept me up at night as I scribbled into my notebook, determined to remember every detail come morning. But I wasn't about to get into that with what felt like an unpaid counselling session.

He looked at me thoughtfully, the lines in his face deepening. "Sounds intriguing. Where did the idea come from?"

I lifted my eyes and found a smile. He wasn't flirting—I

could tell he wasn't. He seemed genuinely interested in what I had written.

"Thanks, I—"

In that moment, my phone rang.

She was alive. I mean, of course she was. Her phone wasn't dead. But somehow, she had "lost track of time" which I found hard to believe. Lila never "lost track of time." She had always been the responsible one–basically The Timekeeper herself.

Her voice was too upbeat for me to be mad at the fact she had wasted Caleb's time and had me worried sick. The important thing was that she was safe and socialising with her friends. That was a milestone itself, and I wasn't about to put a damper on that.

It was almost as though the clouds parted to the news the moment I ended the call. Seconds later a hint of sunlight kissed the windscreen, clearing the windows and my surroundings were back in vision, reminding me that here I was, in a car park, with my daughter's psychologist.

It all suddenly felt highly inappropriate.

With his hand on the door handle, it appeared as though Caleb got the memo.

"I'm glad Lila is safe. I should get back before the rain takes me down again." He stepped out with his umbrella in hand. "Thanks for the shelter."

"Of course. It's no problem," I said already thinking about getting to my daughter. "I'll give Sarah a call and reschedule for another time. Sorry again about today."

"You have nothing to apologize for." His smile was warm, his face gentle and kind. "I'm just glad Lila is ok."

"Me too."

As he disappeared back inside the clinic, I realised I hadn't asked a single question about the man with the Canadian accent.

At least that's what I thought it was.

I sat there for a moment longer, watching the rain patter softly against the windshield, the brief glimpse of sunlight already fading. My mind raced through the events of the past hour. I glanced at my phone, half expecting another call or message from Lila, but the screen remained silent. The relief of hearing her voice had settled into a strange mix of emotions—worry, frustration, and an odd sense of calm.

"Can I speak to you for a moment?"

I had just finished after-school duty and was practically flying back to my classroom to catch my first break of the day—which happened to be at school dismissal. Five minutes was all I was after; just enough time to take a bite of my tuna salad and hope there wasn't a queue for the bathroom from all the other teachers with bursting bladders. I was in the middle of returning my walkie-talkie when Brad appeared out of nowhere.

I don't know why, but my stomach dropped. It never used to drop around him—not since the email blunder I made last month despite years of praise from him before that.

"Absolutely," I said with far more enthusiasm than I felt. I allowed him to follow me to my classroom. With the lanyard around my neck, I took the key and inserted it into the door.

Something was wrong. He was looking down. Brad rarely looked down.

I smoothed my lips, feeling a ripple of nerves take hold. Maybe this was about Luke. Come to think of it, I hadn't filled him in on the conversation I had with the boy at the end of last term. But the past two weeks had been smooth—I was regularly checking in, and it seemed as though everything was relatively back to normal, even if I hadn't gotten to the bottom of why

Ryan had been spreading rumours. Did my unawareness of this make me a bad mum?

"So, how are you, *really*?"

This wasn't good.

Moving a pencil case to the side, I edged myself onto the table. 'I'm fine, thanks, Brad. What's going on?'

"It has been brought to my attention that there have been a few slip-ups with you lately around CORP."

"CORP" was our school's Continuous Online Reporting Program for student assessments. It was basically an online library of assessment criteria and structured comment templates. If there was one thing I was on top of, it was CORP. I basically led the team with anything summative assessment-related—again, teaching terms.

"Slip-ups?"

There had to be a mistake. I wasn't prideful in thinking I was perfect at my job, but surely, I would have known if I had done anything drastic. And why didn't I know about it until now?

"Yes." His voice was firm, strong, although the look in his eyes was nothing short of apologetic.

A sinking feeling came over me.

"It should have been cross-checked, but for some reason, it wasn't. But a series of assessments you released to the parents last Friday followed the same mistake that happened at the end of last term."

Oh. My. Gosh. I had done it again.

Again.

"What? I thought... I mean, I was sure I went back and..." I had gone back over it. I combed my hand through my hair. I hadn't needed it to be cross-checked because I had triple cross-checked it. Maybe even quadruple-checked.

"Data was released." His eyes were on me. But they were filled with more than just a look of pity—he looked uncomfortable. "Look, it's been a stressful season for you," he started, neglecting the details of my mistake. He crossed his hands over his chest and lowered his head. It was obvious that what was about to come next wasn't necessarily something he wanted. "You're tired. You've had a lot on your plate, Maddie. We are aware of that. You know we are here for you, but we also think you need to take some time."

"Time?" My head shot up. I didn't like where this was going. "What do you mean by time?"

Brad sighed. "Take some leave. You have plenty of it. Take some rest. Look after yourself, spend some time with your daughter, and come back in a week or two."

I stared at him. A week or two was as a month in the world of teaching. Surely, I was hearing this all wrong.

"Is this..." I swallowed, almost too scared to say it. "Is this a warning?"

His face softened with compassion as soon as I said it. "Look, what has happened isn't... ideal. But no, of course not. You know you are valued here. You have a permanent position, you know that. This is more of a request."

"Or, an order," I spat out.

"Well..."

"Come on, Brad."

"I suppose let's see it as that."

I nodded. "Is there anything I can do to fix the mess I've made?"

"Oh, Maddie."

I sounded like a child; I knew it. But I was humiliated.

"Go home and put together some notes for a substitute teacher tonight and leave it with me."

"Oh, wow," I said, playing with the zipper on the pencil case. "That soon, huh?"

But he said nothing. He had made his point clear. I let go of the zipper. "Lila is okay to stay though, right? She can stay?"

"Yes, Lila is fine. It's important she's at school."

I nodded, feeling a string of tension tighten around us. We used to banter, Brad and me. Our relationship was light—professional—but always light. He would always trust me to go above and beyond with any work-related matter, and I would deliver. But now here I was, failing him. Leaving him to pick up the pieces.

"She seems happier though, don't you think? More social, which is amazing."

Brad frowned. "More social? In what way?"

"She and Maci seem to be on good terms again. They went for a bit of a shopping spree together on the weekend."

"Well, that honestly surprises me."

My stomach plummeted. Why was he questioning it?

"Oh," I said, realising I never actually confirmed with the girl's mother that that was where she was. Did that make me a bad mother? Come to think of it, I never got her to parade her new clothes. We used to always do that together. "What's going on, Brad?"

He cleared his throat and crossed his arms over his chest. "From what I'm aware, Lila is still sitting on her own in class, and at lunchtime, it's no different, so I've been told. We keep encouraging her, obviously. But yeah, not sure who she is socialising with, but from what I've put together, I find it very surprising if she was with Maci on the weekend."

I was struggling to understand this. My daughter appeared to be upbeat these days, confident, *something*. What else could that possibly mean?

"Do you think it's possible something is going on between her and Ryan? Do you think she has a thing for him?" It was what Caleb had predicted, and for some reason, I voiced it.

"I think that's even more unlikely, taking into account everything, don't you?"

I stood to my feet and stared out the window. It was almost

time to check on her; the way I always did at the end of the day. I had to make sure she was there. "Maybe it is unlikely," I said, feeling anxious as I processed our conversation. Having some time off work meant that our routine would be broken. Now I would have even less control of my daughter's day.

I turned to face him, clarity nowhere in sight. "But when did anything ever really make sense?"

Brad's expression softened. "Just take the time you need, Maddie. We'll handle things here. And maybe this break will help you gain some perspective on everything."

I forced a smile. "Yeah, maybe."

As I gathered my things and prepared to leave, I couldn't shake the feeling of dread that had settled over me. Everything was spiralling out of control, and I felt powerless to stop it. I had to find a way to fix this, for my sake and for Lila's.

TWENTY

Lila

MUM WAS ONTO me; I could feel it.

In fact, I knew it. It was so obvious, it wasn't funny. I don't know where it came from, but the questions started pouring in as soon as she began spending more time at home. Mum had never taken a day off work. That's a lie—she had taken one. And even then, it hadn't been for herself—it had been for me. Grade One. I had fractured my wrist on the monkey bars at school. I still remember being rushed to the hospital. That had to have been the worst pain I had experienced, second to losing Dad.

It still didn't sound right; the whole concept of him being gone.

Maybe that's why Mum was off work. Maybe she was struggling with it as much as I was, but I somehow doubted it. She seemed to be able to function all the time—actually, she never switched off. Apparently, she was using this time to focus on her writing, which was great and all. That's what she had told me when I asked, but I wasn't sure I believed it. She hasn't written since I was basically a toddler. I couldn't see why she would suddenly start now, not when she was stressed out of her mind about getting lessons ready for her sub. The reason why she was taking time off work so soon after the school holidays was unknown to me. As soon as I asked the question, she would give me some aloof answer and divert the attention onto me, and it went something like this:

"What's new with Maci? Maci is welcome here too, you know. You should invite her. What have you girls been working on in dance? Maybe you could invite them over for a movie night sometime."

She had to be suspicious. Maybe she had even heard me on the phone one time. I sure hope not. I couldn't risk Mum finding out about what was going on, especially when she and Sarah were super chummy these days. But there would be times when she would give me a look and I would know. She knew there was a guy. I knew she knew. But little did she know that Ryan wasn't interested in me.

Maybe he never was.

Oh well. Even though she was on my back, at least I didn't have to worry about her checking in on me after school to make sure I wasn't running off anywhere. I knew that she did that too. It wasn't worth the drama even mentioning her daily walk by the common room when she was probably doing it out of love. It was just easier to pretend I was oblivious to it.

Speaking of oblivious, even after the prank I pulled on Saturday, Ryan was still pursuing Ivy. Sadly, he had been off sick the past couple of days and hadn't been at school, but that hadn't stopped him from texting me while I sat in class, finding new ways to try and hide my phone. Keeping true to the timeframe where "Ivy Griffins" was set to land in Melbourne, I had to find a way to make the whole Instagram budding relationship thing more tangible.

So, I had set a date for the two to meet.

Only, of course, I didn't actually show up as Ivy, or myself, obviously. That was never the plan. I just wanted to experience the satisfaction of him being stood up by someone he liked. I wanted him to know how it felt, but it appeared he was in this too deep.

Ivy Griffins had clearly captured his heart.

I went with the whole "my phone died as I was out with my parents and couldn't let you know that I was running late" excuse. He seemed to buy it, or at least if he hadn't, he didn't voice it. In fact, he was super understanding about it all and even suggested trying again this weekend now that I had "settled in." Sometimes I had to catch myself and be reminded that it wasn't me that he was falling in love with, but some random girl from the other side of the world.

Although nothing felt fake about the connection. After all, this was me; my personality, my witty comebacks, my thoughts, my jokes, my perspective on the world that I was so freely throwing into conversations, day in, day out. It felt real, as psychotic as that probably sounds. We would message into the early hours of the morning only to be exhausted the next day, yet we would repeat our message marathons all over again the next night.

And truth be told, I didn't want it to end. I didn't even know if I hated him anymore.

When Maci took me by the arm in the bathroom at school that morning, I knew that things maybe had gone too far.

"I think Ryan is cheating on me."

It was the first thing she had said to me in almost a week and now here she was, looking as vulnerable as ever, confiding in me.

I grabbed a paper towel from the dispenser and did my best to act surprised but at the same time my heart was in my throat. Was I ready for this?

Yes, I was ready for this.

"What do you mean?" I asked, my voice far too animated.

Maci pinched the bridge of her nose as though she was

trying to stop herself from crying. "He's been super distant and," she came closer to me and dropped her chin, so she was right up to my ear, "I noticed he is following this girl on Instagram. He has even liked all her photos. I have no idea who she is or where she came from."

I lowered my head, so it was at level with hers, silently hoping that she hadn't noticed a massive hastening in my breathing.

"I'm so sorry, Maci," I said, almost meaning it. "Do you have your phone on you? Show me?"

She nodded hurriedly and took out her phone, leading me out of the bathroom and down the hallway, away from potential prying eyes. With teachers lurking the halls, the chances of getting a phone confiscated were pretty high. I followed her towards our lockers. She sighed and clicked into the app.

"Here. This is her. I mean, who can compete with that?"

I glanced down at her screen and felt a rush of something shoot through my body, like morphine.

It was her. I mean, of course it was her. But I was still in character, so I had to act surprised.

"Sure, she is pretty. But what proof do you have that he's cheating?"

Her steps seemed hurried now as we powered along towards our lockers even though there were still ten minutes before the bell would go for first period. I found myself performing a little gallop just to keep up with her.

"Well," she swallowed, as though it pained her to reflect. "He must have been messaging us both at the same time and sent me something that was just so obvious that it had nothing to do with what we were talking about."

"Like what?"

"Oh, you know. Making jokes about how crappy the weather is here compared to up north and that she would need to pack an umbrella no matter what the forecast said."

"Talking about the weather? Really? How endearing."

Maci snorted. "I know. But a dead giveaway at that."

"What a jerk. I'm so sorry, Maci."

"Hmm, that's what I thought," she said thoughtfully, then stopped and turned to face me. "If it had gone down that way at all."

There was something in her eyes that changed. There was something behind it. Was it humiliation? Regret? It was too hard to tell. But she was looking at me so carefully, so intently, so… well, I don't know exactly. But I wasn't enjoying this queasiness building up inside of me.

"There's more to it?"

Maci's lip began to quiver, but she stilled it before I had a chance to say more. Sliding the phone back into her pocket, she crossed her hands over her chest, and then, suddenly, her physiology completely changed.

"You tell me."

I wanted to throw up. This was it. I was done.

That's when I looked up and saw Ryan walking towards us, his eyes flicking between Maci and me with something dark, something sinister. I wanted the floor to open and swallow me whole. But there was no time to escape. Whatever this was, it felt orchestrated, and it was closing in fast.

"What do you mean?" My voice came out weak, pathetic even, but I needed clarity. I had to be certain I wasn't imagining things.

"Well, it was a bit of a wild guess at first. I saw Instagram open on your bag at your locker the other day, which struck me as odd because you don't use Instagram," Maci said, sighing heavily. She tilted her head, clearly exasperated. "Then your mum called mine, asking if we were okay after our supposed shopping 'date' on Saturday because she hadn't heard from you."

"Skipped a psych session to play dress-up," Ryan chimed in as he joined us at our lockers. "Except, you could never be her."

"She doesn't exist, remember," Maci hissed.

"Yes and no. She does exist somewhere out there as Ivy Griffins," Ryan said, relishing the moment. His eyes darted between us; his arm casually draped around Maci as if she were his trophy. She flinched at his touch, torn between exposing me and trusting him.

"I don't know what you're talking about," I started, struggling to maintain composure. "That doesn't prove anything."

"Well, you're wrong," Ryan countered with a smirk. "Funny thing is, I was supposed to meet this Ivy Griffins exactly where you told your mum you'd be meeting Maci. At Baskin-Robbins."

Oh no. No, no, no.

"So, what do you think about..." I swallowed hard, trying to steady myself. I could handle this. I could play their game. I turned to Maci. "What do you think of Ryan cheating on you for a whole month? Because that's essentially what he did. He started flirting with her long before he knew it was me."

By now, eyes were turning towards us. I didn't think I was raising my voice, but apparently, I was. But you know what? I didn't care.

"I can't believe you're doing this when Ryan set you up all along. Can't you see that?"

But she wouldn't look at me. Her body slumped, avoiding eye contact. She seemed gutless. Naive and gutless.

"So, you admit to creating a fake account. For what? Are you that sick?" Ryan's voice cut through the tension, distancing himself from Maci. His arm was off her now. Of course it was. He didn't care about deceiving her any more than he did me. What had he said to keep Maci playing along?

"And you?" I shot back. "You think you're exposing me, but you're exposing yourself."

Ryan snorted, crossing his arms. "You really think I didn't know? Of course I knew! We all knew! Remember when Maci came to your locker that time? It wasn't the first time you left your phone unattended."

He was right. Why hadn't I thought to set a passcode? Probably because my parents always checked my phone—it was the house rule, for now at least. Still, I'd been clever enough to remove the app from my home screen each night when I left my phone on the counter, so Mum wouldn't notice. Then, every morning, I'd reinstall it and sign back in.

Wait, backtrack. Ryan and Maci checked my phone? When? I guarded that thing like a hawk.

Ryan laughed maliciously, comforting Maci. Was she crying? It was hard to tell.

Should I be mad or sorry for her? What about the selfies Ryan sent? The late-night calls? Why put in all that effort if he knew all along?

"He's lying. He has to be," I muttered. It was the only way he could keep Maci on his side.

"Should I show Maci the photos and voice recordings? I have plenty," I said, reaching for my phone. But Ryan lunged towards me.

"It's over, Lila. You've done enough damage." His eyes gleamed with menace, a warning. What would happen if I pushed back?

"Yeah, for your reputation, you cheater. I have nothing to lose," I snapped. I tried to catch Maci's eye, but she still avoided me.

"He cheated, Maci!" I persisted, unable to stop myself. "He's been flirting with this... catfish! I have proof, look..."

"Calm down. It was all a game, Lila," Ryan interrupted coolly. "I knew it, Maci knew it. We were just playing along until we had enough proof to catch you. And you do care about your reputation," he added, eyeing me critically. "I mean, look at you. You even changed the way you dress. Do you think you're actually her?"

I wanted to punch him. How dare he blame me? How could Maci be so brainwashed? So easily manipulated? I glared at her, but she evaded my gaze like a yo-yo.

"You're so naive, Ryan," I seethed. "You orchestrated this, but I'll expose who you really are. I have proof you're nothing but a cheat and a liar." I was shouting now, but I didn't care. I was angry, furious. It was time everyone saw his true colours.

Ryan snorted, composed. If he was scared, he didn't show it. "Stop. At first, we pitied you. Now... you've gone too far, Lila."

I don't remember much after that, just a surge of fury that was abruptly halted by two hands gripping my wrists. I couldn't see or think clearly—only feel the vice-like hold restraining my fury. It hung in the air, waiting to be unleashed, until Mr. Borrow, the principal, appeared seemingly out of nowhere, stopping me in my tracks.

The next thing I knew, I was outside, wind cooling my tear-streaked face. I must have run because I wasn't in the locker room anymore. Tears blurred my vision, mixing with the wind to sting my cheeks. How did everything unravel so quickly? Ryan's betrayal cut deep, but Maci's betrayal hurt even more. She was supposed to be my best friend, my confidante since childhood. Yet here we were, torn apart by lies and deceit.

I leaned against the cold brick wall of the school, trying to catch my breath. Mr. Borrow's stern voice echoed in my mind, reminding me of the chaos I'd almost unleashed back in the locker room. What would have happened if he hadn't inter-vened? Would I have confronted Ryan? Exposed his manipula-tions in front of everyone?

The anger that fuelled me moments ago now gave way to a numbing sadness. How could I have been so blind? Ryan, with his charming smile and easy confidence, had played us both like puppets on a string. And Maci... I couldn't understand why she chose to believe him over me.

Mum wasn't impressed that she had to come and pick me up. I couldn't understand it myself; I didn't hit him. I know I didn't. Or maybe I just didn't remember. That scared me–the thought that pockets of my memory were completely void. I felt like I was losing my mind. I wasn't a violent person; in fact, I was pretty much the opposite. But I guess I had never really experienced bullying before, and maybe I wouldn't have to again. The answer was simple: I had to change schools. I voiced this to Mum, and she was horrified.

"That is not the answer, Lila. You need to show some accountability for your actions."

Accountability. It was a joke. Ryan had no accountability. All I did was find a way to expose him, and I did so successfully. Or unsuccessfully–depends on what way you look at it. I did get told to take the rest of the week off and do my schoolwork from home. So, it looked like I was joining Mum.

Maci didn't believe me. But if I sent her the photos, Ryan threatened that he'd report me, and I was terrified of ending up in juvie or having some sort of record. I was pretty certain what I had done was a criminal offense. Or at least, that's what I thought he whispered to me before I apparently punched him. I still find it hard to believe that I did that. I have never taken a swing at anyone in my life. It just wasn't who I was… or was it?

All I recall was the scene afterward when Mr. Borrow brought all three of us to his office. I had never seen Ryan so cool, calm, and collected, with Maci dangling by his side like a dead weight. She looked like a scared little rabbit as the door closed behind us, and we each took a seat on the black leather chairs. Mr. Borrow's patience began to wear thin as he waited for one of us to speak, but none of us came clean. It was as though, in the waiting, in those few seconds that felt like an eternity, an unspoken decision was made. But even then, I didn't trust Ryan to be the one to voice it.

"There was a party on the weekend that I didn't know about..." I started, not really having a clue where I was going with this. I could hear Ryan's feet scuffing on the carpet as his legs curled under his chair.

"And I was lied to about it until I saw photos the day after," I finished with little conviction.

"You not being invited led you to punch Ryan in the face?" Mr. Borrow wasn't buying into this story at all. His eyes narrowed as he studied me like I was some sort of terrorist. He was waiting for more, leaning forward in his chair with the sternest look on his face. He might as well have expelled me right then and there. That's when I froze. I couldn't finish this, not with him looking at me like that. I hated that I was being painted as the bad guy when, really, I was the victim. Come to think of it, I was painting myself this way. What was I doing? No wonder Mr. Borrow was questioning my violent behaviour—even if I don't remember any of it—when Ryan looked like an angel in all of this. I was not going to fold now, not after everything he put me through.

I felt my hands begin to clench, the muscles in my mouth twitching with too many words held captive around it. It was time to let them free. Jail or not, I had all the photos and timestamps to back me up—the lying, manipulative, disgusting cheat...

"In Lila's defence, I did kind of rub it in her face. I took photos, knowing it would upset her, Sir." Ryan shuffled in his seat. "And then I rubbed it in her face again just now at the lockers."

My eyes shot to Ryan as he continued the story. His tough exterior had eroded completely, and now he looked... almost scared. Scared for me? Either way, he didn't have to speak up, he didn't have to say anything. He probably would have gotten out of this if he had kept quiet. My heart softened, just for a second. But then I remembered that this was about Maci. He was scared of losing her, even if it meant sparing me now.

"Can I see the photo, please?"

I inhaled deeply as I waited for Ryan to pull up an image from his phone and present it to the principal. Maci still wouldn't look at me. She wasn't looking at Mr. Borrow either. Or Ryan. She was lost in space.

Whatever he showed him seemed to do the job as Mr. Borrow nodded and passed it back to Ryan, who looked visibly relieved. Who knows, maybe there had been a party. It was a pretty safe guess. Even if there was, I couldn't have cared less if I had been invited or not.

I released my breath and began picking at the skin around my nails. Somehow, this still didn't feel over.

"Please help me understand, Ryan," Mr. Barrows started, a look of knowing coming over him. "Why would you go out of your way to antagonise Lila? Did you want to make her jealous? Was that the goal?"

If the whole scenario had actually been true, then the question might have been a compliment. But sadly, he was so far off the mark.

I had to catch myself in my thoughts. For a split second, I couldn't help but wonder: was I trying to expose Ryan for the lying cheater that he was? Or did I want to remove Maci from the equation because I felt like I was a better match for him? Did I somehow still want Ryan?

It didn't matter the answer because neither option made me feel good. Here I was trying to feel alive, but I had never felt so dead inside.

TWENTY-ONE

Maddie

THOUGHT I WOULD have hated it, having all this time off. But I had been filling my time quite nicely.

I will be honest with myself in admitting that I had put my writing on the backburner over the years, but something inside of me–despite having received the last couple rejection emails–told me to keep plugging away at it. I hadn't refined my craft in short courses, book clubs, or even much reading over the past year, but I couldn't help but be led by the stirring inside of my soul telling me to return to the drawing board.

It was time.

It was both an exciting and terrifying thought–not necessarily about getting back into writing but having the ability to feel something as profound as this.

Or feel anything at all.

Now, being home alone for the first time in a long time, I noticed how much I missed the flowers, particularly the red roses that used to sit on the counter. Their absence was like a silent echo, a reminder of Dylan's love and thoughtfulness. He always made sure I had my flowers. It struck me deeply, realising how much I had taken those small acts of love for granted. Without them, the house felt emptier, and I felt his absence even more acutely.

Pulling myself out of my misery, a surge of courage welled up inside me as I opened my laptop. As soon as I had pulled up the manuscript for *Say It Again,* something took over me and quite unexpectedly, the entire day disappeared. I couldn't remember the last time I had been so focused on anything outside of work, and I must admit, it felt liberating.

Over the course of the week before Lila went off to spend time at her grandparents' house, adamant to do her schoolwork from there, I chipped away at what would have to have been my ninth or tenth draft. Although this time, it felt different. Something pretty close to magic took place as I read over it with a new set of fresh eyes–as though I was looking at the words on the page for the very first time. New ideas flooded my conscious like an incoming tsunami and there was no stopping it. Well, it had all started that way until I got the call from school that quickly killed the flow.

I had never known my daughter to be the jealous type; it simply wasn't the way we raised her. It was beginning to sound questionable, this tension between her and Ryan. I couldn't shake the feeling that there was more to it, but if so, what was it that she couldn't tell me and why? I wanted to understand her, I really did. But the tension was beginning to extend outwards, to the point where it was beginning to affect my friendship with Sarah. We were being fed the same stories, but I could sense that Sarah was beginning to question not Lila, but me as a parent.

"How are you spending quality time together?" "What has been Lila's biggest trigger?" and, "How is she feeling about her sessions with Caleb?" The questions were simple enough, but it was an attack. Or maybe it only felt that way because I had no idea how to answer them, which was ridiculous when this sort of dialogue used to flow like a river between Lila and me.

Now I didn't know how to have a single conversation with her. I didn't even know how to start one. The fact that I was asking myself that question only made me think that Sarah was right– or at least what she was implying with her many questions was right; I had no idea how to connect with my daughter. What was easier than finding a way to break that barrier?

Sending her off to her grandparent's house. And they lived a stone throw away, so that helped.

It's not like I palmed her off; I really didn't. Lila insisted. She was adamant about going, so naturally, I said yes. She had a great relationship with my parents, and she always seemed to have a lot of fun in their company. It had always been that way; my parents were never "old" grandparents. They had better fashion sense than me and the energy levels of a twenty-year-old. They were go-getters–high achievers and the perfect team. No wonder they had accomplished so much, not only with the psychology clinic but with their heart to serve. They had many friends and loved well. They were among the few people I truly looked up to, and everything I had strived to achieve in my own marriage.

Unlike me, they had found a way to connect with Lila after Dylan passed; their relationship never seemed to change. I always wondered how this could be. Maybe because they never changed with her. That was impossible for me. I couldn't pretend for a second that everything was well and chirpy with the world. I wore my emotions, and my daughter could clearly sense that. It was easier to live in a bubble where everything was unchanged than to confront the painful reality. But being with her grandparents gave Lila stability and consistency, something I had failed to provide as a mother. But maybe they didn't have it all together either.

Because when my phone rang, my mother, Heather, was frantic.

"She said she was going to head out but that was over an

hour ago." Her voice was breathless on the other end of the line.

"Head out for what, Mum? Why is she out on her own?" I was trying to sound calm, but it was rare for me to hear her panicking like this.

"She was going to pick up a parcel for me from the post, the one just around the corner," she took a breath. "That was over an hour ago."

"Did you try and call her? Did you go down there?"

"She didn't take her phone. It's sitting here on the bench."

I closed the lid of my laptop and stood to my feet, fear coursing through my veins like wildfire. "Why would you let her go on her own?"

There was a pause on the other end of the line. "It was just down the road—"

"It doesn't matter, Mum. You know she is unstable at the moment."

"Probably wasn't my best move," she said, sounding hurt.

I squeezed my eyes closed and tried to take control of my emotions. Lila was fine. I had to stop freaking out like this. It was ridiculous.

"Sorry." I stood to my feet and made my way down the hall to find my keys. She couldn't be far. We would find her.

"I'm coming Mum, give me ten."

I was already out the door. Turning the card over in my hand, I knew there was one number I had to call first.

I don't know why I was expecting him to pick up. It was the middle of a business day—he would have had clients, after all. But when he did, a knot I didn't even know I had in my chest loosened.

"If you were a fifteen-year-old girl, where would you go if you wanted to escape the world?"

"Hello, Caleb Peters here. Who is it that I'm speaking with?"

My breath hitched. I had lunged in too fast. "It's Maddie. Maddie Evans." My voice wavered. "Lila is missing."

There was a pause. A long one. For a second, I thought I'd lost him. But then his voice returned, calm and steady on the other end, grounding me in a way I hadn't expected.

"How long has she been gone for?"

The question was simple, straightforward, but it made my heart race. "She's staying at my parents' place, but she went out and didn't come back." I swallowed hard, the reality of what I was saying hitting me again. "She doesn't have her phone on her."

I had spent so much time being frustrated at her lately. It was easy to blame her stubbornness, her defiance. But now, with the creeping dread in my chest, I realised maybe I'd missed something. Maybe there was something else going on.

"Why don't you meet me at the clinic? We can figure out where to go from there."

"Go where?" I said, my voice sharp as I fumbled for my keys. "I don't know where she is." I was being rude, but I couldn't control it. My panic was rising, suffocating me. "I don't know what to do."

"It's okay—I do."

The certainty in his voice stopped me cold. He didn't hesitate. He knew. And in that moment, I realised I trusted him more than I thought I did.

I called Mum quickly, letting her know I'd be making a detour, then drove to the clinic, the weight in my chest growing heavier with each passing second. When I pulled up, Caleb was waiting outside, leaning against the doorframe like he'd been there for hours. There was a quiet assurance in the way he stood, and for some reason, it made me feel less alone in this.

I barely shifted into park before he approached, signaling for me to roll down the window.

"I think I know where we can find her."

"Where?"

"The O'Kinley trail."

I blinked, confused. "You think my daughter's at home?" My voice sounded too sharp, too inconvenienced, and guilt twisted in my stomach. He was here, offering his time—again—and I couldn't even be civil. But he didn't seem bothered, his expression staying calm, patient.

"No, I think she might be at the trail. Has she mentioned running there before?"

A chill ran down my spine. The O'Kinley trail. The one she used to run with Dylan. She hadn't been there since... since him.

"Maddie?" Caleb's voice broke through the fog in my mind.

I shook my head, trying to gather myself. "It's too far away. It's back near our house." The words came out jumbled, rushed. I couldn't see how she could have made it out there on foot. Not without a car. It didn't make sense.

He hesitated for a second, brow furrowing as he leaned against the open door. "Do you want me to follow you? I can take my car."

For a moment, I wanted to refuse. I wanted to take control, to solve this on my own. But the truth was, I needed him. And maybe—just maybe—I didn't want to be alone in this either.

"That might be best," I said, finally meeting his eyes. "Are you done for the day?"

"For now, yeah. I've got another client in an hour."

I bit my lip, the guilt creeping back in. "I'm so sorry. I'm taking your time. Again."

"Maddie, you haven't inconvenienced me." His voice was

soft, and the warmth in his eyes eased some of the tension coiling inside me. "I'm happy to help."

I almost smiled at that. Almost. "What are you charging?"

"Luckily, I have a flexible schedule." He let out a light laugh, and for the first time today, I found myself relaxing, just a little.

I flinched at the sound—how could he be laughing when my world felt like it was unraveling? But then, I realised that the laugh wasn't at my expense. It was kind, reassuring, like he was reminding me I wasn't alone in this.

"This one's on me," he said, leaning slightly closer to the window. His steady presence was reassuring, cutting through the chaos in my head. For the first time in what felt like hours, I felt a little more in control.

Everything about the drive was a blur as Caleb followed closely behind. We pulled up together, parking side by side. There weren't many cars around, the cold weather deterring most of the locals. Everything was still soggy from all the rain we had been having. It didn't even occur to me that my white Converse were quickly changing colour as my feet sank into the ground, a layer deeper than normal.

As we approached the pebbled entrance to the trail, I couldn't help but glance over at Caleb. His calm demeanour was a stark contrast to my mounting panic. He seemed to understand the gravity of the situation without needing to ask a million questions.

"I think we should split up," Caleb suggested. "I'll head towards the east side of the trail, and you can take the west. We'll meet back here in half an hour if we don't find her."

I nodded, grateful for his decisiveness. We started walking, the sound of gravel crunching beneath our feet mingling with the rustling leaves and distant bird calls. Memories of Dylan came flooding back, and I could almost hear his laughter echoing through the trees. My heart ached with the loss and the realisation that I had been so consumed by my own grief that I had missed the signs of Lila's suffering.

"Lila!" I called out, my voice breaking the silence. "Lila, it's Mum! Please let me know if you can hear me!"

No response. I quickened my pace, my eyes scanning the trail for any sign of her. My mind raced with worry. What if she was hurt? What if she had run farther than I thought? Panic surged through me, but I forced myself to stay focused.

The trail parted in various directions, vaguely familiar to me. I had never been much of a runner myself, but our bikes had once travelled the path more times than my feet had. I took a left, remembering the giant, distorted eucalyptus tree that draped unapologetically over the narrow track. Instantly, the temperature dropped a few degrees as I moved past it; the shadows of its tangled branches cast a chill that seemed to match my mental state.

As I rounded a bend, I saw a flash of movement up ahead. My heart leaped into my throat, and I broke into what I attempted to be a run. With adrenaline coursing through my veins, I mustered up the stamina despite my lack of fitness, to make the one-hundred-meter stretch. I could already feel a blister coming on as my ankle socks slipped under my heel with every stride.

But it was worth it.

There, sitting on a large rock by the side of the trail, was Lila. Her shoulders were hunched, her face buried in her hands. Relief washed over me, and I slowed down, approaching her cautiously.

"Lila," I said softly, reaching out to touch her shoulder. She flinched but didn't pull away. "It's okay. I'm here."

She looked up, her eyes red and swollen from crying. "Mum, I—I'm sorry," she choked out, tears streaming down her face.

"Shh, it's okay, sweetie," I whispered, pulling her into a

hug. She trembled in my arms, and I could feel her anguish. "You have nothing to be sorry about. I'm just glad I found you. We were so worried."

Why did you take off like that?

I was desperate to know. I still fully couldn't make sense as to why…

"I thought I killed him," she sobbed. " I was so convinced that I killed him. I didn't know he was sick. I thought if I pushed him to keep running, he'd get better. But he didn't, and it's my fault."

My heart shattered at her words even if it didn't ignite any memory.

How could she carry such a heavy burden? "Lila, listen to me," I said, pulling back to look into her eyes. "Your father loved you more than anything in this world. He would never blame you for what happened. He wanted to spend those moments with you because you made him happy. You didn't kill him, sweetie. The cancer did."

She clung to me; her sobs gradually subsiding. "But I feel so guilty," she whispered.

"I know," I said, my voice trembling. "I know. But you don't have to carry that guilt. We'll get through this together, okay? We'll talk to Caleb and figure things out. You're not alone."

She nodded, wiping her eyes. "Okay, Mum."

We stood there for a while, holding each other, finding solace in our shared pain. Eventually, I heard footsteps approaching. Caleb emerged from the trail, his expression one of relief mixed with concern.

"You found her," he said, his voice gentle.

I nodded, managing a small smile. "Thanks, Caleb. I don't know what I would have done without your help."

Lila's eyes danced between the two of us. "What is he doing here?"

"Well…" I started, not entirely sure how I would explain

this. I mean, how do I tell my daughter that I called her psychologist the moment I found out she was missing? I didn't want her to know that he had shared any information about their sessions together. That would only betray her trust. It would put Caleb in the bad books and push me down there even further.

"Your mum accidentally called the clinic," he started, picking up that I was struggling to come up with an answer.

"And Caleb picked up."

"Why did you call the clinic?" Lila parted from me, her eyes boring into mine.

"Grandma called. She couldn't find you. Our call was cut short, but instead of calling her back, I must have tapped one of the recent contacts. The clinic is one at the top." I gritted my teeth at the lie. At least it was the half-truth. And she did need to know that she put her grandmother in a frenzy. It wasn't fair to just take off like that.

"How did you know to find me here?"

"Just a sense."

I wanted to ask how she got out here, but I didn't want things to blow up. Not when she was emotional. For now, it didn't matter. She was here, she was safe.

And she had *hugged* me.

As we walked back to the car, Lila's grip on my hand tightened. I glanced down at her, my heart aching at the sight of her tear-streaked face. She was so young to be carrying such a heavy burden. We reached the car and Lila got in ahead of me.

I turned to Caleb. "Thank you. I can't begin to tell you how grateful I am," I said, my voice breaking.

He shook his head. "You're a strong woman, Maddie. You would have found a way. But I'm glad I could be here."

I smiled and with a little nod, opened the door to the

driver's side. Caleb closed the door behind me before turning to walk back to his own vehicle.

I turned to Lila, brushing a strand of hair from her face. "Are you okay, sweetie?"

She nodded, though her eyes still shimmered with unshed tears. "I'm sorry I ran off, Mum."

I shook my head, reaching for her hand. "Don't apologise, Lila. I'm the one who should be sorry…" I swallowed, feeling a calm wash over me like a breeze. "I should have seen how much you were hurting."

Lila's grip tightened around my hand, her own tears starting to flow. "I miss him so much, Mum. Every day."

"I know, sweetheart, I know," I whispered, pulling her into a tight embrace. "I miss him too, more than words can say. But we have each other, I'm here. I'll always be here for you. I promise. Your dad wouldn't want us to be sad."

As we sat there, the weight of the past few months seemed to lift just a little. We were still broken, still grieving, but for the first time, I felt a sense of unity between us.

TWENTY-TWO

Maddie

I SAT BY THE window, my eyes tracing the horizon as the sun dipped below it, casting a warm, golden glow across the room. The house was quiet, except for the soft hum of the refrigerator and the occasional creak of the floorboards.

Lila was at dance practice. Other than dropping her directly off at the doorstep of the studio, I had achieved very little today. I took a sip of my untouched ginger turmeric tea, trying to fight the flutter of anxiety in my chest. I wasn't used to this, doing nothing. I had vigilantly finished my sub plans sent them off, stressing if they would be followed. It was one of the reasons why I never took time off; it only creates more work when you come back. The holes in the learning and the derailed behaviour from having a routine disrupted takes days to bounce back from.

But I had no choice.

I sat my cold cup of tea down next to the unopened *Robyn Harding* novel on the coffee table, trying my best to push work out of my mind. I had a little over an hour until I had to pick Lila up and I wouldn't be late. I had set an alarm on my phone to be sure of it. I had to keep my eyes on her.

Leaning my head back against the chair, I allowed myself to drift into the memories of Dylan—the way he laughed, the way he held me, and the stories he used to tell. My soul whimpered as I found my mind transitioning from one unrelated memory to the next. I missed him so much. Then one memory surfaced—a conversation we had late one night, where Dylan had opened up about his college years. It was so early in our beginning, yet I was never part of it. A season forgotten, buried as deeply as the grief that accompanied the loss of Dylan's parents.

But there were parts I was let in on, fragments of that chapter that were safe to discuss. And I remember it like yesterday.

It was an autumn evening, and the fire crackled in the hearth, casting a flickering light around the living room. Dylan and I were curled up on the couch, wrapped in a blanket, sharing a bottle of wine. Dylan had a distant look in his eyes, one I had come to recognise as the look he got when he was lost in memories.

"Dylan," I said softly, resting my head on his shoulder, "tell me more about college. I know that time brings up a lot of emotions. What's something about that time I don't know about that you're happy to share?"

He sighed, his breath warm against my hair. "College was... complicated," he began. "Before I was dealing with my own stuff, I had put a lot of time aside to help a friend out."

"Do you want to talk about it?" I asked, gently coaxing him. I knew he had suffered greatly when his parents died in that horrific car accident, but he had never gone into detail about his time in college.

"There was a lot I blocked out," he admitted, his voice tinged with sadness. "But there were also some good times. I had a friend, Kay. He was like... family to me."

I smiled, encouraged by the softer tone in his voice. "Kay? I've never heard you mention him before."

"He was... an amazing guy," Dylan said, a wistful smile

playing on his lips. "Kay was one of those people who could light up a room just by being in it. He had this resilience, this ability to keep going no matter what life threw at him."

"Sounds like someone I'd like to meet one day." I squeezed his hand just as his smile faltered slightly.

"He was definitely likeable. The best of the best. We lost touch after a while, when everything happened. But he was dealing with his own stuff too."

I nodded, understanding how complicated life could be. It didn't mean it was personal.

Dylan returned my squeeze, inhaling. "I'll always remember the holidays we spent together. Spring Break, Fourth of July, Thanksgiving… even Christmas one year. Family was complicated. Especially for him. His grandparents had been his legal guardians since his mom… well, after she left.'

"How old was he when she left?"

"Six, I think. Young."

I felt a pang of sympathy. 'That must have been hard for him.'

"It was," Dylan agreed. 'But he never let it show. He was always the one lifting everyone else's spirits. I remember that one Christmas; I invited him to stay with us. Freshman year, I think. He was hesitant at first, didn't want to intrude, but I insisted. He lived in Wisconsin, and we were living in Lansing at the time, about five hours apart. He made the drive. We had the best time— decorating the tree, being dudes in the snow with these huge mortar snowballs. it was extra. It was just easy with him, you know?"

There was both a joy and sadness in my husband's eyes as he went back. But by doing so, he was taking a step forward.

"Those are the best kinds of people," I agreed.

Dylan took another sip before placing it down more slowly than he had all night. "He was. He was one of the best dudes I got to share a lot of life with."

I didn't want the flashback to end. I wanted nothing more than to be back there, curled up on the couch with my husband. But the memory faded, and I opened my eyes, blinking back tears. I had never heard Dylan speak of "Kay" again after that night, but the tenderness in his voice when he did was something I would never forget. It was clear that this friend, whoever he was, had meant a great deal to him, a bright spot in an otherwise dark period of his life.

I wondered now about Kay, where he was, what he was doing. I never learned his last name. Dylan never spoke about him again after that night. It was either too painful, or it was what it was; the two of them had lost touch and weren't close anymore. If that was the case, Kay probably didn't even know about Dylan's death.

I felt a sudden urge to find out more, to piece together the fragments of Dylan's past that he had left behind. We wouldn't create any more memories together, but I could go back and learn his.

I knew where the best chance was to find them. If they were anywhere, if a photo of the two of them even existed, it would be found in one of our many photo albums. And we had a cupboard full of them. Some neatly arranged and labelled, other albums not. The ones that made the cut were colour coded, representing some of our most fond moments in time; our engagement, wedding... baby photos of Lila along with about ten more albums highlighting basically every waking moment of Lila. You name it, it was there.

Then there were boxes too of photos that never got sorted. And as the years went by, the box had grown, becoming too overwhelming to even begin the project of sorting them. So, we didn't. Then, of course, developing photos started becoming redundant as the digital world grew. The problem was, all of these photos... all of these albums, were stored away in the office. Dylan's office.

And I hadn't set foot in there since before he died.

Was I ready? No, I would never be ready. But with a

curiosity deeper than my fear, I stood to my feet. I didn't know how easy this would be, if I would even find anything. And I would probably need hours to go through it all. I barely had thirty minutes until I had to pick Lila up.

I arrived at the door and took a heavy breath.

It's going to be fine, Maddie.

It had been over a year, and the room was exactly the way it had been left. As I stood at the door, I took in the familiar surroundings. The printer remained in the right-hand corner by the window, unplugged. The reams of white paper, still sitting beside it. The silver metal photo frame of the three of us at the beach three summers ago still prompted up the middle shelf above his desk. His florescent sticky notes to the right of his mouse near his desktop computer.

As I turned my head, I noticed the peace lily plant by the cupboard was still there, standing strong on its golden pedestal. I frowned, wondering how that could be. Plants needed to be watered. But the more I thought about it, it began to make sense. I knew Mum came into the office on occasion when she visited the house. She didn't tell me when she would, but the room doesn't clean itself. Nor do plants water themselves. She must've come in here and dusted every now and then, knowing this room was one I hadn't re-entered.

Bless her.

I expected the pain inside me to twist a little. But my heart kept a steady beat. Maybe it was going to be fine after all.

With the daylight dwindling, I knew I didn't have much time. I had to make this count. My fingers trembled slightly as I grasped the handle of the office door, pushing it open slowly. The room smelled faintly of old books and Dylan's cologne, a scent that hadn't faded even after all these months. I crossed the threshold and flicked on the light, casting a soft glow over the familiar surroundings.

The cupboard where we stored the photo albums stood tall

against the far wall. I approached it with a sense of reverence, my heart pounding in my chest. I opened the doors and was greeted by the sight of neatly stacked albums and several boxes that hadn't been sorted. My hands moved instinctively to the boxes, starting with the top one.

As I sifted through the photographs, memories flooded back in a whirlwind of emotions. Pictures of our engagement, our wedding, Lila's first steps, family vacations—all interspersed with candid moments of laughter and love. Each photo was a reminder of the beautiful life we had built together.

It wasn't long before I found a photo that made me pause. Dylan was in the picture, smiling broadly, with his arm slung around another young man. They were both wearing Michigan Wolverines gear and sunglasses, clearly enjoying a football game. I flipped the photo over, and there it was, written in Dylan's handwriting: *Dylan and Cay, September 2004.*

Spelt "Cay", not "Kay", as Dylan had said. The unusual spelling caught my attention, but what stood out even more was the birthmark on Cay's right forearm—a distinctive smattering of moles, or was it a birthmark?

I stared at the photo, trying to piece together this new fragment of Dylan's past. Who was Cay, really? And why had Dylan never mentioned this particular memory?

I examined the photo more closely. The boys looked carefree, basking in the excitement of the game, the stands behind them filled with enthusiastic fans. The date, September 2004, placed it during Dylan's college years, the time he had spoken about with such mixed emotions. This photo was a testament to their friendship, a snapshot of a moment Dylan had kept close to his heart.

I couldn't help but let my curiosity about Cay deepen. Who was this person who had been such a significant part of Dylan's life, yet remained a mystery to me? And why had Dylan kept these memories hidden away?

I looked back at the photo, studying what I could see of Cay's face again. The sunglasses obscured his eyes, but there was something familiar about him, something that tugged at the edges of my memory. But no matter how hard I tried, I couldn't place him.

I continued to sift through the photos, my eyes scanning each one for more clues. There were shots of Dylan at parties, in class, and even during a spring break trip to the beach. One particular photo caught my eye. It was of Dylan; the other, I assumed, was Cay. But like the last one, I couldn't make out any facial features as the boy's face was turned as they were running under a large oak tree, Dylan's face lit with laughter, their bodies inclined towards each other. But with Cay's arm facing the lens, his birthmark was visible again, and I traced it with my finger, feeling a strange connection to this person I had never met.

After a little more digging, I found a small, leather-bound notebook wedged between the pages of one of the albums. Curious, I opened it and found it was Dylan's journal from his college years. If you would even call it that, with only one entry hidden amongst a bunch of scientific study notes about the brain, mental processes and behaviour.

I hesitated for a moment, feeling like I was intruding on his privacy, but my need for answers pushed me forward.

October 3, 2004

Cay and I had a long talk last night. He opened up about his mom leaving when he was just a kid, and hearing it from him hit me harder than I expected. He didn't go into too much detail—Cay never really does—but the way he described it, I could feel the weight of what he's been carrying. Growing up without a mother... it's something I can't imagine. The more I think about it, the more I realize how much it must have shaped him, though he never lets it show.

What really got to me wasn't just the story itself, but the way he talked about it. So calm, so matter of fact, like it's just a part of who he is now. But I could see the pain, even if he didn't say it outright. There's a lot more to his past than he's willing to share, especially when it comes to family. I hate how complicated things have gotten for him.

We also talked about the future. Despite everything he's been through, Cay's always thinking ahead. He's the guy who's there for everyone else, never asking for anything in return. We joked about how we'd run our own practice one day, helping people the way we've always dreamed of. It's a long way off, but I believe we can do it. I believe in him. We've always balanced each other in a way that feels right, like we're meant to do this together. I've never felt so excited about the future or felt like I could truly dream it. It's exciting.

Tears welled up in my eyes as I read Dylan's words. It was

clear that Cay had been an important part of his life, a source of support and comfort during a difficult time. I felt a pang of sadness for not knowing about this friendship while Dylan was alive. It was as if I had only known half of my husband's story.

I closed the journal, holding it to my chest as I took a deep breath. This new information about Cay added another layer to my understanding of Dylan. It made me appreciate the depth of his compassion and the strength of his friendships. I felt a renewed sense of determination to uncover more about Cay and their time together.

Returning to the box, I found a few more photos of Dylan and Cay. In one, they were at a Halloween party, both dressed as superheroes, striking exaggerated poses. But again, I couldn't see Cay's face as they were both wearing masks. In another, they were studying in what looked like a campus library, their heads bent over books, with Dylan playfully trying to distract Cay. Every photo of Cay seemed to follow a pattern: his face was either covered, turned away, or he was captured mid-action, like dancing down a hallway.

As I carefully placed the photos back in the box, I couldn't shake the feeling that finding Cay might bring me some closure. If he was still out there, I needed to know. I needed to understand why Dylan had never mentioned him again, and what had happened to their friendship.

With renewed determination, I closed the cupboard and turned off the light in the office. I knew that this was just the beginning of a new chapter in my journey of understanding Dylan's past. And maybe, just maybe, finding Cay would help me find a piece of myself that I had been lost with Dylan's passing.

TWENTY-THREE

Maddie

"**B**ABY?"

I ROLLED over, seeking his warmth, and nestled my body closer to his. His breath felt warm against my skin as he gently stroked my arm.

"Hmmm?"" I mumbled, half-asleep, enjoying the soothing sensation of his touch.

"Have I told you today how much I—"

"Love me?" I finished for him, a playful smile tugging at my lips. With my eyes still closed, I lifted my head and pressed my cheek against his. "Yes, hun. You did. This morning, just as I was heading to the bathroom."

He chuckled softly. "I know how to pick my timing."

"You certainly do," I replied, my smile widening. Leaning in, I kissed him deeply. "I'll love you always, Dylan," I whispered as I pulled back.

Those words, vows we made long before saying "I do," were our anchor through every season, especially the tough ones.

Dylan often woke at 2:20 a.m., like clockwork.

"It will get easier, day by day," he whispered, drawing me closer under the duvet.

"Things are so hard," I confessed, feeling tears well up. With my eyes shut tight, tears began to escape. "I don't know how to make it better."

He lifted my chin and planted a gentle kiss on my forehead, always bringing comfort.

"You're so strong, baby. Progress is progress, no matter how little."

I felt a rare calm wash over me, believing his words for the first time in months.

Wait.

Struggling, I forced my eyes open, seeing his silhouette faintly lit by moonlight.

How was this possible?

Reaching for the bedside lamp, we both groaned as the light snapped us awake.

"What's wrong?" he asked, shielding his eyes, concerned.

With my heart racing, I sat up. "How? You're—"

His face softened, a knowing look. "Shhh, baby." He gently brushed away a curl of hair stuck to my cheek.

Tears flowed freely. He gathered me up, laying me back down, kissing my tear-stained face as confusion overwhelmed me. His soft lips hovered over my wet eyelashes.

"But you're... I saw you—" I tried to say, but his lips met mine, silencing me. Slowly, he reached for the light switch, bringing us back to darkness. Peace washed over me once more. No words were needed as we shared an intimate moment, questions forgotten, everything making sense again.

I opened my eyes to a blinding light.

"Babe, can you please turn it off?" I muttered, pulling the duvet over my face.

No response.

Stretching out, I groped around the warm bed, searching for him. Frowning at my lack of success, I wondered how he had moved so quickly. Slowly, I peeled back the duvet, blinking against the harsh light like a hot summer sun. The blinds were open; birds chirped outside.

Panic seized me, hesitating to turn my head. Eventually, I turned left to where Dylan should be—empty. I brought my hands to my face, eyes and pillow wet.

6:14 a.m.

How had time jumped four hours?

"...Mum?"

I turned sharply, seeing Lila in the doorway, concern etched on her face.

"Hey, honey, what's up?" I tried to sound casual.

"Have you been crying?"

"I don't know," I admitted, sitting up. "I must've dozed off."

Lila scrutinised me, nostrils flaring, trying to gauge if I was telling the truth. Vulnerable, she looked at me; —a wreck.

"You dreamed about Dad."

Her statement broke my composure. I nodded, meeting her eyes. The connection was everything.

Unexpectedly, Lila came over, sitting beside me on the bed. I shifted, making room for her.

And as though she had dropped ten years, she curled up next to me.

Her back to me, she reached back, little finger linking with mine. In an instant, the heaviness inside of me dissolved and my heart swelled with warmth.

"Sometimes, I dream about Dad too," Lila murmured softly, her voice barely above a whisper.

Her words hung in the air, heavy with the weight of shared grief. I turned to look at her, seeing the vulnerability etched in her young features. The bedside lamp cast a gentle glow, highlighting the tear tracks on her cheeks.

"You do?" I asked gently, trying to gauge her emotions.

Lila nodded, still facing away from me. "Yeah. Sometimes,

it's like he's right there, like he never left. But then I wake up, and he's gone again."

Tears welled up in my eyes again, not just for my own loss but for hers too. How had I missed this? How had I not been more sensitive to the fact that she carried this pain alongside me?

"Oh, Lila," I whispered, reaching out to stroke her hair. "I wish I could take this pain away from you."

She didn't respond, but leaned slightly into my touch, seeking comfort in the only way she knew how.

We sat in silence for a while, the weight of our grief palpable in the dimly lit room. Dawn was breaking outside, casting a soft, golden light through the window blinds, as if the heavens themselves were reaching into our sorrow.

After a few moments, Lila pulled away slightly, wiping her tears with the back of her hand. "Do you think he knows we still think about him?"

I hesitated, my heart aching with the complexity of grief, dreams, and the mysteries of Heaven. "I... I'm not sure, sweetheart," I whispered, my voice thick with emotion. "But I believe he's with God now, and maybe in ways we can't fully understand, he knows. I think Heaven is closer than we realise."

Lila nodded quietly, her gaze drifting to the window, as if hoping to catch a glimpse of something beyond the horizon. I squeezed my eyes shut and inhaled deeply, feeling the warmth of the morning light. It wasn't everything, but for now, the gentle warmth of this new day would be enough to hold us, enough to remind me that even in our darkest moments, light would find its way back in.

TWENTY-FOUR

Lila

THE FOLLOWING DAY, tension hung in the air as I walked through the school hallways. The confrontation with Maci replayed in my mind on a loop, making me feel more isolated with every step. I avoided eye contact, not wanting to see the judgment in my classmates' eyes.

At lunch, I found a secluded spot in the library. The quiet was a welcome relief from the chaos outside. I pulled out my notebook, hoping to find solace in writing, but my thoughts kept drifting back to Maci. We used to be so close, sharing everything, but now there was a chasm between us.

Just as I was getting lost in my thoughts, my phone buzzed. It was a message from Maci.

Meet me at the bleachers after school. We need to talk.

It was the first time she had texted me in months. My heart pounded as I read the message. I wasn't sure what to expect, but I knew I couldn't avoid this confrontation any longer. I replied with a simple "Okay," and spent the rest of the day in a haze of anxiety.

After school, I headed straight to the bleachers, my heart racing. I quickly texted Mum to let her know I'd be a few minutes late. She wouldn't mind. She probably hadn't even left yet since we lived so close.

Maci was already there, sitting alone with her arms wrapped around her knees. She looked up as I approached, her expression unreadable.

"Maci," I greeted her cautiously.

"Lila," she replied, her voice flat. "Sit down."

I took a seat next to her, the silence between us thick and uncomfortable. After a few moments, she spoke.

"Why did you do it?" she asked, her eyes searching mine. "Why did you create *Ivy*?"

Looks like we were getting straight to it.

I took a deep breath. I would be honest this time. "I was trying to protect you. And I was so angry at you. I saw how close you and Ryan were getting, and I didn't trust him. I thought if I created someone who could catch his attention, I could prove he wasn't who he pretended to be."

Maci's eyes filled with tears, but she quickly blinked them away. "You should have talked to me, Lila. Instead, you went behind my back and made me look like a fool."

"Really? You haven't spoken to me in months. You know that's not true," I said on the defence.

She didn't say anything, but instead, just held her knees tighter.

"I suppose that's fair."

"It is," I agreed. "You wouldn't have believed me."

She sighed heavily. "Ryan told me he knew about Ivy all along. He said he was playing along to catch you out, to humiliate you. Is that true?"

I shook my head, anger bubbling up inside me. "No, it's not true. Ryan didn't know Ivy was fake until the other day. He's lying to you, Maci."

Her face crumpled, and for a moment, she looked like the girl I used to know, the one I shared all my secrets with. "Why would he lie about that?"

"Because he's trying to cover his tracks," I said softly. "He doesn't want to admit he fell for a fake profile. He's trying to save face."

She watched curiously as I took out my phone. I hesitated for a moment, then handed it to her.

"What's this?" she asked, opening it.

"Proof," I said quietly. "Proof that Ryan didn't know about Ivy and that he was lying to you."

She stared at the screen then back at me. "What kind of proof?"

"Screenshots of the conversations I had with him as Ivy," I explained. "And voice recordings of him talking to Ivy. I saved everything before I deleted the account."

Maci's hands trembled as she flipped through the screenshots. Her eyes widened as she read Ryan's messages, seeing the flirty exchanges, the compliments, and the plans he made with Ivy.

"He... he really fell for it," she whispered. "He thought she was real."

I nodded. "He did. And when he found out the truth, he lied to you to save himself."

Tears welled up in Maci's eyes again, but she blinked them away. "Can I listen to the recordings?"

"Of course," I said, turning the volume up for her. "They're all there."

Maci put on her earphones and played the first recording. Ryan's voice came through, smooth and charming, as he chatted with Ivy. I watched her face as she listened, her expression shifting from disbelief to anger to sadness. She passed me back my phone.

"This makes me want to vomit."

I took it from her and tapped my downloads. I clicked on the file, and Ryan's face appeared on the screen, smiling and speaking in a tone I recognised all too well. "Ivy, you're so amazing. I can't believe we haven't met in person yet. I'm really looking forward to it."

Maci's jaw clenched as she watched beside me. "He really thought she was real."

"Yes," I affirmed. "And he was planning to meet her."

Maci's eyes narrowed as she read his words, her anger evident. "He's such a liar," she muttered. "He made me believe I was the only one he cared about."

Same here, once upon a time.

I nodded, feeling her pain. "I know. And I'm sorry you had to find out this way. But you deserve to know the truth."

She continued scrolling through the screenshots, her expression hardening with each message. "He told me that he was falling for me," she whispered, her voice breaking.

"Ugh," was all I could say in response to that. It felt like I had taken a knife to the chest. I guess it meant that his feelings for her still hurt me even though I was sure I hated him.

Maci buried her face in her hands, her shoulders shaking with silent sobs. I reached out, hesitated, and then placed a tentative hand on her back.

"I'm sorry, Maci. I know I've lost your trust, but you deserve to know the truth. Ryan isn't who you think he is. He proved that when he just disappeared."

She looked up at me, her eyes red and swollen. "I feel like such an idiot. I stole him from you, thinking he was worth it, and now…"

I shook my head. "You're not an idiot. You believed in him because he made you feel special. The same way he made me feel special once upon a time. That's not your fault."

Maci sniffled, wiping her nose on her sleeve. "I just don't know what to do now."

"Do you still care about him?" I asked gently.

She hesitated, then shook her head. "Not after this. I can't be with someone who lies to me."

Relief flooded over me. I knew she was smart. "Then you need to confront him," I said firmly. "He needs to know that he can't get away with this."

She nodded slowly, determination replacing the sadness in her eyes. "You're right. I'll confront him with the evidence. If he denies everything, it'll just confirm the truth even more."

It was a good point. Ryan had a chance to come clean and own his mistakes. I had no intention of sharing these screenshots with anyone else; they would stay with me. Unless I wanted a stapler in *my* face.

We sat in silence for a few moments, the weight of our conversation hanging between us. I could see the pain in her eyes, and I knew this wasn't easy for her. Finally, she took a deep breath and turned to face me.

"I miss you, Lila," she said softly. "I miss our friendship."

I couldn't believe this. I could pinch myself. "I miss you too," I replied, my voice barely above a whisper. "I hate how things have been between us."

"Things have sucked."

"You have no idea."

"I miss our late-night talks," Maci said, her face coming alive at the memory. "The ones where we'd laugh about the stupidest things until we couldn't breathe."

"Me too," I admitted. "And our ridiculous dance parties in your room, trying to outdo each other with the worst moves."

Maci giggled. "I think you still owe me a rematch. My 'robot' was unbeatable."

"Oh, it's on," I challenged, playfully nudging her. "Just wait until you see my new and improved 'floss.'"

She laughed, the sound bringing a warmth that had been missing for too long. "I'll hold you to that." A smirk appeared on Maci's face. "I can't believe you downloaded Instagram and faked your identity… or her identity."

"It was a bold move," I agreed.

"A very bold move," she repeated, a hint of laughter in her voice.

I grinned, the tension between us easing just a little. "I was channelling my inner secret agent. You know, for the greater good and all that."

Maci chuckled, wiping her eyes. "Yeah, like a high school James Bond, but with social media instead of spy gadgets."

I laughed. "Hey, Instagram can be a powerful tool. Who needs a license to kill when you have a fake profile and some clever messaging?"

She shook her head, still smiling. "I swear, Lila, only you could turn a mess like this into a covert operation."

"What can I say?" I shrugged playfully. "I've got a knack for drama."

Maci rolled her eyes but couldn't hide her amusement. "Maybe you should join the drama club instead of causing it."

"Maybe," I conceded, my smile widening. "But where's the fun in that?"

She sighed, her smile fading slightly. "Despite everything, I appreciate what you tried to do. It was crazy, but you did it for me."

"Maci," I began hesitantly, "there's something I need to say."

It was time I swallowed my own pride.

She looked at me, her expression wary. "What is it?"

I took a deep breath, my throat tightening. "I know what I did was wrong. Creating Ivy, lying to you… I crossed a line. And I'm really sorry. You were my best friend, and I hurt you. I didn't just betray Ryan, I betrayed you too. I should have talked to you instead of trying to handle things on my own."

Her eyes softened, but I could see the pain lingering. "You did hurt me. But… I can't pretend like I didn't hurt you too."

I nodded, swallowing the lump in my throat. "I guess we both messed up. I let my anger and jealousy get the best of me, and I pushed you away when I should've just told you how I felt."

Maci looked down, her voice barely above a whisper. "I'm sorry too, Lila. I should've never gone after Ryan, especially when I knew how much you liked him. That was wrong. I just hope one day you can forgive me."

I reached out, placing my hand gently over hers. "I already do."

TWENTY-FIVE

Maddie

THE FINAL DAY of my leave was slipping away, and tomorrow I would be back at work, faced with the routine I had temporarily escaped. Each passing moment felt like sand slipping through my fingers, a reminder of the normalcy I had to return to, whether or not, I was ready. The house was quiet, with Lila at school and my mother out running errands. This rare moment of solitude gave me the perfect opportunity to focus on something I had been meaning to do for a while: find a book on healing and managing tragedy.

I couldn't help but feel the weight of my impending return to work. The thought of stepping back into that environment, where every task seemed monumental, and every decision carried the potential for mistakes, crushed me. And Brad would be watching me. I resolved to be more careful moving forward. There were clearly parts inside of me that were having a hard time completing things that had always been second nature. I needed to find a way to navigate my grief without letting it interfere with my professional life.

This moment of quiet was a gift, a chance to seek out guidance and solace in the words of those who had walked this path before me. I needed to find something that would help me manage the turmoil inside, something that could offer me a blueprint for healing.

Because I clearly didn't have it all figured out on my own.

I grabbed my laptop and settled onto the couch, my fingers flying across the keyboard as I logged onto Amazon. The familiar interface greeted me, and I quickly navigated to the search bar. The search for books about grief and healing brought up countless results. Titles like "*Grief Recovery Handbook*" and "*Finding Meaning: The Sixth Stage of Grief*" filled the screen, each promising some form of solace or guidance. I was overwhelmed by the sheer number of choices, each title representing a potential lifeline in this sea of grief I was navigating. The descriptions and reviews blended, making it hard to decide which book might hold the answers I was so desperately seeking.

As I scrolled, a particular book caught my eye: *The Psychology Blueprint: Mapping Human Behavior*. The author was Caleb Peters. My curiosity was piqued. Could this be the same Caleb Peters who was Lila's psychologist? It seemed unlikely, but I clicked on the title anyway.

The cover of the book was professional and intriguing, featuring a brain with various pathways and connections illuminated. I navigated to the "About the Author" section, my heart beginning to race with a strange sense of anticipation.

Caleb Peters is a licensed psychologist with over a decade of experience. He specialises in cognitive-behavioural therapy and trauma recovery. He holds a doctorate from the University of Michigan...

My eyes widened in shock. *University of Michigan*. The same college Dylan went to. The same college where he met "Cay." I scrolled down further, reading every word carefully.

Originally from Michigan, Dr. Peters now resides in
Melbourne, Australia, where he practices psychology
and writes. He is passionate about helping individuals
navigate their mental health journeys.

He wasn't Canadian, as I had assumed. He was American.
From Michigan.

How had I got his accent so wrong?

I leaned back on the couch, my mind racing. The name
"Cay" echoed in my mind, bouncing around like a relentless,
haunting refrain. Dylan had never mentioned a Caleb Peters,
never given me any reason to suspect that Lila's psychologist
was anything more than a compassionate professional. But the
realisation that Caleb could be Cay—the elusive friend Dylan
had spoken of only in passing—clawed at my insides.

Could it be a coincidence, or had they known each other?
My thoughts swirled with a mix of disbelief and anxiety. I
tried to steady my breathing, but the unease was spreading,
seeping into my bones. My fingers tingled with a cold dread
as I stared at the words on the screen. The possibility that they
had known each other, that Caleb had been a part of Dylan's
past, unleashed a torrent of questions and uncertainties.

I felt a tightening in my chest, a suffocating grip of betrayal.
Had Caleb been keeping this from me deliberately? And if so,
why? My heart pounded as I remembered the photo of Dylan
and Cay at the football game, the easy camaraderie between
them. The idea that Caleb, the man I had entrusted with my
daughter's emotional recovery, had shared a significant part of
Dylan's life yet never mentioned it to me—it was almost too
much to bear.

I could almost hear Dylan's voice, his laughter from those
days, now tinged with an edge of mystery. How could he have
kept this from me? Or was it Caleb who had chosen to remain
silent about their connection? Each possibility was like a sharp

needle, pricking at the trust I had placed in both of them. The unease gnawed at me, growing into a relentless, gnashing beast.

My hands trembled as I closed my laptop, the room suddenly feeling colder and more alien. I tried to gather my thoughts, to push through the fog of confusion and suspicion. The weight of the discovery pressed down on me, heavy and inescapable. I felt like I was standing on the edge of a precipice, looking down into a dark abyss of secrets and half-truths.

I closed my eyes, trying to calm the storm raging inside me. But the unease persisted, an insidious whisper in the back of my mind. Could it be true? Could Caleb really be the same Cay that Dylan had known and trusted? And if so, what did it mean for Lila and me?

I opened my eyes, my gaze falling on the familiar surroundings of my living room. The walls seemed to close in, the space suddenly too small to contain the enormity of my discovery. The gnawing unease had grown into a full-fledged dread, a sense that my world was shifting in ways I couldn't yet comprehend.

I stood up, my legs feeling unsteady beneath me. I had to find out the truth, no matter how unsettling it might be. The questions that now plagued me would not be silenced until I had answers. As I walked down the hallway, I couldn't shake the feeling that my life was about to change in ways I had never anticipated.

The office where Dylan's photo albums and yearbooks were kept beckoned me like a magnet. I hadn't been back in there since a couple of days ago, and the room still carried an aura of Dylan's presence that was both comforting and painful.

With a deep breath, I opened the door. The familiar scent of old books and Dylan's cologne greeted me. Whether I noticed last time, I couldn't remember. All I knew was that right now, my senses were heightened.

I switched on the light, casting a warm glow over the room.

My heart pounded as I approached the cupboard where I had begun recovering some of the photo albums and other memorabilia. I had to know if Caleb and Dylan had crossed paths.

I pulled open the cupboard doors and reached for the bottom shelf, where the yearbooks were stored. After shuffling through a combination of mine and Lila's, the 2006 University of Michigan yearbook was at the back, covered in a thin layer of dust. I carefully pulled it out and laid it on the desk, my hands trembling slightly as I opened it.

Flipping through the pages, I searched for the psychology department. My eyes scanned over countless faces, names blurring together as I frantically looked for any mention of Caleb Peters. And then I found it—Caleb Peters, staring back at me from his headshot. His face was unmistakable, even without the distinctive mole on his right forearm that I had seen in the photograph.

I stared at his picture, feeling a mix of emotions—confusion, anger, betrayal. There he was, clear as day, a part of Dylan's past that I had never known about. The realisation hit me like a punch to the gut: Caleb Peters, Lila's psychologist, was "Cay.: The same friend Dylan had spoken of with such fondness and sadness.

Why hadn't Caleb said anything? Why had he kept this a secret? I felt a surge of mistrust and anger. All this time, he had been working with Lila, helping her navigate her grief, and he had never mentioned knowing Dylan. What was he hiding? And why?

I flipped through more pages of the yearbook, searching for any other clues. There were several group photos, each one a window into the past. I saw students posing in front of academic buildings, at social events, and even some candid shots of them laughing and talking. But none of these photos showed Dylan and Caleb side by side.

The absence of their shared moments made me feel like

I was looking through a keyhole into a room full of secrets. I found a group photo of the psychology department, and there they were, standing among their peers. Dylan and Caleb were not next to each other, but both were present. I scrutinised the image, trying to decipher the dynamics between the students. Dylan's relaxed posture and easy smile contrasted with Caleb's more composed and serious expression.

I closed the yearbook, my mind swirling with questions and emotions. I felt like I was drowning in a sea of unknowns, each wave bringing a new piece of information that left me more unsettled than before. I needed answers.

Desperate to find more clues, I returned to the box of loose photographs I had been sifting through the day before. I pulled out the photo of Dylan and Cay at the football game, examining it more closely now. The birthmark on Cay's forearm was something I had yet to see in person. Even as we were heading into spring the weather had been too cold to wear anything less than a sweater.

I sat back on my heels, clutching the photo in my hand. What was I supposed to do with this information? Confront Caleb? Demand answers? My head throbbed with the weight of it all. The room felt smaller, the walls closing in as the gravity of my discovery settled over me.

I inhaled sharply, trying to steady myself. I needed to think clearly. Confronting Caleb without understanding his reasons would only create more chaos. But how could I continue to trust him with Lila's care, knowing he had kept this secret?

As I sat there, I scanned the office, seeking solace in the familiar objects that surrounded me. Dylan's favourite books lined the shelves, their spines worn from years of reading and re-reading. A framed photo of our wedding day sat on the desk, capturing a moment of pure happiness. I felt a pang of longing for the days when life was simpler, when I didn't have to question the motives of those I trusted.

As the sun dipped lower in the sky, casting long shadows across the room, I felt a sense of urgency. Time was slipping away, and I needed to act. But what should I do? I couldn't let this revelation go unaddressed, yet I had to approach it with care.

Desperate to find more, I returned to the cupboard and began sifting through the albums with renewed determination. I pulled out another album from Dylan's college years, flipping through pages filled with pictures of him and his friends, campus events, and everyday moments. I analysed each photo, looking for any sign of Caleb, any further evidence of their connection.

The memories captured in the photographs brought a mix of emotions—joy at seeing Dylan's happy moments, and sadness at the thought that he was no longer here to share them with me. My fingers traced the edges of the photos, lingering over his smiling face. Each image was a fragment of a life that I was now piecing together with new and unsettling information.

I pulled out another box of photos, this one containing a haphazard assortment of snapshots. I found myself returning to the photo of Dylan and Cay at the football game. I studied it again, focusing on the details—their broad smiles, the sun glinting off their sunglasses, the crowd in the background. They looked so carefree, so connected.

I placed the photo beside me and continued searching through the box. There were more pictures from that same football game, some of Dylan with other friends, some of the game itself. But none of these photos showed Caleb. I was starting to feel like I was chasing shadows, trying to grasp something just out of reach.

My mind kept circling back to the same question: Why hadn't Caleb told me? What was he hiding? The uncertainty gnawed at me, eroding the trust I had in him. I had to know more.

I took a deep breath and turned my attention back to the yearbook. Maybe I had missed something. I flipped through the pages again, slower this time, examining each photograph, each caption. I reached the section on extracurricular activities and clubs. There, among the list of psychology club members, was Caleb's name. And Dylan's.

They had been part of the same group, shared the same interests. It was another piece of the puzzle, another connection that deepened my suspicion and unease.

I needed to confront Caleb, but I also needed to be careful. I couldn't let my emotions drive me to rash decisions. Lila's well-being was at stake, and I had to think of her first. But I couldn't ignore the burning questions that now consumed me.

I gathered the photos and the yearbook, placing them back in the cupboard with deliberate care. Each movement felt heavy with the weight of my discovery. The pieces of Dylan's past, once just fragmented memories, now formed a clearer picture, yet left me with more questions than answers.

As I closed the office door behind me, the gravity of my discovery weighed heavily on my shoulders. The familiar scent of Dylan's cologne lingered in the air, a poignant reminder of the man whose secrets I was only just beginning to uncover. The realisation that Caleb had known Dylan, that there was a hidden connection between them, gnawed at my thoughts. Why had Caleb kept this from me? What else did he know about Dylan that he hadn't shared?

The past had resurfaced in a way I had never anticipated, and now I had to deal with the consequences. This wasn't just about Lila's psychologist anymore; it was about uncovering the truth that had been buried with Dylan. The intertwining threads of their lives, now revealed, forced me to confront a reality I wasn't prepared for. With a heavy heart and a mind swirling with uncertainty, I knew what I had to do. There was no turning back now. I had to know. I had to know right now.

TWENTY-SIX

Lila

I WAS IN UNUSUALLY high spirits when Mum picked me up from school today. I couldn't stop smiling. Things with Maci were finally starting to feel right again, like they used to. We were on the brink of being friends again, and it felt amazing. But there was more to it than just that. Maci had broken up with Ryan. Like predicted, he didn't own his part, but that was to be expected. To be honest, I think he knew it was coming. Even though I had done my best to avoid him at school, having known his routine a little too well, already I could tell that he was starting to show interest in another girl. A seventh grader, Lizzie Cutler.

But of course, I would never tell Maci that.

Anyway, the whole thing was like a weight had been lifted off my shoulders, and for the first time in weeks, I felt like I could breathe again.

As I climbed into the car, Mum immediately noticed my upbeat mood. "Well, someone looks happy today," she said, her eyes bright with curiosity. "Did something special happen at school?"

I buckled my seatbelt and grinned. "Yeah, actually. I had a

great day. Things with Maci are starting to feel normal again. It's like we're getting back to how things used to be."

Mum's smile widened. "That's wonderful news. I'm so glad to hear that. I know you've been missing her a lot."

I nodded, feeling a surge of relief. I was ninety-nine percent sure that Mum had no idea about the whole Ryan debacle, or the social media thing, but she had known something was off. I could tell. Apparently, it was a *mother's instinct.*

"Yeah, I really have. It's nice"

Mum looked over at me, her eyes warm with concern. "You've seemed so much happier lately. It makes me really happy to see that."

I knew she was sincere, but there was something in her expression, just beneath the surface, that I couldn't quite place.

We lapsed into a comfortable silence as Mum drove. The sun bathed everything in a golden light, and for the first time in a while, I felt a sense of peace. It was a welcome relief from the weight that had been hanging over me. And it was nice that the weather was finally getting warmer.

When I walked into Caleb's office, the familiar sight of the place was almost comforting. I greeted Caleb with a bright smile, and he smiled back warmly. I didn't even mind that the yellow couch was gone. For the first time, the white clinical replacement didn't bug me. Even Caleb's habit of crossing and uncrossing his legs didn't bother me today.

"Hi, Lila. How are you today?" Caleb asked, his eyes twinkling with genuine interest.

"I'm… good," I replied, feeling a hint of excitement in my voice. "Maci and I are friends again."

Of course, I hadn't told him the details of the circumstances that led us there. I couldn't risk him ever telling Mum about the Instagram incident. I wasn't allowed to have it until I was sixteen as it was.

"That's wonderful news," Caleb said, his smile widening.

"Friendships can be really important, especially when you're going through tough times."

His smile was genuine, and I could see the warmth in his eyes. I nodded eagerly, feeling the happiness inside me bubble over. "Yeah, you're right."

In the corner of my eye, I couldn't help noticing a book on his shelf that caught my eye. It had a royal blue cover with striking yellow accents, standing out among the other books. The title, *The Psychology Blueprint: Mapping Human Behavior*, was written in bold, captivating letters. For a split second, I thought it was pretty cool that I knew published author writer.

I leaned forward, squinting to get a better look at the spine. "Is that your book, Caleb?"

Caleb followed my gaze to the shelf and smiled modestly. "Yes, it is. I wrote it a few years ago."

"Really?" I said, feeling a surge of curiosity. I stood up and walked closer to the bookshelf, my fingers tracing the letters of his name on the cover. "Caleb Peters," I read aloud. "That's really cool. I didn't know that about you. That you're an author."

He chuckled softly. "Well, I guess you could say it's part of the job. Writing helps me organize my thoughts and share my insights with others."

"What's it about?" I asked, turning the book over in my hands, feeling the weight of it.

"It's about understanding human behaviour and the various factors that influence our actions and decisions," Caleb explained. "It covers a range of topics, from personality development to coping mechanisms."

"Sounds interesting," I said, feeling a spark of admiration for Caleb. It was strange to think that someone I saw regularly had achieved something so significant.

Caleb's expression turned thoughtful, and he leaned forward slightly. "Thank you, Lila. But let's get back to focusing on you and what's on your mind today."

I nodded, placing the book back on the shelf. The brief detour left me feeling a bit more connected to Caleb. It was like I had glimpsed another layer of who he was, beyond just my therapist. As I returned to my spot on the couch, the conversation shifted back to our session, but I couldn't shake the newfound respect I had for him.

I couldn't help but think about the few details he shared about himself as a kid and his own struggles. It might have been out of line, but I was feeling more confident these days. Besides, I felt like I was starting to get to know this man.

"Caleb," I began hesitantly, "you mentioned your own struggles before. How did you deal with them?"

Caleb's expression softened. "Well, it wasn't always easy. But talking about my experiences, like we're doing now, helped a lot. It's important to have someone to share your thoughts and feelings with."

His words resonated with me. The more I learned about Caleb, the more I felt understood and supported. And I never thought I would think that. I mean, the guy did come to my rescue with Mum out on the trail the other week.

What an emotional wreck I had been.

"I was thinking about what you asked me in our first session, weeks ago."

Caleb's interest was piqued, and he leaned in slightly, his posture open and inviting. "Oh? What was that?" He crossed his legs. Like he always did.

"You asked me about one thing I wished my mum had done differently," I said, my voice taking on a more serious tone. "Back then, I didn't really know how to answer. I was just so confused and overwhelmed. But now, I think I've figured it out."

Caleb raised his eyebrows, encouraging me to continue. "I'm listening."

I took a deep breath, gathering my thoughts. "I wish she

had told me what was going on with Dad sooner. If she had, maybe I could have helped more or at least understood better. I felt like I was kept in the dark, and that made everything so much harder."

It was true. That's why I went to the trail, to relive that memory with Dad and try to make sense of it all. I hadn't realised how much of my anger was directed at Mum because of it. She had known that day, when Dad was struggling to breathe during our run, when he was hunched over in pain. She had known about his diagnosis, yet she had still let him go with me on that run.

Caleb's expression grew thoughtful. He nodded slowly, as if weighing my words carefully. He uncrossed his legs and lifted the other. "It's normal to feel that way, Lila. Sometimes, adults make decisions with the intention of protecting their children, but it can often feel like you're being left out or kept at a distance."

I fidgeted with my hands, unable to keep still. The frustration and sadness I had felt over the past weeks seemed to come rushing back. "You personally mentioned before that you wished your mum had done more to keep you close. What did you mean by that?"

It was the question I had been building to.

Caleb's eyes softened, and there was a flicker of something in his gaze that I couldn't quite place—regret, maybe, or nostalgia. "Well, my situation was a bit different. My mom, who I've told you about, left when I was six years old."

My eyes widened, my heart skipping a beat. "She left? Why did she leave?"

Caleb seemed to look far away for a moment, his gaze distant and contemplative. It was like he was reliving a memory that was both painful and complex. "It's complicated, Lila. Sometimes, adults have their own struggles and difficulties that can make it hard for them to be the parents they want to be. It's not always as simple as it seems."

I processed this slowly, the weight of his words sinking in. I could feel a knot tightening in my chest, a mix of empathy and sadness for both Caleb and me. "I'm really sorry, Caleb."

"I appreciate that," Caleb said gently, his voice calm and reassuring. "Talking about these things can be really important. It helps us understand ourselves and each other better. Sometimes, opening up can bring us some clarity and comfort."

I nodded, feeling a strange mix of relief and melancholy. The conversation had touched on things I hadn't fully acknowledged before—my own feelings of being left out and Caleb's experiences of loss and longing. It was like we were both peeling back layers of our own struggles, trying to make sense of them.

Caleb leaned back in his chair, the gentle smile returning to his face. "You know, Lila, it's important to remember that even though these experiences are painful, they can also be opportunities for growth. Understanding where we come from and what we've been through can help us shape who we want to be and how we relate to others."

I looked at Caleb, my heart full of mixed emotions. "It's hard to think about it that way sometimes. It feels like it just hurts too much."

"I know," Caleb said, his tone soothing. "It's okay to feel that way. It's part of the process. But remember, you're not alone in this. We're working through it together, and that makes a difference."

I managed a small smile, feeling a bit more at ease. "Thank you, Caleb. I appreciate it."

He nodded, his eyes reflecting a deep well of compassion. "Anytime, Lila. It's what I'm here for."

As the session ended, I felt a mix of emotions—relief from having shared my thoughts, sadness from reflecting on the past, and a glimmer of hope for the future. Caleb's kindness and understanding had made a difficult conversation feel a little more manageable, and for that, I was grateful.

When it was time to leave, I gathered my things, feeling a sense of quiet resolution. Caleb's words had resonated deeply, and although the road ahead still seemed daunting, I felt a little more equipped to face it.

Caleb walked me to the door, his smile warm and encouraging. "I'm looking forward to our next session, Lila. Take care until then."

"Thanks, Caleb," I said, feeling a renewed sense of hope. "I will."

I was content to focus on the small victories in my life—like the renewed friendship with Maci and the progress I was making in understanding myself and my feelings.

When my session ended, I was surprised to find Mum waiting right outside the door. She never usually came in, let alone met me at the clinic. Her smile looked forced, and her eyes immediately flicked to Caleb. They lingered on him longer than they ever had before, studying him in a way that made my skin prickle.

"Hey, Lila. Ready to go?" she asked, her voice bright but hollow.

"Yeah… Mum, I guess." I gave her a curious glance, but she wasn't paying attention to me at all. Her gaze was fixed on Caleb.

Something was off. I felt it immediately.

The air had thickened, and a strange tension hung in the room. My excitement about the session started to fade as Mum's expression shifted, her smile tightening. Her attention was locked on Caleb's arm—on the birthmark there, something I had noticed before but never thought much about. To me, it was just a birthmark. But Mum's eyes widened, her focus sharp as if she was piecing together a puzzle only she could see.

"Maddie," Caleb said softly, acknowledging her presence, but he didn't sound as calm as usual. There was a crack in his voice.

"Thank you, Caleb," Mum replied, her tone surprisingly composed. But her eyes stayed glued to that mark. "Or should I say, Cay?"

I saw Caleb flinch. The name she used hit him like a slap, his reaction almost imperceptible, but I caught it. His face tensed, and the room felt like it had suddenly shrunk.

"Mum?" I interrupted, unsure of what was happening. "What's going on?"

Mum blinked, as if waking from a trance, and turned to me, her voice gentle but firm. "Lila, sweetheart, can you wait outside for a minute? Caleb and I need to talk privately."

The request caught me off guard. "Why? What's happening?"

Her expression softened, but there was an urgency beneath it, something that made my heart race. "I promise I'll explain later. I just need to speak to Caleb alone right now."

I wanted to argue, to demand answers, but the serious look in her eyes told me this was not the time. I nodded, feeling a knot of anxiety tighten in my chest. "Okay. I'll wait outside."

The door closed behind me, and I found myself in the sterile hallway, the faint hum of the office too quiet to distract me from the thoughts swirling in my head. Why was Mum acting like this? What was so important that I couldn't hear it?

I picked up a magazine, but my mind wasn't focused on the glossy pages. Every sound from the room behind me made me tense, straining to catch bits of their conversation. I pressed my ear to the door.

Mum's voice was muffled, but I could hear the sharp edge in it. "How do you know him?" she asked, her words tight with emotion.

Caleb's response was quieter, harder to make out. "It's not what you think, Maddie."

There was a pause, and then I heard Mum again, louder this time. "Dylan. You knew him, didn't you?"

My chest tightened. Dad. Why was Mum talking about Dad? I felt the floor drop out beneath me as my thoughts raced. Caleb knew my dad?

I pressed my ear harder to the door, my heart hammering in my chest. Inside, Caleb's voice was low and strained, as though he was choosing each word carefully. "I didn't want to bring this up...it's complicated."

"Complicated?" Mum's voice trembled with anger. "Why is this the first time I'm hearing this? How could you keep something like this from me?"

The conversation grew more intense, the muffled sounds of their voices blending with my growing anxiety. Every time I thought I had a grasp on what they were discussing, another word would throw me off, leaving me in the dark again. I hugged my arms around myself, trying to quiet the storm of emotions swirling inside me.

Caleb's voice broke through again, quieter, almost pleading. "I thought it would be easier if—"

"Easier?" Mum's voice cracked, and I could hear the anguish seeping into her words. "Easier for who, Caleb?"

I heard a faint sob and my heart sank. The tightness in my chest was unbearable now. I wanted to burst through the door, demand they tell me what was happening. Why was Dad's name coming up? What had Caleb been hiding?

The silence on the other side of the door stretched on until I could barely stand it. Then the door opened, and Mum stepped out, her face blotchy, tears staining her cheeks. She looked older, smaller, somehow more fragile than I'd ever seen her.

"Lila," she said softly, her voice thick with unshed tears. "Let's go home."

I wanted to ask her what had happened, to demand answers,

but something in her eyes stopped me. The grief there was too raw, too deep. I nodded silently and followed her out, my heart heavy with the questions that swirled in my mind.

As we walked to the car, the silence between us was suffocating. I had never seen her like this. Not this angry. Whatever Caleb had said, whatever secret had been revealed, I knew it was about Dad.

But why? And why now?

The drive home was tense and silent, the car engine's hum the only noise as unanswered questions weighed heavily on me. My fingers clenched around the seatbelt, my mind fixated on one burning thought: What was Caleb's connection to my father, and why had they hidden it for so long?

TWENTY-SEVEN

Maddie

MY STOMACH LURCHED as I made my way briskly through the secluded park, my heart pounding so hard I could feel it in my throat. Questions raced through my mind, each sharper and more painful than the last. The setting sun cast a golden glow over the trees, creating long shadows that danced on the path before me.

I would meet Caleb any minute now.

I thought I could wait a day or two to have this conversation, but my emotions were too heightened. I had demanded to see Caleb as soon as he got off work, just hours after confronting him. I needed answers. I had waited my entire marriage to learn about a man who had shaped my husband's entire college experience. I had too many questions.

Questions my parents weren't ready to answer.

I had called them on the drive to pick up Lila from her appointment, probably racking up a speeding ticket or two in my outrage.

"Caleb Peters. You've known who he is for a long time, Mum. You and Dad hired him! You hired him knowing that he was Dylan's friend. He was so loyal that he followed Dylan here all these years later... from America. Who does that? That's not normal. Especially after they had lost touch. How could you keep that from me?"

The more I thought about it, the more unsettled I felt. It was hurting my brain just trying to make sense of it all. Their friendship, their silence, the timeline…

"I understand that you're upset, Maddie. Have you spoken to Caleb about it? Have you talked it out?"

"I'm picking up Lila now from the clinic." I inhaled, trying to steady myself. "I don't even know if I want to hear it, Mum."

There was a sigh on the other end of the line. "Talk to him. It will all become clearer when you do."

"I'll try to catch him after he finishes work tonight. And then I'm coming over to talk to you and Dad. It might be late."

"That's fine, dear. We will be waiting for you."

I spotted Caleb standing by a bench, looking contemplative. As I approached, I felt a surge of anger and confusion. How could Dylan have kept such a significant part of his life from me?

"Caleb," I called out, my voice sharper than I intended.

Caleb turned to me, his expression softening into a tentative smile. "Hey, Maddie."

I didn't return his smile. "We need to talk."

We sat on the bench, the silence between us thick with unspoken words. I clenched my fists, trying to steady my breathing. I had to know the truth.

"Why didn't Dylan ever tell me about you?" I demanded, my voice shaking.

Caleb sighed, running a hand through his hair. "Dylan and I were close in college. We were like brothers for the best part of it." His eyes glistened as he spoke. "But after his parents died, he changed. He started blocking out that part of his life, including our friendship."

It was true. I had experienced it firsthand. But something

didn't add up. I felt a pang of sympathy, but my anger quickly resurfaced. "He blocked it out? What does that even mean?"

Caleb met my gaze, his eyes filled with sadness. "Dylan went through a lot of trauma when his parents died. It was a dark time for him. We used to spend holidays together, every single one of them… but after their death, those times became too painful for him. He stopped inviting me over, stopped talking about the past. He didn't even want to talk about his parents' death even though it affected me too. He was mute at the funeral, Maddie. He wouldn't look at or talk to anyone. I had never seen anything like it. He was really depressed."

I glanced away, feeling the sting of tears in my eyes. "I knew losing his parents hit him hard, but he never really opened up about it. Not even with me. It was something we both went through… but…" He shifted, then locked his gaze back on me. "And then he left the country. Ended up here."

I shook my head, caught somewhere between vulnerability and wanting to keep my guard up. I wasn't going to confide in this man. "I never realised he was hiding so much."

I never thought I would say that about Dylan, but between the lines of silence was a tale longing to be told. It just wouldn't be told by him.

Caleb's voice was gentle. "He wasn't hiding it to hurt you. He just… couldn't handle the pain. Moving to Australia with you was his way of starting fresh, away from all the reminders."

I took a deep breath, trying to process everything. "So, how did you end up here? At the clinic?"

It was a huge chunk of the story that didn't seem to add up.

"When Dylan got sick, he reached out to me… after all those years of silence. He found my book online and realized I was in Australia, although I was living in Sydney at the time for work. I had five months left of my contract, so the move to Melbourne wasn't going to happen immediately," Caleb explained. "Why did I come to Australia? Well, the money was good, and I had no ties back home… not after my grand-parents died. This was about three years ago now. I came on a sub-Class 186 visa if that means anything."

It didn't.

"My grandparents were the ones who raised me." He scratched his brow, contemplating his next thought. I could barely make sense of my own thoughts as I waited.

"Like Dylan, I was an only child. My mum left me when I was six. Substance abuse… she died an addict. Finding that out as a freshman in college didn't make for the smoothest start. I was alone, I had never met my father, I had lost my mother… my grandparents had health issues themselves as much as they did their best to be there for me. I didn't really have anyone."

"Until Dylan."

Caleb smiled, gently nodding. "He was always there. I had always found making friends hard, especially as a kid, without parents that were present. It made it hard for playdates. It was easier just to avoid them altogether."

He may have had a smile, but his body sagged as though the weight of the past was too much. The breeze picked up, sweeping a layer of defensiveness off with it.

"I can't imagine." And I meant it. I was blessed with parents who not only deeply loved and cared for me but set me up for the future. I couldn't imagine having a family in the capacity that Caleb did. Yet look what he had achieved. He was so successful.

Which led me to my next jumbled thought.

"So, Dylan discovered your book, got in contact with you and you came here for an interview at the clinic? My parents interviewed you?" I asked, gritting my teeth.

Caleb looked at me, his eyes full of something else… pity … or maybe it was remorse.

"Yes, Dylan reached out to me, and we finally reconnected. It was brief. It was only for a couple of hours, at that Italian joint around the corner from the clinic. It was before I went in for my interview." His eyes narrowed. "I knew he was sick, Maddie, but I didn't know what time frame we were dealing with. There was always a part of him that kept things so private."

I blinked back tears, feeling the load of it all. Dylan had withheld information from both of us that day.

"When was this? When did you meet up with him?"

"April, I think it was… yes. Shortly after Easter."

Just weeks before he died.

We sat in silence for a moment. No amount of time could make that reality any easier to bear.

"How did you know that he passed, if you didn't know he was sick?"

"I didn't at first."

"My parents didn't tell you?"

"No." He shook his head with conviction. "They didn't know my connection to Dylan."

I let that sink in.

"Are you telling me… that they hired you without knowing your personal relationship with my husband?"

He nodded. "Yes, Maddie. That's right."

Caleb shifted, his eyes clouded with something deeper. He took a long breath before he finally spoke.

"Dylan and I weren't just friends, Maddie."

His words hung in the air, something inside me twisting tight. "What do you mean? What are you saying?"

Caleb's gaze locked onto mine, the silence between us stretching painfully long before he finally spoke. "We were cousins. Our mothers were sisters, though they didn't have a relationship. My grandparents… were also his grandparents."

Cousins.

The word hit me like a punch to the chest. "Cousins?" I repeated, my voice thin with disbelief. This was another layer. "Dylan never told me—"

Caleb nodded slowly, his eyes heavy with regret. "He didn't want to. His mom and mine... they weren't close. My mom was an addict, Maddie, in and out of rehab. She brought shame on our family. Dylan's mom cut her off and tried to keep me out, too. But when my mom died, his parents took me in. That's why Dylan and I were so close."

I stared at him, my mind spinning, trying to grasp this new reality. "You're telling me that all this time, you were family? And he never said a word?"

"I know it's hard to understand," Caleb said softly. "But Dylan had complicated feelings about our family, about the past. He wasn't trying to hurt you."

I could feel the weight of it all pressing down on me. "But you knew, Caleb. You knew I was Dylan's wife from the start, and you never told me."

Caleb's expression twisted with guilt. "By the time I realized who you were, it was too late. We were already deep into Lila's sessions, and I didn't want to make things worse for you."

I stood abruptly, pacing as the world tilted beneath me. It was too much, all of it. My breath came in sharp bursts as the ground spun beneath my feet.

"He kept so much from me. Dylan kept so many secrets—his sickness, his family, and now you. How could I have missed it all?"

Caleb rose, watching me carefully, hands at his sides, helpless. "I should have told you sooner, but it wasn't my story to tell. I didn't want to pile more pain on you."

"Burden me?" I let out a harsh, bitter laugh. "You've both kept me in the dark. You've been lying by omission this entire time."

Caleb stepped closer, his voice low but steady. "I didn't lie, Maddie. Dylan loved you. He just couldn't face the past. He thought hiding this was protecting you."

Tears streamed down my face, but I didn't bother to wipe

them away. "Protecting me? He robbed me of the truth. This is something I had the right to know from the beginning."

Caleb's shoulders sagged, defeat written across his face. "I know. And I'm sorry. Dylan was trying in his own way to start fresh with you. He didn't want you tangled in his past. He thought it would only make things harder."

"But keeping this from me—" My voice cracked. "How can I trust anything now?"

Caleb's eyes softened. "I don't expect you to trust me right now. But Maddie, I'm here. I want to help you make sense of all this. For Dylan. For Lila. And for you."

"How do we even begin?" I whispered, my voice hollow.

Caleb stepped closer, offering the smallest sliver of reassurance. "We take it one step at a time. We talk. We remember. And we heal."

The drive to my parents' house felt interminable, each minute stretching into eternity as Caleb's revelation echoed in my mind.

Cousins.

Dylan and Caleb had been cousins, a truth Dylan had kept buried from me our entire marriage. The betrayal gnawed at me, raw and unrelenting. My parents had been part of this, knowingly or not, and I needed answers.

I pulled into their driveway, gripping the steering wheel so tightly my knuckles turned white. Their cosy house, always a place of comfort, felt unfamiliar under the weight of the storm inside me. The porch light flickered in the gathering twilight, its soft glow doing little to calm the fury brewing in my chest. I sat there for a moment, staring at the door, willing myself to find the strength for this confrontation.

When I finally knocked, the door swung open almost immediately. My mother, Heather, stood there, worry etched in every line on her face. "Come in, sweetheart."

Her voice was gentle, but it scraped against my raw nerves. I stepped inside, the warmth of the house in stark contrast to the cold tension building inside me. My father, Gareth, was in the living room, his expression mirroring my mother's concern. They looked older, wearier, as if the weight of recent events had aged them.

"Here, get comfortable." Dad said, gesturing to the couch.

But I couldn't. I remained standing, arms crossed tightly against my chest as if they could hold me together. "I spoke to Caleb," I said, my voice sharper than I intended.

Mum's eyes darted to Dad before she looked back at me. "And?"

"And he told me something—something I should have heard from Dylan, or from you," I continued, my voice thick with emotion. "Why didn't anyone tell me that Caleb and Dylan were cousins?"

Mum's face paled, and her hand went to her chest. "What?"

I pressed forward, the words tumbling out before I could stop them. "Caleb told me that his mother and Dylan's mother were sisters. Sisters, Mum. That means Dylan and Caleb were cousins, and no one thought to tell me?"

Mum's mouth opened and closed a few times before any words came out. "I... Maddie, we didn't know. Dylan never told us."

I shook my head, the frustration bubbling up, ready to spill over. "But you knew Caleb. You knew he was important to Dylan's past. How could you not make the connection?"

"Maddie, we didn't know the extent of their relationship," Dad interjected, his voice low and measured. "We hired Caleb because he was the best candidate for the job. We didn't know he was connected to Dylan until after he started working with us."

The sincerity in their voices gave me pause, but the rage simmering beneath the surface wouldn't be quelled so easily. "So, you're saying this is all just a coincidence? You had no idea?"

Mum nodded, her voice soft but steady. "We had no idea, Maddie. Dylan never mentioned Caleb to us—not until the very end, just before he passed."

The weight of her words settled on me like a stone, heavy and unyielding. I sank onto the couch, my body finally giving in. "He kept so much from me. It's hard to understand why."

My parents exchanged a pained glance, their faces drawn with regret. "Dylan was a very private person," Dad said quietly, leaning forward. "We knew he had his anxieties, but he never let us in completely. We didn't realise how much pain he was carrying."

I buried my face in my hands, my fingers digging into my scalp as tears slipped through. "He was so broken... and I didn't even know the half of it. How could he live with so much pain and not let me help him?"

Mum sat beside me, pulling me into her arms as my shoulders shook. "I don't know why he kept that from you, but I do know he was always deliberate in his actions. In my heart, I believe he meant well, sweetheart. He just didn't want to weigh you down." "But it is burdening me," I whispered, my voice shaking. "It's burdening me now more than ever."

"We're so sorry, Maddie," Dad said, his voice thick with emotion. "If we had known, we would have done things differently."

I looked up at them, the anger mingling with the deep, aching sadness inside me. "I just feel so betrayed. By Dylan, by you, by everything I thought I knew."

"We understand," Mum said softly, squeezing my hand. "And we're here for you, whatever you need."

I nodded, wiping at my tears with the back of my hand. *Cousins.*

Caleb and Dylan were cousins. The words still felt foreign, as if saying them would make them more real. "Caleb said Dylan was trying to protect me, but it doesn't feel like protection. It feels like abandonment."

"Dylan loved you more than anything," Dad said firmly. "I hope you know that. He did what he thought was best, even if it was misguided."

"I just wish he had trusted me enough to share his pain," I said, my voice breaking. "We could have faced it together."

Mum's eyes glistened as she held my gaze. "It's not too late, Maddie. We can still honor Dylan's memory by understanding his pain and finding a way to heal."

I took a deep breath, the whirlwind of emotions inside me slowly starting to calm. "Caleb seems to want to help. He said we should take it one step at a time."

"That sounds like a good idea," Dad agreed. "Caleb can offer insights we might not have, and together we can piece together the parts of Dylan's life that we don't know."

I nodded slowly, the initial shock and anger giving way to a weary acceptance. "I think I need that. I need to understand why Dylan made the choices he did, even if it hurts."

The silence hung between us, thick and uncomfortable. After what felt like too long, I stood, the weight of the conversation pressing down on my shoulders. Mum and Dad rose too, hesitant but watching me closely.

"We're here, Maddie," Mum said quietly, her hand brushing my arm before dropping away.

I gave a slight nod, not trusting my voice to hold steady. I turned and stepped outside. The cool air hit my skin, sharp and bracing. I paused, closing my eyes for a second, letting the cold ground me. The future felt just as murky as before, but standing still wasn't an option. Not anymore.

TWENTY-EIGHT

Lila

THE SUN FILTERED through the slatted blinds in Caleb's office, casting soft, golden stripes on the floor. I sat on the same white couch that I always internally made a mockery of as I fidgeted with the hem of my shirt. My mind was racing with thoughts I had been gathering for days. Today's session felt different, heavier, as if the air itself was charged with the weight of what we'd learned.

Caleb sat across from me, his posture relaxed but his eyes keenly observing my every movement. He had sensed the shift in my demeanour the moment I walked in, and I knew today's session was going to be significant. The revelation of his connection to Dad had left our last session in a tumultuous state, and I could tell that Caleb knew I had a lot on my mind.

"Hi, Lila. How are you today?" Caleb asked gently, his voice comforting in the swirling sea of my thoughts.

I took a deep breath, trying to steady my racing heart. "I'm okay. I've been thinking a lot since... well, since everything happened."

Caleb nodded, his expression encouraging. "I figured as

much. It was a lot to take in. I'm sure you have some questions for me."

I nodded, biting my lip as I gathered the courage to speak. "I do. I've been trying to piece things together about Dad… about who he was. I feel like there's this huge part of my life that's just… missing even though I wasn't born when… you know, when you and Dad spent a lot of time together."

Caleb's eyes softened, and he leaned forward slightly, his hands resting on his knees. "I understand, Lila. Your father was a complex and wonderful person. We were close, more so in college. We used to run together almost every morning when most people our age at the time would sleep in. It was our way of staying grounded amidst the chaos of university life."

I looked up, my curiosity piqued. "Really? What was he like back then?"

A gentle smile played on Caleb's lips as he reminisced. "Your dad was always the first one up, ready to hit the pavement. He had this infectious energy about him, always pushing me to go just a bit further. He was fiercely determined but also had a great sense of humor. There was this one time we decided to race to the top of this huge hill on campus. I thought I had him beat, but at the last second, he sprinted past me, laughing the whole way."

I found myself smiling, picturing the scene. "That sounds like him. Mum always said he never gave up on anything."

"That's true," Caleb said, his eyes distant as he recalled the past. "He was passionate about everything he did. He was always so supportive, always believed in me, even when I doubted myself."

I leaned in, wanting to absorb every detail. "What else do you remember?"

Caleb paused, taking a deep breath. "There was this one night during our junior year that stands out. We had a big exam the next day and your dad was stressed out beyond belief.

He was working two part-time jobs, trying to keep up with his coursework, and dealing with some family issues. We decided to take a break and go for a midnight run. It was pitch dark, and we ended up at this old, abandoned amphitheatre on the edge of campus."

I didn't know what junior year meant, but I listened intently, hanging onto every word.

Caleb continued, a soft smile on his face. "We climbed up onto the stage, and your dad started goofing around, pretending to be a rock star performing to an invisible crowd. He sang at the top of his lungs, completely off-key, but it was the most carefree I'd seen him in months. Then he sat down on the edge of the stage, feet dangling, and opened up about how he felt like he was being pulled in a million directions. He was worried he was failing everyone, including himself."

I could almost see the scene in my mind, the darkness, the stage, and my dad's voice echoing in the empty amphitheatre.

Caleb's eyes grew distant, his voice filled with emotion. "I remember sitting there, listening to him, and feeling this profound respect for how much he cared. After he finished talking, we just sat there in silence, looking up at the stars. He told me that night that no matter what happened, he was going to give it his all, because that's what mattered. Not the grades, not the jobs, but the effort and the people he loved."

"My dad was so talented."

"He was brilliant."

A tear slipped down my cheek, and I wiped it away quickly. "I wish I could have known him like that."

Caleb reached out, placing a comforting hand on my shoulder. "You know, Lila, in many ways, you do. He lives on in you. His determination, his spirit, his kindness—they're all a part of who you are."

I nodded, feeling a mixture of sorrow and gratitude. "Thank you, Caleb. For sharing this with me. It means a lot."

Caleb smiled warmly. "Anytime, Lila. Your dad was an incredible person."

There was a silence as we both reflected, in different ways.

"What else is on your mind?" he asked after a while.

I bit my lip, my eyes flickering to the bookshelf where Caleb's book, its spine cracked from use, called out to me. "Well…" How was I going to bring this up? "I want to talk about your book, of all things."

The Psychology Blueprint: Mapping Human Behavior stood out prominently from where it was standing now that I knew it was there. "I've been… processing. There's something I want to talk to you about."

Caleb followed my gaze to the bookshelf and then back to me. "Of course, Lila. This is your space to share whatever you need to."

I hesitated for a moment, gathering my thoughts. "I noticed your book again," I began, my voice tentative. "I think it's really cool that you've written a book. It made me think about my mum… and her writing."

Caleb's expression softened as he listened. I'm not sure what dad had shared with him about Mum, but if he knew about her writing, he didn't show it. "Your mom's manuscript is really important to you, isn't it?"

I nodded, my expression softening with a hint of nostalgia. "Yeah, it is. She's had this unpublished manuscript that she's been working on for years. But this one, well, it's been through a lot of changes, and she's had a few rejections from publishers. But she hasn't written anything new in a long time. As far as I know, she kind of gave up on it."

Caleb leaned forward slightly, his attention fully on me. "That must be tough for her. Writing can be a very personal and sometimes painful journey, especially when faced with rejection."

My eyes glistened with unshed tears. "It is. She was always

so passionate about it. And… my dad, Dylan, he was her biggest fan. He always believed in her. He believed in me too. I love writing, and he was always so supportive. But ever since he… passed away, it's like a part of her just shut down. She hasn't been the same."

Caleb's face softened. "I'm really sorry, Lila. Losing someone you love can be incredibly hard, and it affects everyone differently."

I nodded, wiping away a tear. I had come a long way in our sessions. I felt less stubborn, freer to let out all of my suppressed emotions. Maybe this counselling thing was finally working.

But after today, I wouldn't be back. This was it. Despite the trust I had in Caleb, the revelation of his connection to my family made it a conflict of interest to continue. It wasn't that I was deeply shaken or distrusting—quite the opposite. I respected him even more for his honesty. But confiding in someone with such close ties to my family was no longer appropriate.

"Yeah. I miss him every day. But that's not why I brought this up. I wanted to ask you something."

Caleb's eyes softened. "Go ahead, Lila. You can ask me anything."

I took a deep breath, steeling myself for what I was about to do. "I have my mum's manuscript in the car. It's all crinkled and old, and she has probably totally forgotten that it's there, but I brought it with me. I was wondering if you could read it. Not just read it but tell me if you think she has a shot. If it's good enough to be published."

Caleb's eyes widened in surprise. He hadn't expected this, but he could see how much it meant to me. He also remembered seeing the manuscript and knew how important it was. "You want me to read your mom's manuscript?"

I nodded fervently. "Yes. I know it's a lot to ask, and I know it's not your job, but… it would mean so much to me. And to her, even if she doesn't know it yet. She's been so discouraged, and if someone like you, someone who understands writing and publishing, could give her some hope, maybe she would start writing again. Maybe she would find that part of herself she's lost."

Caleb felt a lump in his throat. He admired my determination and my love for my mother. "Lila, I appreciate you advocating for your mom. It's a beautiful thing you're doing. I can't promise anything, but I'd be honored to read her manuscript and give you my honest opinion."

My face lit up with a mixture of relief and gratitude. "Thank you, Caleb. Really. It means the world to me that you would even look at."

Caleb smiled warmly. "You're welcome, Lila. We may need a plan for how I can get this back to you, seeing as we won't be meeting like this again in the near future."

"I know. I've thought about that." I hesitated, looking down at my hands. "There's something else. Mum doesn't know I'm doing this. She doesn't know I brought the manuscript. I just… I want to help her. She's been so sad, and I thought maybe this could give her some hope."

Caleb nodded, his expression turning more serious. "I understand, Lila. It's very brave of you to take this step for her. I'll handle it with care and discretion."

I nodded eagerly and dove into my tote bag. I handed it to Caleb with a sense of reverence, as if I were passing on a treasured family heirloom.

Caleb took the manuscript carefully, feeling the weight of the years it had spent in limbo. He glanced at the title page, and then turned a couple of pages. *To Dylan, my rock and my inspiration.*

He looked up at me, as I watched him with hopeful eyes. "What a beautiful dedication. I'll read this, Lila. I promise. And I'll let you know what I think."

I smiled, a weight visibly lifting off my shoulders. "Thanks. I know this is a lot to ask, but it's really important to me."

Caleb nodded, placing the manuscript on his desk. "I understand. And I want to help in any way I can."

I hesitated for a moment, then spoke again. "There's one more thing. I know this is my last session with you."

"I know, Lila. I'm going to miss our sessions."

My eyes filled with tears again, but I held them back. "Me too. And believe me, I never thought those words would come out of my mouth."

Caleb chuckled. "Look how far we have come!"

"Who would have thought," I said with a smile and a sigh, all at once. "And I guess… there's one more thing."

"Okay, I'm listening," Caleb replied, leaning in with an attentive expression.

I lifted a finger. "This might be a stretch."

"I'll be the judge of that," he said, his tone gentle but playful, though I could sense a seriousness behind his eyes.

"Well…" I tucked my hair behind my ears and shifted forward on the couch. "Let's just say, hypothetically, if my mum's manuscript has potential, maybe you could help her get it… you know, published." My gaze dropped to the floor, avoiding his eyes as embarrassment crept up on me. "I noticed you're with *Big Sky Publishing*, so you've probably got an agent or something, right? A direct line… a shoo-in kind of thing."

His smile wavered, and the silence that followed felt heavy. He scratched the back of his neck, clearly uncomfortable. "You were right, that is a stretch," he said, his voice still light, but something about his expression told me he was holding back. His fingers drummed quietly on the armrest.

"I knew it," I mumbled, already regretting asking. But I wasn't giving up that easily.

He didn't look away, though I could see the hesitation etched in his features. "So, you're saying your mom isn't aware you're asking me this? She hasn't given her approval for me to read her work?"

I swallowed, trying to find the right words. "Not exactly… but she would never ask for this kind of help herself. She's been working on that book for years. It's more than just a story to her—it's everything she poured into it when things got hard with Dad and after he passed. This manuscript, it's like… her lifeline. And I know she'd want someone like you to take a look, even if she's too proud to admit it."

Caleb frowned slightly, his gaze softening but still uncertain. "I get that. But if she hasn't given me permission to read it, I'm not sure it's right to do so. You understand why that might be a problem, don't you? I don't want to break her trust, or yours."

I leaned forward, my heart racing. "You wouldn't be breaking her trust, Caleb. I promise. She doesn't have to know. It's not about making decisions behind her back—it's about giving her a chance she won't take on her own. If you see potential in it, maybe that will be the push she needs to believe in herself again."

He rubbed his jaw, clearly torn. "I just… I don't want to step over any boundaries."

I didn't blink, determined to sway him. "You don't have to promise anything about the publishing part. Just… read it. That's all. And if you think it's worth something, you can help her figure out the next step. You don't even need to tell her that you've seen it. She won't know unless you think she's ready to hear it."

His brows furrowed, and for a long moment, he was quiet; the conflict evident on his face. "Lila, if I do this… she'll have to know at some point. I'm not comfortable keeping it a secret from her."

I gave a small nod, knowing full well I wouldn't tell Mum until it was necessary. But Caleb didn't need to know that. "Of course, I'll tell her when the time is right," I said smoothly, hoping he wouldn't press further. "I just want her to have a chance at something good after everything she's been through."

He sighed, his internal struggle still playing out, but the earnestness in my voice must have gotten through. Slowly, he nodded, though his discomfort was clear. "Alright. I'll take a look. But you need to talk to her at some point, okay? This must turn out the right way."

Relief flooded through me, and I smiled, my heart lighter. "Thank you. That's all I'm asking for."

He gave a small, resigned smile, though the wariness lingered in his eyes. "No promises, Lila. But I'll do what I can."

It wasn't everything, but it was more than enough for now. Mum didn't need to know just yet—and I was confident that once Caleb saw her work, everything would fall into place.

He gave me a warm smile, and the room seemed to lighten just a bit. "You know, Lila, you've come a long way since we first started these sessions. You've got a real knack for making the impossible sound reasonable."

I grinned, feeling a mix of gratitude and sadness. "Guess I learned from the best."

"Flattery will get you everywhere," he said with a wink. "Seriously though, you've grown a lot. I'm proud of you."

His words hit me hard, and I felt a rush of emotions. It was something a parent would say, and it meant more to me than I could express. A lump formed in my throat as I tried to hold back tears. "Thanks, Caleb. That means a lot. By the way, do you know you've crossed your legs one hundred and seventy-two times since we started these sessions?"

He raised an eyebrow, a playful smile spreading across his face. "One hundred and seventy-two times, huh? You've been keeping track?"

"Of course," I said with a mock serious tone. "I have to keep myself entertained somehow, right?"

He laughed, shaking his head. "I guess I'll have to work on my leg-crossing habits then."

I paused, sensing the gravity of the moment. This was our final session since the recent revelation, and I was uncertain about what would come next.

Would I ever see him again?

"But, what happens now? How will I get your feedback on my mum's manuscript if we don't have any more sessions together?"

Caleb's smile softened. "I can provide feedback through email. I'll make sure to keep you updated on that. Just because our sessions are ending doesn't mean I won't help where I can."

I nodded, feeling a bit more at ease. "Okay, that sounds good. Thank you, Caleb."

He walked me to the door. "Remember, just because this is our last session doesn't mean you're alone in this. You've got your mum, Maci, your other friend, what was her name again?"

"Ellie."

"That's right. Ellie, and a whole network of people who care about you."

"I know. And I've got my head on a bit straighter now, thanks to you."

As I walked out of Caleb's office, feeling a bittersweet mix of emotions, I moved past the reception area where Sarah, Ryan's mum and an old family friend, worked. Sarah was finishing up her shift, her warm smile from the past now replaced with a curt nod. The tension was palpable; our relationship had strained ever since I had gotten Ryan into trouble.

"Have a great evening, Lila," Sarah greeted me briefly, her tone neutral.

"Thank you. You too," I replied with a slight nod, not wanting to linger.

Just then, I noticed Ryan hovering near the front door. My heart skipped a beat. This was the first time I had seen him face-to-face since everything had gone down with Maci. The fake Instagram profile, the betrayal, and the aftermath that had nearly shattered my friendship with her all rushed back to me. Ryan had once had a lot of power over me, but now, seeing him there, he looked different. Almost nervous.

Almost scared.

Ryan's eyes met mine briefly, and I could see the flicker of fear. He quickly looked away, shifting uncomfortably. The silence between us was thick, filled with unspoken words and lingering resentment. I felt a surge of disdain, remembering how he had manipulated both Maci and me.

Sarah sensed the tension and continued to pack her things, clearly uncomfortable with the encounter. "I'll be right there, Ryan," she said, her voice strained.

His eyes lifted. Surprising myself, I offered him a small, sincere smile. It wasn't a smile of forgiveness, not yet, but it was a step toward it. A gesture that, although I wasn't ready to let go completely, I understood the necessity of moving forward. For myself.

Ryan seemed to understand the message, his tense shoulders relaxing slightly. Caleb had told me that we need to forgive to create space and freedom in our hearts. This moment, this smile, was my first step toward that.

As I stepped outside into the warm sunlight, I felt a sense of closure. This brief, silent encounter had closed the door between Ryan and me for good. I was willing to put the past behind me and move forward, focusing on my friendship with Maci and the new chapter of my life. The weight of the old wounds felt lighter now, and as I walked away from the building, I knew I was ready for whatever came next.

Ryan had no place in my future. The quiet confidence I had gained through my sessions with Caleb gave me the strength to leave the past where it belonged. With each step, I felt more empowered, embracing the freedom and hope that lay ahead.

TWENTY-NINE

Maddie

S ITTING AT MY kitchen table, I stared at the untouched cup of coffee in front of me. The events of the past weeks had left me reeling, struggling to make sense of the tangled web of connections between my family and Caleb. I've always been a person who needed answers, clarity, and control. But now, faced with the enigma of Caleb and his connection to Dylan, I felt unmoored.

Inviting Caleb into my home was a big deal. I rarely allowed anyone into this sanctuary, a place filled with memories of Dylan, where Lila and I had tried to rebuild our lives. But today was different. I needed to understand Caleb, to see the man behind the psychologist, and to grasp his place in our lives. Lila had a sleepover planned with Maci and Ellie at Ellie's house, giving us the privacy and time to delve into the past without interruptions.

The doorbell rang, and my heart skipped a beat. I took a deep breath, steadying myself before opening the door. Caleb stood there, holding a small, worn leather-bound photo album. His eyes were soft, and there was a hint of vulnerability I hadn't noticed before. He looked different outside the clinical environment—more relaxed, almost casual, wearing jeans and a light blue button-down shirt that brought out the colour in his eyes. His hair, usually neatly combed, had a slight tousle to it, adding to the relaxed aura.

"Hi, Maddie," his gentle voice greeted me.

"Hi, Caleb. Come in," I replied, stepping aside to let him in. As he crossed the threshold, I felt a mixture of apprehension and hope. This was my space, and now he was part of it.

We moved to the living room, a cosy space filled with family photos and mementos of happier times. Caleb looked around, taking in the warmth of the room.

"This is a lovely home."

"Thank you. It's been our safe haven," I responded, guiding him to the couch. "Can I get you anything to drink? Coffee, tea, water?"

"Water would be great, thanks."

I walked to the kitchen, my mind racing with thoughts about the conversation ahead. Returning with a glass of water, I handed it to Caleb and sat down opposite him.

"Thank you," he said, taking a sip. "So, how have you and Lila been holding up?"

"We're managing," I replied. "It's been a rollercoaster, but we're getting through it one day at a time."

Caleb nodded, his expression empathetic. "I can imagine. It's a lot."

There was a brief silence, comfortable yet charged with unspoken thoughts. I decided to lighten the mood a bit before diving into the deeper conversation.

"So, do you always carry around old photo albums, or is this a special occasion?" I asked with a teasing smile.

Caleb chuckled, the tension easing from his shoulders. "Only for special occasions. I thought it might help today."

"I appreciate it. It's nice to have a glimpse into your past. Makes you seem more... real."

He smiled warmly. "I'm glad. Sometimes it's easy to forget that psychologists have their own stories too."

We chatted a bit more about mundane things—work, the weather, a funny story about a neighbour's dog. The small talk was comforting, a way to bridge the gap between us and build a sense of normalcy.

After a few minutes, I felt more at ease. Caleb's presence was calming, and the initial apprehension I'd felt began to melt away. I decided it was time to address the reason I'd invited him over.

"Caleb, I wanted to talk about... everything. About you, Dylan, and how all of this connects."

He nodded, placing the album on the coffee table between us. "I understand. I brought this. It's a collection of photos from my past. I thought it might help you understand a bit more about who I am and where I come from."

I looked at the album, curiosity mingling with hesitation. "I'd like that."

Caleb opened the album, revealing the first photo—a picture of a young boy, around six years old, with a bright smile and a mischievous glint in his eyes.

"That's me, before everything changed."

I leaned in, my interest piqued. "You look so happy."

"I was, until my mom's addiction took over our lives. She was a wonderful person when she was sober, but those moments became fewer and farther between."

He flipped the page, revealing a photo of a woman with striking features, her eyes mirroring Caleb's.

"That's my mom. She struggled with drug addiction for most of her life. She tried to get clean so many times, but it never stuck. My grandparents... our grandparents protected me from a lot that was going on. Not that I really understood much at six."

The woman, even in her struggle with addiction, had an air

of quiet beauty that was hard to miss. She had long, dark hair that fell in soft waves around her face, a bit dishevelled but still framing her delicate features. Her eyes, a deep shade of blue, held a mixture of warmth and sadness, reflecting the battles she fought within herself. There were faint lines around her eyes and mouth, etched from years of hardship, but they couldn't overshadow her naturally kind expression.

A pang of sympathy hit me. The stories Caleb shared mirrored the stories Dylan used to tell—of family, resilience, and loss. But now, knowing they were cousins, those stories felt more like puzzle pieces falling into place. Dylan had always been private about his extended family, and I'd never pressed. Now I wished I had.

"I'm so sorry, Caleb. That must have been incredibly hard."

"It was, but I'm so grateful I had them. They took me in and raised me. They were my rock, my stability."

He turned another page, showing a photo of an elderly couple holding a young Caleb between them. Their smiles were warm, full of love.

"They did their best to give me a normal life. They encouraged my education, supported my interests. They were amazing people."

Growing empathy for Caleb filled me. His story was filled with loss and resilience, much like my own. "They sound wonderful."

"They were. They passed away almost ten years ago now."

I nodded, taking it all in. "Thank you for sharing this with me. It helps me understand you better."

A faint smile played on his lips. "I'm glad it helps."

We spent the next hour going through the photos, Caleb sharing stories from his past. I listened, feeling my trust in him grow with each story. He spoke of his struggles and triumphs, his journey to becoming a psychologist, and his unexpected reunion with Dylan.

"There's one more thing I want to show you," Caleb said, reaching the final page of the album. He gently pulled out a loose photo tucked into the back cover, handling it with care. The image showed two young men, arms around each other, grinning at the camera, standing in front of what looked like a cabin in the woods.

I stared at the photo, tears welling in my eyes. "I've never seen this picture before."

"I found it in my old things. I thought you might like to have it."

I took the photo, my fingers tracing the faces of the two young men. They both looked so carefree, so full of life. Dylan's eyes sparkled with the same mischievous glint I remembered from our early years together. There was a sense of adventure in their stance, their arms slung around each other in camaraderie.

"That's me and Dylan. We were like brothers back then."

"Or cousins," I said with a teasing smile, glancing up at Caleb.

He chuckled softly, a warmth creeping into his expression. "Right. Or cousins." He shook his head lightly, still smiling. "But back then, we didn't think much about family labels. We were just... close."

"I can see that," I said, feeling a tug in my chest. "You two really did seem like you had the world figured out."

"We thought we did," Caleb said, a hint of wistfulness in his tone. "But you know Dylan. Always making everything seem like an adventure, even if we had no clue what we were doing."

"Yeah, that sounds exactly like him," I replied, a soft laugh escaping me. "Even when things went sideways, he'd just... keep going."

Caleb smiled, his gaze distant for a moment. "He always had a knack for turning chaos into something fun. I guess that's why we clicked so well." He paused, looking at me. "Must have shared some DNA or something."

I met his eyes, feeling the weight of that word in ways neither of us were ready to unpack just yet. "Cousins…family," I added softly, as we both sat in the shared space between memory and the present.

Caleb nodded, taking out another picture. "This was taken during one of our summer breaks. We went camping in Michigan, just the two of us. It was right after a tough semester, and Dylan knew I needed to get away. We spent a week out there, fishing, hiking, just being kids. He taught me how to make a fire without matches. I'll remember it forever."

His eyes softened with the memory. "We had this little tent that barely fit the both of us. I remember one night, we stayed up late just watching the stars. Dylan had this knack for telling the most ridiculous ghost stories, and he managed to scare me silly, even though I knew he was making it all up."

I couldn't help but smile, picturing Dylan weaving his tales by the light of a campfire. "That sounds just like him."

"Yeah," Caleb continued, a hint of amusement in his voice. "And then there was the time we decided to go fishing at dawn. Neither of us had much experience, and we ended up with our lines tangled more often than not. But Dylan was determined. He wouldn't give up until we caught something."

"Did you?"

"We did, eventually. A tiny, scrappy fish that was barely worth mentioning, but you'd think we'd caught a trophy with how proud Dylan was. We cooked it over the fire that evening, and it tasted terrible. But it didn't matter. It was the experience, you know?"

I nodded, feeling a warmth spread through me. "He always had that spirit. It wasn't about the end result for him, but the journey."

"Exactly. And he had this way of making every moment

feel significant. Like the time we tried to hike up this small mountain. It was more of a large hill, really, but to us, it felt like Everest. About halfway up, we realized we'd taken a wrong turn and were completely off the trail. But instead of panicking, Dylan just laughed and said it was an adventure."

"How did you find your way back?"

"Dylan pulled out this old, beat-up compass he had in his pocket. He'd bought it from a thrift store for a couple of dollars. It probably didn't even work properly, but he pretended it did. He led us back, making up stories about how he was an intrepid explorer guiding us through the wilderness. It took us twice as long, but we made it back to camp eventually."

I chuckled, imagining the scene. "He had a way of making everything seem less daunting."

"Yes, he did. And that week, despite the mishaps and the less-than-perfect conditions, was one of the most carefree times I can remember. We were just two friends, away from the pressures of school and life, living in the moment."

Caleb's voice grew softer as he added, "Those were the moments that shaped our friendship. Dylan was always there, bringing light and laughter, no matter how tough things got."

I felt a lump form in my throat, the bittersweet ache of remembering Dylan mingling with gratitude for Caleb's stories. "Thank you for sharing this with me, Caleb. It's comforting to hear about Dylan from someone who knew him so well."

Caleb smiled, his eyes reflecting the same mixture of sadness and fondness I felt. "I'm glad I could. Dylan was something else." He turned the page of the album and lifted his eyes. "And he left a mark on everyone he met."

We sat quietly for a moment, the weight of shared memories settling between us like a bridge between the past and present. From where we sat, I could see the gazebo Dylan had built just peeking into view. For a second, I considered showing it to Caleb, but something held me back. The timing wasn't right—Caleb was still caught up in his storytelling, and this moment felt like enough for now.

Caleb finally broke the silence, his voice lighter. "I remember the time we tried to make s'mores but forgot the chocolate. Dylan used leftover granola bars instead. It was awful, but he swore they were gourmet."

I laughed, the sound easing the tension. "I can just picture him doing that."

"Yeah, he always had a solution, even if it wasn't the conventional one. He made the best of every situation, and that's something I've always admired about him."

The conversation continued, filled with laughter and tears, as we delved into more memories of Dylan. Each story brought him closer, made him feel more present. It was as if through Caleb's words, Dylan was there with us, sharing in the moment.

I felt a wave of emotions crash over me. The photo was a testament to the man Dylan was, the friend he had been, and the life he had lived before we met. It made me feel connected to him in a new way, and it made Caleb's presence in our lives make more sense. He wasn't just a psychologist; he was a link to Dylan's past, a part of our history that had come full circle.

"Thank you, Caleb. This means a lot to me."

He smiled, a genuine, heartfelt smile. "I'm glad it does."

The afternoon light filtered through the windows, casting a warm glow around us. In that moment, I felt a sense of peace I hadn't felt in a long time. I knew there would be challenges ahead, but with Caleb by my side, I felt ready to face them.

We continued to talk, sharing more stories and memories. Caleb mentioned a time when he and Dylan had decided to build a makeshift raft to sail on a nearby lake. The raft had fallen apart halfway across, and they ended up laughing hysterically as they swam back to shore.

"That sounds exactly like something Dylan would do," I chuckled. "He always had these grand ideas, didn't he?"

Caleb grinned. "Absolutely. And most of them ended in some kind of disaster, but those were the best times. We didn't care about anything else but the moment."

Our conversation eventually turned to lighter topics. Caleb shared more amusing anecdotes about their college days—their attempts at cooking elaborate meals in their tiny dorm kitchen, the late-night study sessions that often devolved into watching bad movies, and the impromptu road trips to nowhere in particular.

I laughed. "Dylan never mentioned half of these things. It's nice to hear about him in a different light. Makes me miss his spontaneity even more."

Caleb shook his head, smiling. "He always had a way of making everything an adventure, even if it didn't turn out as planned."

As the golden hues of the afternoon gave way to the deep blues of evening, Caleb reluctantly stood to leave. He lingered at the threshold, a pensive look in his eyes, as if searching for the right words to convey the whirlwind of emotions inside him.

"Thank you, Maddie," he said softly, his voice tinged with sincerity and a hint of melancholy. "For welcoming me into your home, for allowing me to revisit these memories. Some of them I hadn't touched in years. Sharing them with you today… it means more than I can express."

I looked at him, feeling the sting of tears behind my eyes. The weight of his words settled over me, a poignant reminder of the past we shared through Dylan. "It was a gift, Caleb," I replied, my voice breaking slightly. "To hear about Dylan, to see him through your eyes… it brought him closer to me. And to Lila."

We stood there in shared silence, the air thick with unspoken emotions and a newfound sense of connection. I could feel the depth of Caleb's gratitude and the unhealed wounds we had both exposed today. As he finally turned to leave, I realised that today had marked the beginning of something new in our lives, offering a sense of closure and understanding I hadn't known I needed.

232

THIRTY

Lila

THE LATE AFTERNOON sun streamed through the living room windows, casting a warm glow over the cosy space. I sat on the couch, nervously fidgeting with my phone. The weight of the USB drive in my pocket was a constant reminder of my secret mission. I knew I had to act quickly and discreetly.

Mum walked into the room, a steaming cup of tea in her hand. She looked relaxed, more so than she had in a while. The lines of stress that usually creased her face seemed softer, and there was a rare tranquillity in her eyes. I took a deep breath, ready to set my plan into motion.

"Hey, Mum, I left my laptop at school today, and I have some homework to finish. Can I use yours for a bit?" I asked, trying to keep my voice casual.

She looked at me, her eyebrows slightly raised in surprise. "You left your laptop at school? You never do that."

I forced a laugh, shrugging. "Yeah, I know. I guess I was just distracted. Must have left it in my locker."

Mum looked thoughtful for a moment, then nodded.

"Alright, just be careful with it. You know how much I rely on that thing."

"I will. Thanks, Mum."

She handed me the laptop, and I watched her retreat upstairs to her room. Once I was sure she was out of sight, I opened the laptop and quickly navigated to her desktop. I found the folder labelled "Final Drafts" and clicked on it. I felt a pang of guilt but pushed it aside, knowing this was for a good cause.

I inserted the USB drive and copied the manuscript file onto it. As the progress bar moved slowly, I listened carefully for any sound from upstairs. Each second felt like an eternity, my heart pounding with the fear of being caught. The transfer completed, and I safely ejected the USB drive, slipping it back into my pocket just as I heard Mum's footsteps descending the stairs.

Quickly, I opened a random document and pretended to be engrossed in my homework. Mum walked into the room, her expression softening as she saw me working.

"How's it going?" She sat down beside me, her presence a mix of comfort and pressure.

"Good, just finishing up a few things," I said, glancing up with a reassuring smile.

Mum took a sip of her tea and leaned back into the couch, her eyes scanning the room thoughtfully. "It's nice to see you so focused on your homework. Do you need any help?"

Mum was going above and beyond these days. She hadn't offered to help me with my homework since I was about twelve. Not because she didn't care, but because I had always been super independent with that kind of stuff. Nevertheless, I appreciated how intentional she was being.

I shook my head, feeling a mix of relief and nervousness. "No, I've got it. Thanks, though."

She nodded, her eyes lingering on me for a moment

longer before she picked up a magazine from the coffee table and began flipping through it. I turned my attention back to the screen, my heart pounding as I pretended to work on my homework. I had to make this look convincing. The minutes seemed to stretch into hours, each one filled with the tension of my secret mission.

As I typed, my mind drifted to the stories Caleb had shared about Dad. His words had painted vivid pictures of Dad's life, and it made me feel closer to a man whose childhood I had never heard stories of. Caleb's anecdotes brought a warmth to my heart, imagining Dad as a vibrant young man, full of life and ambition.

Eventually, I closed the laptop and joined Mum on the couch. We sat in silence for a while, the living room filled with the soft sounds of the evening—Mum's occasional page turning, the distant hum of the refrigerator, and the faint chirping of birds outside. It felt surreal, sitting here with such a heavy secret while Mum was unaware. I knew I had to be careful not to raise her suspicions.

Mum looked up from her magazine, her eyes softening as she watched me. "I'm really proud of you, Lila. You've been handling everything so well lately."

Her words sent a pang of guilt through me. I forced a smile, trying to hide the turmoil inside. "Thanks, Mum. I feel… a lot more in control of my emotions these days."

She reached out and squeezed my hand gently. "You really are. And I appreciate it more than you know. I love you, honey."

"I love you, too."

The weight of my secret mission pressed down on me. I wished I could tell her what I was doing, how I was trying to help her in the best way I knew how. But I knew it had to stay a secret for now. This mission, this desperate act, was my way of giving her a piece of the hope and passion she had lost.

As the evening wore on, the room grew darker, the sun

sinking below the horizon and casting long shadows across the walls. I glanced at the clock, noticing it was almost time for dinner.

"I think I'm done for now," I said, stretching and trying to sound casual.

Mum smiled and set her magazine aside. "Perfect timing. I was just about to start dinner. How about you join me in the kitchen?"

"Of course," I replied, getting up to follow her. Cooking dinner together was something we always did, and I hadn't realised how much I missed it until now.

As we prepared one of our regular meals of Spaghetti Bolognese, I tried to focus on the present moment, pushing aside the anxiety about my covert operation. Mum chatted about her day, and I found comfort in the normalcy of our routine. It was a reminder of why I was doing this—for her, for us.

"Lila, could you pass me the garlic?" Mum asked, her voice bringing me back to the moment.

"Here you go," I said, handing it to her. I watched her expertly chop it, the familiar scent filling the kitchen and mingling with the other aromas. This simple act of cooking together, something we did often, felt grounding amidst the whirlwind of my thoughts.

We continued cooking, the kitchen filled with the sounds of sizzling and chopping. As we worked, I couldn't help but feel a sense of hope. Maybe this small step would be the beginning of something new for Mum. Maybe, just maybe, she would find her way back to the passion she once had.

Dinner was ready, and we sat down to eat, the familiar comfort of our routine wrapping around us like a warm blanket. We talked about our day, about school and work, about little things that filled the spaces in our lives. But underlying it all was the secret I held, the hope that what I had done would help bring Mum back to herself.

After dinner, I excused myself and headed back to the laptop. I opened it again, my hands trembling slightly as I navigated to the email application. Composing a quick message, I attached the file and hovered over the send button for a moment, taking a deep breath to steady myself.

With a final, resolute click, I hit "send." The email disappeared from the screen, leaving me with a mixture of hope and anxiety. Whatever happened next, I knew I had taken an important step.

I closed the laptop and returned to where Mum was tidying up.

Later, after the dishes were put away, we sat together in the living room. The soft glow of the lamps cast a warm light over us, and for a moment, everything felt peaceful. I knew the road ahead might be difficult, but I also knew that I had taken an important step toward helping Mum find her way back to herself.

As the evening drew to a close, I felt a sense of calm settle over me. I didn't know what the future held or what would come from my actions, but I knew that sometimes, taking a step—no matter how small—was all you could do. And for now, that was enough.

As I lay in bed that night, staring at the ceiling, the weight of everything I'd done and everything I hoped for pressed down on me. What if it didn't work? What if Mum never wrote again? The doubts crept in, gnawing at the edges of my resolve.

Yet, amidst the uncertainty, a flicker of determination burned bright. I couldn't predict the future, but I could influence it. I'd done my part, taken that leap, and now I had to trust that it would make a difference. Maybe Mum would find her passion again, maybe she wouldn't, but at least I would know I tried.

Sleep eventually claimed me, my dreams a mixture of past memories and future hopes. I saw Dad, young and vibrant, laughing with Caleb as they ran through sunlit fields. Their camaraderie and joy were palpable, a glimpse into a past I had never experienced but longed to understand. The scene shifted, and I saw Mum, sitting at her old wooden desk, the one she used to write at before everything changed. She was writing with a serene look on her face, her eyes focused and her fingers moving effortlessly over the keyboard. In my dream, the words flowed from her like a river, smooth and unbroken, carrying her passion and creativity with them.

The room around her was bathed in soft, warm light, and I could almost feel the energy and satisfaction she emanated as she wrote. It was a vision of Mum that I hadn't seen in years, a reminder of the person she used to be and could be again.

As I drifted deeper into sleep, the dreamscape morphed into a collage of images and emotions. I saw snippets of my counselling sessions with Caleb, each one a step on my journey of healing. His office, with its slatted blinds and white couch, became a sanctuary where I could lay bare my fears and hopes without judgement. His guidance and understanding had been a lifeline, helping me navigate the turbulent waters of my emotions.

In the dream, Caleb's voice echoed softly, blending with the sounds of my past and future. "You're stronger than you think, Lila. Your dad would be proud of you." His words, though imagined, brought a sense of closure and affirmation. The scenes shifted again, and I saw myself standing at a crossroads, looking ahead with a sense of determination and hope.

I realised just how much I would miss Caleb and our sessions. They had become an integral part of my life, a place where I could explore my feelings and connect with my family's past. But now, it was time to move forward, armed with the hope that I had done the right thing for Mum and for myself.

As the dream faded and morning light began to seep into my room, I woke up with a sense of peace. The doubts and fears of the night before had lessened, replaced by a quiet confidence. I believed that somehow, everything would turn out okay. I had taken a step, made a choice to help Mum rediscover her passion, and even if the path ahead was uncertain, I knew I had to trust in the actions I had taken.

Lying there, I felt a mixture of emotions—gratitude for Caleb's help, a bittersweet sadness at the end of our sessions, and a hopeful anticipation for what was to come. It was a new day, and with it came the promise of new beginnings, for Mum, for me, and for the hopes that would carry us forward.

THIRTY-ONE

Lila

THE KETTLE WAS boiling, its whistle a gentle reminder of the comforting routine Mum and I had established since Dad passed. I stood in the kitchen, staring out at the garden in full bloom. It had been almost a year since Dad's passing, and while Mum had shown incredible strength, I knew she still struggled with her grief.

But recently, something had shifted. Mum seemed lighter, more energised. It couldn't have come at a better time—especially after I'd secretly given her manuscript to Caleb, hoping his agent might take a look at it. She had no idea, of course, but I felt a surge of excitement knowing that this was all falling into place.

The timing couldn't be more perfect.

Just as I was lost in thought, Mum walked into the kitchen with a perplexed look on her face.

"Lila, have you seen my manuscript? The one that was in the back of the car?" she asked, her brow furrowed.

I felt a pang of guilt but managed to keep my expression neutral. "No, Mum, I haven't seen it. Maybe it's buried under some stuff in the car?"

Mum shrugged. "It's okay. I have a digital copy. I'll just print it out again. I was thinking of giving it another go, you know? Maybe try to get back into my writing."

I could barely contain my enthusiasm. "Really? That's fantastic, Mum! I think that's a great idea."

She smiled back, a hint of excitement in her eyes. "Yeah, I think it's time."

I couldn't have been more thrilled. Not only was she ready to write again, but soon she'd find out what I'd done—and hopefully, she'd be in the best possible place to receive the news.

The next day, Mum and I entered Dymocks, the familiar smell of books and coffee surrounding us. I could barely contain the knot of anxiety in my stomach. I hadn't told her. Caleb had trusted me to explain everything to Mum before he read her manuscript, but I couldn't. I chickened out.

After grabbing drinks, I casually led her past the self-help section where Caleb's book was displayed. Trying to act natural, I grabbed it off the shelf and handed it to her.

"Look, Mum! Caleb's book. Imagine if your book was right here too."

Mum laughed, shaking her head. "That would be something, but getting published isn't that easy."

I grinned nervously, unable to keep the tension from bubbling up. "Actually, Mum, I think you might want to hear what Caleb and I have to say."

At that moment, Caleb rounded the corner. His expression was calm, but I could see the tension beneath the surface. His eyes flicked to me, and I knew we were both about to enter dangerous territory.

Mum's face shifted, her smile fading as her eyes narrowed. "Caleb, what are you doing here? What's going on?"

I looked at Caleb, urging him silently to start talking. But as soon as his gaze met mine, I could see the anger flicker there. He was holding back, trying to stay composed. This wasn't just about telling Mum the good news anymore.

"Maddie," Caleb began, clearing his throat, "your manuscript... my agent wants to meet you. They loved your book."

Mum blinked, her confusion evident. "Wait... my manuscript? How did you... Lila, what did you do?"

I froze, guilt crashing down on me. "Mum, I gave it to Caleb. I thought—"

"You gave it to him? Without telling me?" Her voice cut through the air, sharper than I expected. "You... You didn't even think to mention it?"

There it was—the sting I'd been dreading. I couldn't face her, my eyes darting between Mum and Caleb.

Caleb stepped in, his voice steady but with a hint of tension. "Maddie, I was under the impression that Lila was planning to talk to you about this soon." He gave me a quick, reassuring glance before continuing. "I wanted to make sure you were aware before I went ahead with reading the manuscript."

Mum's eyes narrowed slightly, sensing the unspoken tension between us. "So, you thought I knew all along? Were you two working this out together?"

I opened my mouth, but the words got stuck in my throat. "Mum, I... I was going to tell you. I swear. But I didn't know how. I didn't want you to say no."

Her jaw tightened. "You didn't give me the chance to say no."

I shifted uncomfortably, feeling Caleb's silent frustration next to me. But even though I knew he was upset, he still jumped in, trying to protect me.

"Maddie, look," he said, his voice a little calmer, "I get why this feels like a betrayal. But your manuscript... it's extraordinary. I wouldn't have taken it to my agent if I didn't believe in it. I just thought..." He paused, glancing at me, clearly holding something back. "I thought Lila would have told you."

The last part stung. I knew he had every right to be angry. I'd made promises, and I hadn't kept them. And yet, here he was, still trying to make this moment about Mum and her opportunity, rather than my mistake.

Mum's gaze softened for a moment, but the tension between us wasn't gone. Her voice softened, but the weight of her words lingered. "You made decisions without me," she said quietly. "I wasn't prepared for this."

I finally found my voice, shaky but determined. "Mum, I'm sorry. I should've told you. I know that now. But I believed in your writing. Just like Dad did. I couldn't let it sit in the back of a car forever."

Mentioning Dad softened her further. She looked down, biting her lip as if trying to swallow her emotions. I could tell she wasn't just angry. She was scared—scared of believing in something again.

Caleb exhaled, taking a step closer. "Maddie, I know it wasn't the best way to go about things. But you need to know, my agent... he's not easy to impress. When he read your manuscript, he was blown away. He said it was one of the most compelling stories he'd read in years. He wants to meet you."

Mum's breath hitched, her anger shifting into something else. "He said that?"

Caleb nodded, his voice gentler now. "He did. And trust me, he doesn't say that lightly."

There was a pause, a thick, uncomfortable silence. Mum glanced between us, her face a mixture of anger, fear, and disbelief.

"I'm still upset," she finally said, "but... I don't know, this is... it's amazing."

The tension in my chest loosened, but only slightly. I reached for her hand, my voice soft. "Mum, no... *I* messed up. This was on me. But please, don't let that keep you from seeing this for what it is. You deserve this."

Mum's eyes flickered with a swirl of emotions before she let out a heavy breath. "Alright... I mean, I'm curious to hear what he thinks."

As Mum's words trailed off, I saw her mind drift. She'd told me so many stories about Dad encouraging her writing, but this memory was different. I could tell. It seemed to reach deeper, into a part of her that she didn't share often. Mum blinked back tears as she returned to the present, her face softening as she turned to me. "Your dad always believed in me."

I squeezed her hand, my voice steady but full of emotion. "He'd be proud of you, Mum. I know it."

She swallowed hard, her eyes shining with the tears she was holding back. After a long pause, she nodded. "Alright. I'll do it. I'll meet the agent."

Caleb exhaled quietly, a small but genuine smile crossing his face. "That's all we're asking, Maddie. Just give it a chance."

As we left the bookstore, the reality of what had just happened began to sink in. The air felt lighter, but there was still a tension hanging over us—an unspoken acknowledgment that things had changed.

We walked to the car in silence until Caleb glanced at me, shaking his head slightly, though there was a small grin tugging at the corner of his mouth. "You really didn't tell her?"

I gave him a sheepish look. "I was going to... but I panicked."

He rolled his eyes. "You're lucky I didn't throw you under the bus back there."

"I know. I owe you," I muttered.

Caleb smirked. "Yeah, you do. Big time."

Mum looked between us, her eyebrows raised. "You two can cut the act. I know I'm not getting the full story."

Caleb chuckled softly, keeping things light. "Maybe. But for now, let's focus on you. This is your moment."

Mum shook her head, the weight of the situation finally settling. "I can't believe you two pulled this off. I'm still mad, but... I'm also impressed. I'll give you that."

We climbed into the car, the tension slowly dissolving into something else—something closer to excitement. And as we drove home, the reality of what we'd done began to sink in. Mum was about to meet an agent, and her manuscript was finally getting the attention it deserved.

Caleb leaned over, his voice low. "You know," he muttered just loud enough for me to hear, "next time, maybe try honesty. It's less stressful."

I grinned, nudging him lightly. "Yeah, yeah. Noted."

Mum, smiling faintly, glanced at us through the rearview mirror. "And Lila?"

"Yeah?"

"Next time... just tell me."

I let out a breath, relief washing over me. "I will, Mum. Promise."

THIRTY-TWO

Two months later
Lila

"Hey Mum, what do you want to do for your birthday this year?" I asked casually, glancing over my shoulder as I sent an email from my laptop.

Mum looked up from her book, her body tensing slightly. She took a deep breath before responding, her voice tinged with sadness. "I haven't really thought about it to be honest. This is the first one without your dad, so I was thinking maybe just something quiet."

I nodded, sensing her hesitation and the weight of her words. "Yeah, that makes sense. But we could still do something special, just the two of us."

She managed a small smile, though it didn't quite reach her eyes. "Maybe," she replied softly, her gaze drifting back to her book. "We'll see."

I returned to my laptop, typing quickly.

Hey Caleb,

Mum's birthday is coming up next week. Do you think you could help me plan something special?

I hit send and sighed, hoping Caleb would have some good ideas. He had become a great support over the past few months, even though our contact was mostly through email now. Since we had to stop our counselling sessions, Caleb had made a point of checking in regularly. His emails were always thoughtful and encouraging, offering advice on how to handle Mum's grief and my own stress. He even helped me navigate some tough decisions about school and personal projects, giving me the confidence I needed to move forward. I missed our face-to-face sessions, but I was grateful for his continued presence in our lives.

A few minutes later, my phone buzzed with a new email notification. I opened it eagerly.

Hi Lila,

I think it's a great idea to plan something for your mum's birthday. How about a small gathering at your grandparents' place? It would be more casual and relaxed.

I grinned, feeling a rush of excitement. A gathering at Grandma and Grandpa's place sounded perfect. I quickly typed a reply.

That sounds amazing! Let's do it. I'll handle the decorations and food. Can you bring the cake and balloons?

Lila

It was a bit of a reach, but it couldn't hurt to ask, could it?

A few minutes later, another email from Caleb appeared. I loved that he was replying straight away. In a way, this was even better than a counselling session.

I mean, it was free.

Lila, are you sure it's okay for me to be there? I don't want to intrude on a family occasion. Maybe I should just help with the preparations and leave before the party starts.

I bit my lip, thinking for a moment before responding.

Caleb, you're part of our lives now. I'm sure Mum would love to have you there. It won't be the same without you. Please stay.

I was still learning him, but I only got good vibes. Caleb had always had a way of bringing calm. His presence seemed to put Mum at ease, helping her open up and express her feelings. I could see the weight lift off her shoulders, even if only a little, whenever Caleb was around. Which hadn't been often, but still. I knew Mum would appreciate having him there, especially on a day that would be so emotionally charged for her.

The days leading up to Mum's birthday were filled with a whirlwind of activity. Since Mum and I lived just a kilometre down the road, I could set things up without relying on her to take me. I spent hours carefully selecting decorations, wanting everything to be perfect. Streamers and fairy lights were meticulously placed around Grandma and Grandpa's living room, creating a warm and inviting atmosphere. I made a playlist of Mum's favourite songs, each one chosen for its special meaning.

My grandparents were thrilled to host the celebration. It had been a long time since we all gathered together, and their presence would mean the world to Mum. I wanted this birthday to feel normal, and that meant not bypassing it but celebrating it well, like we always did for one another's birthday.

That's what dad would want.

On the morning of Mum's birthday, I woke up early, my heart racing with a mix of excitement and nervousness. Mum seemed content to spend the morning reading, which was pretty normal, so I used this as an opportunity to put the plan into action.

"Hey Mum, I was thinking, why don't we visit Grandma Heather and Grandpa Gareth this morning? They'd love to see you on your birthday," I suggested casually.

Mum looked up from her book, a hint of surprise on her face. "That sounds nice, Lila. I could use a bit of a change today."

"Great! I'll let them know we're coming," I said, feeling a surge of relief. I quickly sent a text to Grandma Heather, letting her know the plan was on.

We got ready and headed over to my grandparents' house. On the way, I kept the conversation light, talking about anything and everything to keep Mum from suspecting anything.

When we arrived, Grandma Heather and Grandpa Gareth greeted us warmly, their excitement barely contained. Mum didn't notice the knowing glances we exchanged.

"Come on in, Maddie," Grandma Heather said, ushering us inside. "We've got something special for you."

As we walked into the living room, Mum's eyes widened, glistening with surprise and tears. The room was beautifully decorated with streamers and fairy lights.

"Oh my goodness, this is wonderful! You all did this for me?" she asked, her voice trembling with emotion.

"Of course, Mum," I said, pulling her into a tight hug. "You deserve it."

"Thank you, everyone," Mum said, her voice filled with heartfelt gratitude. "This means so much."

I glanced at her, thinking she probably believed I was treating today like any other day, completely unaware of the surprise I had planned for her.

Just then, the doorbell rang. I exchanged a quick, knowing glance with Grandma Heather and hurried to answer it. Standing there, holding a beautifully decorated cake and a bunch of colourful balloons, was Caleb. He looked a bit nervous, his usual confident manner slightly subdued, and I noticed he had dressed nicely for the occasion, wearing a crisp shirt and well-fitted pants. It was clear he had put effort into his appearance, which struck me as both thoughtful and surprising.

"Hey, Lila." He greeted me with a warm smile that didn't quite mask his nervousness. "Where should I put these?"

"Hi, Caleb! The cake can go on the dining table, and the balloons can be tied to the chairs," I said, feeling a surge of excitement. The sight of him, so willing and present, filled me with a warm, bubbling joy. "Thanks for bringing everything."

Caleb looked around, a bit unsure. "Uh, where exactly is the dining table?" he asked, glancing around the unfamiliar house.

"Oh, right! Just follow me," I said, leading him through the hallway. As we walked in, Mum stayed in conversation with Grandma Heather and Grandpa Gareth, her laughter filling the room. But when she glanced over and saw Caleb, her eyes widened, glistening with surprise and perhaps a bit of happiness too.

Caleb, sensing her surprise, turned to Mum with a gentle smile. "Happy birthday, Maddie. I hope you don't mind me crashing your celebration."

Mum's eyes welled up, but this time it was joy that spilled over. She stepped forward, her voice unsteady. "Caleb, I… I don't even know how to thank you. This is beautiful."

With a soft smile, he placed the cake on the dining table, setting down something else I couldn't quite make out, and tied the balloons to the chairs with steady, gentle hands. "It's my pleasure, Maddie. You deserve this."

I noticed Mum's gaze linger on Caleb. He'd always been the steady presence, easing the storms in our lives. But seeing him now—slightly nervous, deliberate in every gesture—felt different. It was strange, but not in a bad way. In fact, I think I liked it. There was something comforting in knowing that even Caleb, with all his calm confidence, was trying so hard to make everything perfect for her.

THIRTY-THREE

Maddie

As I LOOKED around the room, my eyes landed on Caleb. I can't say I expected to see him, but at the same time, I was glad he had come. Seeing him standing there with a beautifully decorated cake and a bunch of colourful balloons brought a lump to my throat. A complex wave of emotions washed over me. Initially, there was a flicker of surprise, quickly replaced by an overwhelming sense of gratitude and warmth. His presence was like a balm to my heart, which had been aching from the absence of Dylan.

Over the past couple of months, Caleb had become more than just a supportive figure in Lila's life; he had quietly become a friend to me as well. After our counselling sessions had to end, Caleb was always respectful and gentle in his approach. He never initiated contact, waiting instead for me to reach out. It was this patience and understanding that made his support feel genuine and unintrusive.

There were a few times when I felt overwhelmed and found myself dialling his number. He always answered, his voice calm and reassuring, never rushing me to speak. One particular evening, when the weight of Dylan's absence felt unbearable,

I called Caleb. We ended up talking for hours. He listened as I poured out my heart, sharing stories and memories, and for the first time in a long while, I felt a genuine connection. It was easy, I didn't have to calculate my words but let them run freely.

And that was freeing.

His quiet presence on the other end of the line brought me a sense of peace I hadn't felt in months.

During these phone calls, I couldn't help but want to learn more about Dylan's past, particularly his parents. Caleb was his family, after all. I found myself curious about the in-laws I never had the chance to meet. Caleb would share stories about Dylan's parents, his uncle and aunt, painting vivid pictures of the kind, loving people they were. He spoke of their warmth and generosity, the values they instilled in Dylan, and the deep love they had for their son. These stories helped me feel closer to Dylan and understand more about the family that shaped him into the man I loved.

Caleb's gestures were always considerate and well-timed, never overstepping. The more I think about it, he would always wait on me. He would respond with thoughtful emails with words of encouragement and advice, understanding the delicate balance of offering support without being overbearing.

It was amazing to see how well Lila responded to Caleb as well. In the beginning, she had loathed her sessions with him, resisting every attempt to open up. But over time, his gentle and patient approach won her over. I knew he occasionally emailed Lila too, as she wanted to learn more about her dad. It was heartwarming to see her taking an interest in her father's past and finding a way to connect with him through Caleb's stories.

So, seeing him here today, dressed nicely and clearly having put effort into his appearance, made perfect sense. He was not just here for Lila; he was here for me too. The sight of him, so willing and present, filled me with a warm, bubbling joy.

I realised that his presence today was more than just a kind gesture—it was a testament to the quiet, unwavering support he had offered us over the past months.

Caleb noticed me too, his eyes meeting mine with a warmth that made my heart skip a beat. I still couldn't believe that he never married, that he didn't have a wife. It was a thought that had crossed my mind often since learning more about him. How could someone so kind, so understanding, so gifted not have someone special in his life?

As he placed the cake on the dining table and tied the balloons to the chairs, his movements calm and reassuring, I felt a sense of peace settle over me. I found myself feeling appreciation for Caleb's efforts. He had gone out of his way to ensure that my birthday was special, and his thoughtfulness…

Well, it touched me.

As the celebration continued, I found myself drawn to Caleb's easy laughter and genuine kindness. His ability to connect with my family, making them feel at ease, put me at ease. It took the pressure off the feeling like I had to entertain or ensure that everyone was okay. I could just be.

As we sat down to eat the cake, I noticed the intricate details before even taking a bite. The cake was beautifully adorned with delicate sugar flowers, each petal carefully shaped and dusted with a subtle shimmer that caught the light. Its three layers were perfectly frosted, the smooth vanilla buttercream gleaming under the soft glow of the room. Caleb must have paid close attention to the details because the cake looked like something straight out of an artisan bakery.

As I cut into it, the rich scent of almond filled the air—my favourite. Caleb had chosen an almond sponge cake with a hint of orange zest, just as I always loved. The cake itself was moist, with thin layers of raspberry filling adding a perfect balance of tartness. Caleb leaned back in his chair, casually watching as I took the first bite, and I saw the flicker of pride in his eyes. He hadn't baked it, but he had certainly picked the right one.

"So, Caleb," I said, a mischievous glint in my eye, "Did you bake this cake yourself, or did you have some help?"

Caleb chuckled, shaking his head. "I'd love to take credit, but I'm afraid the bakery down the street did most of the work. I just made sure to pick your favorite."

I raised an eyebrow, amused. "And how did you know it was my favourite?"

He glanced at Lila with a warm smile. "I had a little help from someone who knows you well."

Lila beamed, clearly pleased with herself. "I thought it would be a nice surprise."

I laughed, feeling a surge of affection for them both. "Well, you two make a great team. This really is perfect."

Mum leaned over, giving Caleb a playful nudge. "You know, Maddie always did have a sweet tooth. She used to sneak cookies from the jar when she thought no one was looking."

"Oh, Mum, don't embarrass me in front of everyone!" I laughed, feeling a lightness in my heart that I hadn't felt in a long time.

Dad joined in, a twinkle in his eye. "Remember that time you tried to bake a cake for your eighth birthday and ended up with a kitchen disaster?"

Everyone laughed, and I felt a wave of gratitude wash over me. This was exactly what I needed—a reminder of the love and support that surrounded me, even in the absence of Dylan.

As the evening progressed, I found myself in the kitchen with Caleb, putting away the leftover cake and chatting easily. The connection between us felt natural, effortless. The low hum of conversation and laughter from the living room provided a comforting backdrop.

"Thank you for today, Caleb," I said, handing him a dish to dry. "You really made it special."

"I'm glad I could help," he replied, his eyes warm. "You deserve to feel special, Maddie."

I hesitated for a moment, then decided to be honest. "It's been hard without Dylan. Sometimes I feel like I'm just going through the motions."

Caleb nodded, his expression understanding. "Grief is a tough journey, and it's different for everyone. But you're surrounded by people who love you. It's okay to have good days and bad days."

I smiled faintly, feeling a sense of comfort in his words. "Thank you for being part of that support system. You've been a great friend to both Lila and me."

Caleb paused, drying the dish thoughtfully before placing it on the counter. "Maddie, I've admired your strength. You've managed to hold everything together, and Lila... she's thriving because of you. Seeing her happy today, seeing you smile, that's something."

I looked at him, my heart swelling. "Lila really has come a long way, hasn't she? It feels like just yesterday she was so resistant to opening up to you."

He chuckled softly, nodding. "Yes, I remember those early sessions. But she's resilient, just like her mom."

There was a moment of silence, filled with unspoken understanding. The kind of silence that feels full rather than empty.

"Caleb," I began, my voice wavering slightly. "I've been thinking a lot about what you've told me about Dylan's parents. It means a lot to hear about them, to know the kind of people they were. It's like... I'm piecing together parts of Dylan I never knew."

His eyes softened, and he stepped closer, the warmth of his presence comforting. "They were wonderful people, Maddie. And they would be incredibly proud of you and Lila. I'm sure Dylan felt the same way."

I took a deep breath, feeling a warmth in my chest that I

hadn't felt in a long time. "Would you like to stay for a while longer? I think Lila and I would both enjoy your company."

His eyes met mine, and for a moment, I saw something deeper, something unspoken. "I'd like that very much," he said softly.

We rejoined Lila, Heather, and Gareth in the living room, the five of us settling into comfortable conversation. Caleb fit in seamlessly, his presence feeling welcome and reassuring. It was a comforting feeling to have him there, adding a sense of warmth to the evening. As we all chatted and laughed together, I found myself appreciating his quiet support and the way he effortlessly became part of our gathering.

Later in the evening, as the night was winding down, I found myself alone with Caleb on the back porch. The stars were scattered across the sky, twinkling like tiny diamonds. We sat in silence for a moment, the cool breeze carrying the sounds of laughter and conversation from inside. The warmth of the day was giving way to the coolness of night, and the quietness of the porch felt like a refuge from the emotions that had surfaced throughout the evening.

"It's beautiful out here," Caleb said, breaking the silence. He leaned back, looking up at the sky. "It's been awhile since I've taken the time to just sit and look at the stars."

I nodded, following his gaze. "There's something comforting about them, isn't there? A sense of continuity, I guess. No matter what happens, they're always there, shining away."

Caleb smiled. "Yeah, it's like they're silently watching over us, reminding us that we're just a small part of something much bigger."

I glanced at him, the starlight reflecting in his eyes. "You know, we always talk about me and Lila, but what about you, Caleb? Tell me something about yourself."

He looked a bit surprised, then thoughtful. "Well, there's

not much to tell. I've always been more of a listener than a talker."

I laughed softly. "Come on, there must be something. What do you do when you're not busy being the supportive friend?"

Caleb chuckled. "Alright, you got me. I love hiking. There's something about being out in nature that clears my mind. I try to go every weekend if I can."

"Hiking, huh? Do you have a favourite spot?"

"There's a trail called the Olinda Heritage Walk. It's a beautiful path, with a mix of forest and open areas. On a clear day, you can see for miles," Caleb explained, his eyes lighting up as he spoke.

I smiled, enjoying seeing this side of him. "That sounds amazing. I've never really done much hiking, but maybe I should give it a try sometime."

"You should. I think you'd love it. There's something about reaching the end of a trail that makes everything else seem... smaller, more manageable," he said, his tone thoughtful.

We sat in silence for a few moments, the night enveloping us in its quiet embrace.

"Do you hike alone, or do you have a group you go with?" I asked, genuinely curious.

"Mostly alone," Caleb admitted. "It's my time to think and unwind. But sometimes I go with friends. It's nice to share the experience with others too."

"Well, if you ever need a hiking buddy, let me know," I said, surprising myself with the offer. I wasn't even sure if I meant it, but the words had come out before I could stop them. "I think I could use a new challenge."

Caleb's expression brightened, a look of genuine pleasure on his face. "I'd like that, Maddie. It would be great to have you along."

We sat there for a while longer, talking about lighter things—favourite books, places we'd like to travel, even our favourite movies. The conversation flowed easily, and for the first time in a long while, I felt truly relaxed.

As we rejoined the others inside, I couldn't shake the feeling that something had shifted between Caleb and me, though I couldn't quite pinpoint what it was. For the first time, I felt like I was truly seeing the person behind the professional.

We shared stories and laughter late into the night. The casual, relaxed atmosphere at my parents' house made the celebration feel even more special. Despite the underlying ache of Dylan's absence, I found myself genuinely enjoying the company of loved ones. Caleb's presence felt natural, and his easy banter and kindness added a wonderful layer to the evening.

As I sat there, a memory of a past birthday with Dylan surfaced. It was my thirtieth birthday, and Dylan had gone all out to make it unforgettable. He had secretly organised a garden party in our backyard, inviting close friends and family. I remembered walking into the garden, stunned by the twinkling fairy lights strung through the trees, the soft music playing in the background, and the beautiful arrangement of red roses—my favourite flowers—on every table. Dylan greeted me with that mischievous grin of his, holding a bouquet of red roses just for me.

Throughout the evening, Caleb was the perfect host, effortlessly balancing conversation, laughter, and making sure everyone was enjoying themselves. But Caleb, true to form, never let too much time pass without checking in on me, a steady presence that made me feel more anchored than I realised I needed to be. It was one of those subtle gestures that said more than words could—he was there, without making a show of it.

Then, when I thought I'd seen all of his surprises for the night, he pulled me aside. We wove through the lively chatter to a quiet corner of the garden, where soft fairy lights twinkled gently above us. There, as if it had been waiting for this exact moment, stood a small table with a pavlova he'd baked himself.

Now, anyone who knows Caleb would know that baking isn't exactly his forte, but that made it all the more endearing. The pavlova was slightly lopsided, the center having caved in just a bit, but it was the kind of imperfection that made it perfect. Very Australian of him, a touch homespun and undeniably heartfelt.

But that was hardly the point.

What mattered more was the thought behind it, and the way his eyes lit up when he presented it to me, like a proud chef revealing his masterpiece. He had poured himself into it, into every moment of the night. And then, as if I wasn't already completely floored, he began singing "Happy Birthday." His voice was unmistakably off-key, but full of such warmth and affection that I couldn't help but burst into laughter, doubling over as my sides ached from it. Caleb wasn't the type to fuss over grand gestures, but that made his quiet efforts—his perfectly imperfect pavlova, his terrible singing—all the more meaningful. He was full of surprises, and just when I thought I had him figured out, he'd show me another layer.

As the night drew to a close, I hugged Lila tightly. "Thank you, sweetheart. You made today very special."

"I'm glad, Mum," she said, her eyes shining with love. "You deserve it."

My parents approached, their expressions warm and supportive. "We're so proud of you, Maddie," Mum said, her voice soft. "You've been so strong through everything."

Dad nodded in agreement. "You've raised a wonderful daughter, and you have a great friend in Caleb. You're not alone."

And I truly felt that.

I smiled, feeling tears prick at my eyes again. "Thank you. Both of you."

Just then, Caleb walked over, a playful grin on his face. "Alright, Maddie, it's time for your birthday quiz. I hope you're ready."

"Oh, a quiz, huh? You think you can stump me?" I replied, matching his playful tone.

"Oh, I know I can. Question one: What year did you first start sneaking cookies from the jar?" Caleb teased, holding up a card from the stack Lila had organised.

Heather laughed. "I can answer that! She was five. She thought she was so clever."

Caleb pretended to look surprised. "Sounds like you've been a troublemaker from the start, Maddie."

I shrugged, grinning. "What can I say? Some habits die hard."

Lila joined in, her eyes sparkling with excitement. "Next question: What was Mum's favourite subject in school?"

Caleb raised an eyebrow, glancing at the card. "Hmm, I'm going to guess... English?"

I nodded, feeling a surge of pride. "You've been paying attention."

Caleb's smile deepened, his eyes twinkling. "Hard not to, especially now that the world is about to see what you're capable of."

My breath caught.

THIRTY-FOUR

Lila

WE STOOD TOGETHER at Dad's grave, the three of us, united by our love for him. The red roses in my hand trembled as I knelt, the cold, damp earth beneath my knees grounding me. Grief tightened in my chest, familiar but no longer overwhelming. This was Caleb's first time here since he'd moved back to Melbourne. I had been the one to suggest we come together, and now that we were here, it felt... right.

I glanced at Caleb, standing beside Mum. For the first time, it didn't feel like I was betraying Dad by having him here. Caleb wasn't trying to replace my father. He wasn't filling that space, but he didn't have to. His presence felt comforting, like an extension of the love Dad had for us—steady, quiet, and always there when we needed it. Dad would have wanted this. He would have wanted us to lean on each other.

I shifted on the wet ground, running my fingers over the stem of the rose, trying to find the words. "Hi, Dad," I whispered, my voice barely louder than the wind moving through the trees. "It's Lila. I miss you so much." My throat tightened, but I didn't fight the tears this time. They felt okay, like part of the process. "I wish you were here to see how amazing Mum is. You always believed in her, and now... she's going to be a published author. Caleb's agent loved her book, and they're going to publish it." I smiled, a real one this time. "She did it, Dad. Just like you always said she would."

I placed my rose down on the grave, the cold stone beneath my hand anchoring me in the moment. "I miss our runs together. I'm so unfit now—you'd definitely beat me if we raced." A soft laugh slipped out, and this time, it felt genuine.

Mum stepped forward, her voice trembling. "Dylan, I brought Caleb with me today. I know you'd be okay with that." She glanced back at him, a look passing between them that I couldn't quite explain but that felt... natural. Caleb nodded, his expression filled with emotion, and for the first time, I didn't wonder what Dad would think. It felt right, like Dad would have understood.

Mum's voice was soft as she spoke to Dad, telling him about her book and how much she missed him. I stayed quiet, letting her words fill the space. She sounded different—like she had finally accepted that moving forward didn't mean leaving Dad behind. It was something I hadn't fully grasped before. I wasn't ready to completely let go, but I was starting to understand that it was okay to hold on to both the past and the future.

Caleb stepped forward then, his voice steady but thick with emotion. "Dylan, I wish we could have had more time. But I know how much you loved Maddie and Lila. They're remarkable, and I'm honored to be a part of their lives. You'd be so proud of them." His words didn't feel like an intrusion. Instead, they felt like a bridge—connecting the part of me that missed Dad with the part of me that was ready to move forward.

I knelt beside Mum, resting my head on her shoulder. We sat there together, the three of us, the wind moving through the trees and the sound of birds in the distance. The grief was still there, but it felt different now—softer, like something we could carry together.

Caleb stayed by the grave, staring down at the stone. When he spoke again, his voice was low, almost a whisper. "I've never really said goodbye, Dylan. But standing here now... I miss you, man. You were my family." His voice cracked, and he took a shaky breath. "You always will be."

The rawness of his words hit me, but instead of pushing me further into grief, they offered me something else—closure. Dad would never walk me down the aisle or teach me to drive, but the love he had for us lived on in the people he left behind. In Mum. In me.

And even in Caleb.

Caleb's hand rested gently on my back, and for the first time, I leaned into his touch. He wasn't trying to take Dad's place—he was just here, steady and real, offering the kind of support that Dad would have wanted for us.

"Mum," I whispered, my voice small but sure, "do you think we're going to be okay?"

She looked down at me, her eyes soft but filled with something strong—something unbreakable. She squeezed my hand. "Yes, Lila. We're going to be okay. I'm sure of it."

For the first time in what felt like forever, I believed her.

THIRTY-FIVE

Dylan

As I finish the final lines of my letter to my beautiful wife, a sense of calm washes over me. The words, carefully chosen and painstakingly written, are my last gift to her. I sit back, the pen slipping from my fingers, and take a deep breath. The air feels heavy with the weight of unspoken thoughts and emotions, yet there's a lightness in my heart that I haven't felt in a long time.

I glance at the photograph on my desk—Maddie, with her radiant smile, holding Lila in her arms at the Grampians. It was a moment captured from our last summer together, a day filled with hiking and laughter. Even though Lila preferred the beach, she had embraced the adventure, her curiosity piqued by every new sight and sound. Maddie's smile in that photo is one of pure joy, a reflection of the love and happiness we shared.

My mind drifts back to that day. The sun was warm on our backs, and the air was filled with the sounds of nature. Maddie had looked so alive, her cheeks flushed with excitement as she pointed out different birds to Lila. We found a secluded spot by a waterfall, and as we sat there, the three of us, I felt a profound sense of peace. Maddie's laughter echoed in the air, blending with the sound of the water, and Lila's eyes sparkled with curiosity and joy. It was one of those rare, perfect days that stay with you forever.

Caleb.

His name echoes in my mind, a constant reminder of the promise I made. "Cay" was more than a friend to me; he was my cousin. We shared so much—our dreams, our fears, and countless miles on those morning runs. He was there for me during some of the toughest times, always ready with a word of encouragement or a shoulder to lean on.

Yet, as I sit here, I'm filled with uncertainty. Was it right to keep Caleb's existence a secret from Maddie? I did it out of love, wanting to protect her from the complexities of my past. But now, I wonder if I made the right choice. Caleb is a good man, and I believe with all my heart that he would look after Maddie and Lila in ways I can only imagine. But would they find each other?

I trust in the unfolding of the future, even if I can't see the entire picture. Life has a way of bringing people together at the right moment. I have to believe that Caleb and Maddie will meet when the time is right, that they will find a connection that transcends the boundaries of time and distance. Caleb will know what to do. He's always had an innate sense of understanding, a way of seeing into the heart of things.

I remember our last conversation, the one where I made him promise to look out for my family. He didn't hesitate, didn't flinch. His eyes met mine with unwavering resolve, and I knew I could count on him. But I never told him how to do it, never laid out a plan. It was a promise built on trust and faith, not instructions.

In these final moments, I find solace in the belief that love has its own logic, its own path. Maddie and Caleb will meet. They will connect. It might not be immediate, and it might not be easy, but it will happen. And when it does, they will both understand the depth of the bond that ties us all together.

I close my eyes and picture them—Maddie, with her resilient spirit and boundless love, and Caleb, with his strength and kindness. They will make an incredible team. They will support each other, learn from each other, and together, they will honor the legacy of the love we've shared.

My time is running out, and the reality of my situation is unavoidable. I call Maddie's mom into the room, the letter clutched in my hand. Her eyes are filled with tears, but she nods, understanding the gravity of what I'm about to ask.

"Please," I say, my voice barely above a whisper, "give this to Maddie when the time is right. Discreetly. She'll need it."

She takes the letter from me, her hands trembling slightly. "I promise," she whispers back, her voice choked with emotion.

I squeeze her hand, my own eyes brimming with tears. "Thank you. Tell her... tell her that I love her more than anything. And tell Lila... that her daddy is always with her. Always."

In this emotional moment of reflection, I realize that this letter is not just a goodbye. It's a bridge to the future, a guidepost for the path ahead. It carries my hopes, my dreams, and the silent promises that will continue to guide them even after I'm gone.

The future is uncertain, but it's full of hope. I've done all I can to ensure Maddie and Lila are cared for. Now, I leave the rest in God's hands. If I'm lucky, perhaps I'll have a glimpse from Heaven to watch it all unfold the way it was always meant to—naturally.

As I seal the envelope, a sense of peace settles over me. My journey is coming to an end, but theirs is just beginning. And in that, I find comfort. The love we have shared will continue to grow and flourish, carried forward by those closest to my heart and the heartbeat of my family. Silent promises, after all, are the ones that last forever.

EPILOGUE

Maddie

As I sit on the worn, but familiar chair in Dylan's old office, my fingers brush against the edges of a letter I've just now discovered. It's a letter I knew nothing about, and I wonder how I've never noticed it before. The prologue to this chapter of my life, written in my husband's handwriting, speaks to me in a way his voice used to, full of love and gentle reassurance.

My breath catches in my throat as I carefully unfold the paper, the creases and folds showing signs of its age. Dylan's familiar handwriting brings a rush of memories, each word a testament to the life we shared and the deep love that bound us together. As I begin to read, the room around me fades, and it feels as though Dylan is here with me, whispering these words into my ear.

My dearest Maddie,

I know this time is hard for you. I know you're struggling even though you silence me the second I question you on that. It fills me with hope yet breaks my heart to see you so optimistic. Even now. You don't have to pretend with me, darling.

I know you.

I know that the longer you try and hold it all together, the harder it's going to be on the other side of this when I'm not there to comfort you the way I promised I always would.

I don't need another cup of tea, another disappointing Netflix series, or for my feet to be propped up two levels too high. I need you to collapse into my arms and just stay there for a little while. Can we please do that? You don't have to keep a brave face. You don't have to hold it all together.

Not now. Especially not now.

I know you think I need your strength, but I don't. Please just bring your head to mine and let those emotions of yours run free. Grieve with me. I need you to grieve with me, baby.

Please don't be afraid. I've got you—I've got both of you. You and Lila. I know you can't see it yet, and you won't for some time. But I've got you. You have my word.

I will love you forever.

Tears blur my vision as I finish reading the letter. The raw emotion in Dylan's words pierces through the numbness that has surrounded my heart for so long. Each sentence is a plea for me to allow myself to feel, to break down the walls I've built and let the grief pour out. He knew me so well, better than I knew myself at times. He understood my need to be strong for everyone else, to keep pushing forward even when I felt like crumbling inside.

For over a year, I avoided this room for the most part, unable to face the memories it held. My mother had taken over the task of keeping it clean, respecting my need for distance while quietly ensuring that Dylan's space remained untouched. I never questioned her motives, never thought to look deeper. Now I understand—she was waiting for me to be ready, to find this letter when I could truly absorb its meaning.

The letter trembles in my hands as I press it to my heart, closing my eyes and allowing the tears to flow freely. This room, once a source of unbearable pain, now feels like a sanctuary. Dylan's presence is almost tangible, his love enveloping me, easing the pain. I take a deep breath, feeling the weight of my grief start to lift, replaced by a steady calm and a gentle reassurance.

I stood quietly, tracing the edges of the letter, its weight heavy in my hands. After a moment, I placed it next to my book, *Say It Again*, the cover catching the soft light. Seeing them side by side made it all feel real—what had once been a distant dream was now tangible, something I could hold. I stepped back, taking it in. The room holds its silent promises, and for once, I'm ready to believe in them. The past still lingered, but its weight had lifted, leaving me with a sense of lightness, as though I could finally breathe again. Ready for whatever came next. Ready to keep writing—not just stories, but the life waiting ahead of me.

*Thank you for taking the time to
read my novel!*

I really appreciate all of your feedback, and
I love hearing what you have to say.
Please leave me a helpful review on Amazon and Goodreads,
letting me
know what you thought of this novel.
I am truly grateful!

Jessica

Acknowledgments

Fɪʀsᴛ ᴀɴᴅ ꜰᴏʀᴇᴍᴏsᴛ, I must express my deepest gratitude to my husband, whose unwavering support and encouragement reignited my creativity after a four-year hiatus. His belief in me rekindled my passion for writing and pushed me to continue.

I am profoundly grateful to Sami, my brilliant cover design artist, whose exceptional talent and meticulous attention to detail beautifully conveyed the essence and tone of this story.

Leilani, your editorial expertise and insightful feedback were instrumental in shaping this book.

Thank you to the countless friends and mentors who have supported my dreams and opened doors along the way.

To my loyal readers—it is because of you that I dare to dream. It is because of you the pages continue to turn.

Finally, I thank God, the ultimate author and source of all creativity and insight, through whom all inspiration flows. I am excited to share that I have many more stories in the pipeline and won't be stopping anytime soon.

Love and light,

Jessica

About the Author

J ESSICA LEED HAILS from Victoria, Australia, and has called the United States home since 2021. An elementary teacher, former dancer, and fitness professional, she now lives in Nashville, Tennessee with her husband and two beloved cats. Jessica finds joy in books, coffee, long walks, the beauty of autumn, and cooking hearty breakfasts.

facebook.com/jessicaleedauthor
@jessicaleedauthor (Instagram)

NINE YEARS

You would think Sienna Henderson had the perfect life. She has a successful career, a loving family and is engaged to be married. From the outside she appears to have it all together, yet on the inside she is coming undone.

Caught inside a dysfunctional relationship and with her work environment intolerable, she finds herself slipping further from the life she has envisioned.

After reuniting with a man from her past, Sienna's life is turned upside down in a way that has her questioning everything she has ever known.

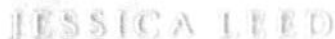

HERE I STAND

Healing from the past is difficult. Especially when it has a way of following you everywhere you go.

New beginnings are of ten faced with challenges. But not in the way Sienna Henderson could have ever anticipated when she comes face to face with an unexpected truth that will change her life forever.

www.ingramcontent.com/pod-product-compliance
Lightning Source LLC
Chambersburg PA
CBHW022107310726
48972CB00007B/1925